Qinmeartha and
the Girl Child LoChi

&

The Tomb of the Old Ones

Qinmeartha and the Girl Child LoChi

John Grant

&

The Tomb of the Old Ones

Colin Wilson

Cosmos Books

Qinmeartha and the Girl Child LoChi

&

The Tomb of the Old Ones

Published by:

Cosmos Books, an imprint of Wildside Press
PO Box 301, Holicong, PA 18928-0301
Www.wildsidepress.com

The Tomb of the Old Ones was first published in The Antarktos Cycle,
ed. Robert M. Price, Chaosium, 1999. Copyright © 1999 Colin Wilson.

Qinmeartha and the Girl-Child LoChi is original to this book.
Copyright © 2002 John Grant.

Cover art copyright © 2002 by audre.
Cover design copyright © 2002 by Juha Lindroos.

For more information, contact Wildside Press
www.wildsidepress.com

ISBN: 1-58715-504-4 (trade paperback)
ISBN: 1-58715-505-2 (hardcover)

Qinmeartha and the Girl Child LoChi

John Grant

Tarburton-on-the-Moor — just another sleepy Dartmoor village. Or so it seems to Joanna Gard when she comes to stay there, until the fabric of the village begins to come apart. As archetypes drawn from the human subconscious play out their incomprehensible rituals, the familiar becomes unfamiliar and the mundane distorts into ever-increasing strangeness, and she is forced to realize that a duel of wills between eternal forces is being played out — that nothing, herself included, is what it seems to be.

In this uncomfortably disturbing tale of clashing realities Hugo- and World Fantasy Award-winning author John Grant adds a new and startling element to the fantasy cosmology developed in many of his earlier works.

Acknowledgements

Dave and Bogna Hutchinson gave me board, lodging, succour and their own excellent company during the long and torrid time that saw the birth of this monster; to them my sincere thanks for this and for having been such true friends for so many years. My daughter Jane kindly read the text and suggested some changes, but overall pronounced it acceptable; thanks, Jane. And my wife Pam did the difficult job of putting up with me not just as I finalized the text for this edition but in general.

Dedication

This is for Hutch and Bogna,
with love,
and as always for Pam,
like life itself.

see LoChi
girl child LoChi
her back bends not for the heaviest load
she is
starwatcher
she is
cloudrider
she is
she who seeks to the ends of roads

— fragment found in West Street, afterwards

I

Qinmeartha

Looking out the window across Tarburton, Joanna caught sight of the reflection of her own face in the glass. Behind her Aunt Jill, sitting in the old yellow armchair that had come down through perhaps too many generations of the family, was neatly framed by the reflected image.

Joanna smiled. The juxtaposition seemed to be telling her that she and Aunt Jill were the last of a kind.

The bells of St Leonard's began unmelodically to lurch into sound. Ever since arriving in Tarburton—full name Tarburton-by-the-Moor—three years back, Aunt Jill had been fighting a losing battle against the bell-ringers, who practised every Tuesday night and Thursday night, very loudly, and apparently to no beneficial effect. Today the peals should have been in their Sunday best, but they sounded much as usual.

The reflected Aunt Jill was making little irritated movements, and Joanna turned away from the window.

"Bloody bells," muttered Aunt Jill. "Bloody, bloody bells." It was the strongest oath she ever used. She got to her feet and gestured at the littered tray in front of her. "More tea?"

"I'll make it," said Joanna, glad for something to do. They'd run out of things to talk about, but Joanna had said that she'd leave about five, and couldn't now say she'd go at four. She was awash with cups of tea drunk in a brittle silence interrupted by doomed attempts to find new topics of conversation.

In the little kitchen, waiting for the kettle to boil, she wondered what it was that had created this new distance between herself and her aunt. Joanna had been only fifteen when her father had died in a light-aircraft crash, eleven years ago, and two years after that her mother had died also—of grief, according to all the family friends, although Joanna knew there had been quite a deal of alcohol mixed in with the grief. Aunt Jill, her mother's spinster elder sister and Joanna's sole surviving relative, had moved into the family home, just off Seymour Street, near Marble Arch, and had taken over Joanna's life. She must have done a good job: Joanna's GCSEs had been screwed up by her father's death, but her A-level results were excellent. In a way, Joanna reflected now, Aunt Jill had been more of a mother to her than her real mother had been.

Except this weekend. Something was bothering Aunt Jill, and Joanna couldn't find out what it was. She'd tried subtle hinting and got nowhere. She'd tried unsubtle interrogation: likewise. The old woman—not that old, but a lot older than Joanna's twenty-six—would volunteer the information in her own time. Maybe.

Could Aunt Jill have got herself a boyfriend? That might be it. She was the other side of sixty, but life didn't stop then—at least, according to all the over-sixty-year-olds Joanna knew. But surely Aunt Jill would have told her? *Maybe*, Joanna thought as she poured the steaming water into the pot, *maybe it's somebody "terribly unsuitable".*

She grinned. Aunt Jill always seemed to get a bit of a kick out of Joanna's more unsuitable lovers, to be full of questions that often tottered over from the personal into the distinctly tasteless. It'd be funny if she came over all coy just because she'd fallen madly, passionately in love with the local poacher or someone.

The grin faded. No—it couldn't be that. However much they might pretend to each other, no two people ever know each other completely, but Joanna was certain she knew Aunt Jill well enough to be able to read that much in her. It was something more serious than—Joanna found herself subvocalizing the words in a pompous tone—an "embarrassing liaison".

The tea was ready. There was no excuse for not going back into the drawing-room.

Aunt Jill looked up as Joanna entered, a polite smile on her face, as if everything between them were just fine. "It's been a good weekend, hasn't it, Joanna?" she said brightly, for at least the tenth time in the past hour.

"Yes. A lot of fun."

"I never thought these old legs would take me to the top of Hay Tor . . . "

Joanna smothered a sigh as she poured a thin stream of tea into the too-small, too-fragile cups. She was already bored with the subject. All weekend Aunt Jill had been busily prattling away about superficialities, anxious to bar the conversation from heading into deeper waters. She was running out of those superficialities now, repeating herself.

"I'll really have to get moving soon. The weather might get rough up nearer London." The excuse was valid, but didn't sound any the better for that.

Aunt Jill obviously recognized it as well, but seemed relieved. "Yes," she said, putting down her hardly touched cup abruptly, sloshing some tea into her saucer. "There might be rain. Or mist."

It seemed odd to be talking of mist when the sunlight was washing in through the window. Down here in Devon, October sometimes saw periods of weather that were better even than the summer, as if the world had arranged things so that the locals, swamped by grockles all through June, July and August, should be rewarded for their tolerance by some fine weeks to share among themselves. Joanna shivered at the prospect of London, which always seemed grey to her at this time of year.

"You've packed," said Aunt Jill. "Sure you haven't forgotten anything important."

Nothing except to talk properly *with you*, thought Joanna. "I've got everything," she said. "Doesn't matter anyway, you old fusspot. I'll be back down here soon."

Which was a lie, and they both knew it. Joanna always intended to come to Tarburton every fortnight or three weeks to make sure Aunt Jill was getting on all right, but somehow things got in the way—commitments, overloads of work, things like that—and she was lucky if she made it down here three times a year.

Aunt Jill collaborated in the lie. "Yes," she said, "of course you will be. There's always that to look forward to."

#

The bells were still filling the sky with discord as the two women stood by Joanna's Mini in front of the Crafts Centre, Tarburton's main centre of social life apart from the pubs. It sold bad coffee, expensive wholemeal food, and a place where you could sit and talk.

"Are you sure you've got everything?" said Aunt Jill yet again.

"Everything," Joanna said, patting the roof of the car as if it were a parcel she'd just finished tying up. "Aunt Jill . . . "

She paused, not knowing if she had the courage to press further.

"Yes, dear?"

"Is there anything"—Joanna found she was twisting her hands together, like people did in books—"anything you want to talk to me about?"

"What do you mean?" That dreadful artificial brightness again.

"Is there anything . . . well, you know, *wrong*?"

"No, darling!" Aunt Jill was attempting to pass it off with a laugh. "What could there be to be wrong? We've just had a lovely weekend, and I'm happy because you're looking so well. Of course there's nothing the matter."

Her aunt, smelling of some perfume that Joanna was certain was no longer manufactured—something with a lot of lavender in it—leaned forward in the sunlight and kissed her on the cheek. Was the hug she gave a little too vigorous? Was Joanna's imagination simply running away with her?

"All right," Joanna said, rummaging in her jacket pocket for a cigarette. "Just so long as everything's OK. I do worry about you, Aunt Jill."

"I'm flattered."

"I love you very much, you know." Joanna found her cigarettes but her matches were playing harder to get. "It matters to me that you're all right. Do take care."

"Of course I shall," said Aunt Jill, looking up crossly towards the spire of St Leonard's. "Those bloody, bloody bells. I'll be all right, dear. You'll see. I'm a tough old boot, you know. I got through the war. I'll be all right."

Joanna shrugged. The lady was maybe protesting too much, but it was easier to believe her than to worry about it.

"OK," she said, climbing into the Mini, gripping her cigarette between her teeth, feeling vaguely inadequate but not knowing what to do about it. "So long as you're sure."

"Do call me when you get home, just to let me know you're safe."

Standing in the evening sunlight, Aunt Jill suddenly looked smaller than Joanna had seen her before.

"I will," said Joanna through the open window. "I promise."

2

Girl Child LoChi

It would be Easter in a couple of weeks.

Joanna had had a good drive down from London, and was feeling relaxed rather than tired by it. Slowing down as she came in off the A38 onto Regent Street—the road that led into Tarburton's centre from the east—she wondered for the first time how much of what had happened in the past six months she could tell Aunt Jill, how much would have to be censored. *Quite a lot,* she concluded. *There are some things that don't cross the generation gap, however much Aunt Jill is supposed to have been a bit of a goer in her young days.*

She parked the red Mini in Ham's Lane, just in front of the Crafts Centre, as usual. Climbing out of it, she looked up at the windows of her aunt's flat, just above the Blue Horse. They were blank, like eyelids closed against the sunshine. Aunt Jill would be watching her from there, so she waved cheerfully, then dived into the back seat to fetch out her squashy grey bagful of clothes.

Greta appeared at the door of the Crafts Centre, smiling uncertainly. She was of middle age and looked it, despite a lifetime spent eating nothing that came out of a packet or tin. She claimed to cook everything served in the Crafts Centre from raw materials, no shortcuts, but her neat blue designer apron never seemed to show any food-stains.

"Hi," said Joanna.

"Hello," said Greta slowly. "You'll have come to see your aunt again?"

"Yes," Joanna said. It was an obvious question, and for a second it worried her. Greta wasn't exactly a conversational expert, but she wasn't usually as dim as this either. "It's been a while."

"Been a while," Greta echoed. She turned and went back into her shop.

Joanna hefted the bag onto her shoulder and crossed the road. The Blue Horse was open, even though it was the middle of the afternoon—Jas must have decided the grockle season had begun—and Joanna was briefly tempted to push her way in through the swing doors to the cool, friendly darkness. No—Aunt Jill must have seen her arrive. Later on, perhaps, Joanna would be able to drag her out of the flat for a drink or three.

The flat's entrance was through a concrete corridor and up a little flight of stairs at the back. Listening to the bell's ping-*pong*, Joanna saw that the tiny garden was a mess, with weeds already growing in a tangled mat across the earth. She frowned. Aunt Jill wasn't an enthusiastic gardener, but she was determinedly dutiful. Had she been ill sometime during the winter, and not said anything—not wanted to bother Joanna? It would be like her.

Ping-*pong* again.

Not that Joanna could have done much about it, even if Aunt Jill had told her. There had been too much going on in London, too many emotional quagmires that had to be either navigated or circumnavigated. The things she wasn't going to be able to talk to Aunt Jill about.

The symmetry of the situation struck her as she stood waiting on the doorstep. When last she'd been here in Tarburton she'd been aware that there was something Aunt Jill was withholding from her. Now it was the other way around. Splitting up with Mike—well, that would be OK: Aunt Jill had shown something akin to impatience when Joanna's relationship with Mike had entered its third year, as if Aunt Jill herself, in her youth, would have ditched the man months before, just on principle. Yeah, and it'd be all right to talk about Peter, too—about most of it.

Ping-*pong*.

How long had she been standing here? Couldn't be more than a couple of minutes. Maybe Aunt Jill had gone to the loo after seeing her arrive. *Don't worry about things so much*, thought Joanna, pulling a battered pack of cigarettes from her handbag. *You're getting to be as bad as Aunt Jill. A fussbudget, Peter would call you . . .*

Yes, it'd been a bit of a mess with Peter, hadn't it? Three years of Mike had reduced everything to familiarity. Peter had seemed a good option—although, when Joanna thought about it, she realized angrily that a lot of what had made him seem so glamorous was just that he had a faster car. They'd driven north one day, up almost as far as Manchester, and in between being terrified of police speed-traps Joanna had felt as if she were throwing off the shackles of her staid, quasi-respectable relationship with Mike.

Peter had driven away very quickly indeed when she'd told him she was pregnant.

Ping-*pong*.

And the odd thing was, she'd hardly blamed him.

"Joanna, darling," said a voice at her elbow.

She turned to find the door had opened. A pale face looked at her out of the gloom.

"Aunt Jill?" she said hesitantly.

"Who else would it be?"

"Yes, but . . . "

"I've lost a little weight since you were last here, that's all. Come in, child, come in. Don't just hang around there. There's a chilly draught, if you hadn't noticed."

Following Aunt Jill up the inside stairs, Joanna found her mind in a turmoil. If she'd met her aunt in the street she wouldn't have recognized her. Aunt Jill couldn't be more than half the weight she'd been last October, and she seemed twenty years older. This was somebody's grandmother who was pointing her into the drawing-room—somebody's rather old and decrepit grandmother.

"Aunt Jill," Joanna began helplessly, "you look so . . . "

"So *what*?" There was still a strong light in the blue eye that peered up at her.

"So . . . *changed*," said Joanna.

"I'm six months older, that's all." Aunt Jill settled herself into the yellow armchair, leaving Joanna to sort herself out however she would. "It's been a long six months. I don't suppose you've had too much time to think about your poor old aunt—not with all the things you young folk get up to in the city."

"I'm sorry it's been so long . . . "

"No, don't apologize to me, Joanna." Aunt Jill waved a frail hand in dismissal. The skin between the fingers was pale-yellow parchment. "I was young, too, you keep forgetting. A long time ago."

"Not all that long," said Joanna brusquely, dropping the squashy bag and plonking herself down in the window seat. "You're not all *that* ancient, Aunt Jill." But she looks it. *She looks as if she's not far from the grave. She doesn't look sixty . . . sixty-three, I think . . . or is it -four?*

"Long enough. Tea? You'll have to make it for us both, if you could. I seem to have been standing half the day."

Joanna put the kettle on, scuttled upstairs briefly to the loo, then filled the pot. The kitchen, normally as neat as one of those pictures in the colour supplements, was like the garden out the back: it gave the impression of being overgrown.

"What was Peter like, then?" said Aunt Jill as Joanna came back into the room, carrying the tray. "You never told me much about him on the phone."

She didn't sound very concerned. In fact, she sounded as if she were finding it an effort to formulate the words, like an actress suddenly thrust into a part without having been given the script, just told to muddle along as best she can.

"Not much to tell," said Joanna. And there wasn't. He had been fun to be with, but now it was an effort to conjure up even the image of his face or the sound of his laughter. Their brief fling had been somehow affectless, even at the time. And then, of course, he'd been abruptly out of her life—business had suddenly, by some astonishing coincidence, necessitated his departure to Glasgow for the next two years.

Leaving her, and a fetus developing inside her. And Mike—except Mike hadn't really come into it. Oh, he'd been *there*, of course: hanging around like a faithful spaniel, over-eager that they remain best friends, even though they were no longer lovers.

She hadn't had the heart to tell him that the child was actually his, not Peter's: he might have offered, in his gallant way, to marry her, or something embarrassing and *confining* like that. So instead she'd quietly arranged for an abortion.

She'd been surprised by how much of an argument the doctors and nurses had put up, pointing out that an abortion was a permanent thing: you couldn't change your mind about it afterwards. And then she'd been surprised by how completely they'd acquiesced as soon as they'd realized that her mind was set. She got the feeling that, even if she'd had second thoughts an hour before the op, they'd have been overridden by those now-impersonal persons.

The biggest surprise was the guilt, afterwards. It was as if it was only once the bond between them had been sundered that she could start to recognize the fetus—the dead fetus, which she wasn't allowed to see—as a fellow human being. She didn't think of herself as a murderess, not quite; but she did have the haunting sensation, whenever she woke up in the night, that perhaps she'd run someone over in the car and forgotten about it. Which was illogical, silly, a notion not to be entertained. But a notion which, alas, had gate-crashed, and showed no signs of departure.

Joanna didn't respond to her aunt's question. The *old* Aunt Jill would have seen her preoccupation, but the new one—this grandmother—didn't even seem to be interested.

"I had a good drive down," said Joanna. "The countryside always looks so gorgeous this time of the . . . "

"You're looked after in my will," said Aunt Jill. "As you must have known you'd be. Say no more about it, now. Just so long as you know."

"Auntie!" She'd left the sugar in the kitchen. "Whatever brought that up?"

"I'm not as young as I used to was."

"You're not *old*."

"Amn't I?"

Looking at the pale face, with the bones of the cheek and jaw clearly demarcated beneath the wrinkled paper skin, Joanna could find no answer. Yes, whatever had happened in this past half-year, Aunt Jill was now indisputably old. No argument.

"I'll get the sugar," she said.

"As you wish, child." This time the arm on the worn yellow chair only half-rose, leaving the little dismissive wave uncompleted.

When Joanna located the sugar-lumps, tucked away near the back of the cupboard for the cleaning powders and washing-up liquid, she found they were stained and spotted with what she hoped was just old tea. On the spur of the moment she dumped them in the overflowing pedal bin.

"You're out of sugar," she said, back in the drawing-room. "I'll get some for you, later."

"Oh, don't worry about 'later'. Tell me something about what's been going on."

A little of the vitality had returned to the old woman. She'd pulled herself more upright in the chair, and was drinking her tea black and sugarless.

"Well, they sacked me." When Joanna had first told her aunt on the phone there had been a shocked sucking-in of breath: in the old days people never got sacked unless it was for some gross breach of conduct. "They called it making me redundant, but it felt just the same as being sacked."

She'd been working for a publishing company, Rolfe & Baldwin. Mainly they published glossy novels with lots of pages and lots of sex in different countries and in unorthodox locales and positions that sold hardly at all in hardback but gained big paperback advances. Joanna had been an assistant editor for nearly five years, all the time telling herself that she was wasting her time—that sooner or later the *right* job would turn up at OUP or somewhere respectable, and then she'd be on her way. Instead, as Dave Rolfe had told her, the bottom had fallen out of the soft-porn market, and they were having to cut back. She'd got six months' salary and a big bunch of over-ripe red roses.

"Well," said Aunt Jill, "you were never very happy there anyway. Not a great loss."

All at once Joanna felt an upsurge of fury. The last few months had been hell—Mike, Peter, the abortion, the redundancy, everything—and surely it was her entitlement to have some older person she could lean on, someone whose shoulder she could weep into, just like she'd wept into her mother's shoulder as a child. For almost a decade Aunt Jill had been that person: it was her *job* to be a sort of mother confessor, and she was failing to fulfil it just at the time Joanna most needed her to.

I should be sympathetic, she told herself sternly. *I shouldn't be thinking about my own interests at all. I shouldn't be being so selfish. Aunt Jill's ill—she must be, and here am I worrying away about my own trivial concerns.*

It was good advice, but the anger didn't go away. She watched her hand clenching on her knee.

"I'll go and make up my bed," she said. "And then I'll do some shopping. And clean the kitchen. You've been letting things get out of hand, I think. Have you seen a doctor?"

Aunt Jill produced a thin imitation of a snort.

"Doctor Grasmere? He gave me a prescription. The same prescription he gave me last year for my rheumatism. I think it's a special sort of medicine that's designed to make elderly biddies go away and stop pestering him."

It was the nearest to the old Aunt Jill that Joanna had seen since arriving here. She looked for the smile that should have accompanied the remark, but it wasn't there.

"I'll go and make up my bed," she repeated.

#

Aunt Jill was too tired to go out for a drink that evening—too tired to do anything much except keep her feet up in front of the television, not even clucking over the usual dreadful news about rioting in Kuala Lumpur and further slaughter in the Balkans. Joanna, who had done some shopping, cleaned the worst of the kitchen and concocted a casserole to throw in the oven—all in a state of righteous fury—had no choice in the matter: she *needed* the drink, not for its own sake but just to get away from the funereal flat and its morbid occupant.

It's like the baby all over again, she thought as she clattered too noisily down the stairs. *I'm already beginning to think of Aunt Jill as someone completely isolated from me, rather than just . . . Aunt Jill.*

The Blue Horse smelt of stale cigarette smoke and spilt beer, just the way it always did—but there the semblance of normality ended. It wasn't ever a *noisy* pub—not like the Customs House in Regent Street, where the yobbos with bikes and leather jackets hung out—but this evening it was almost silent, as if the air were too thick to carry sound. The lights— fake gas-lamps that Jas had put in to replace the fluorescents his predecessor had installed— likewise seemed muted. There were a few other drinkers already there, one or two of whom she recognized enough to exchange nods with, but only Jas himself had any words for her.

"Miss Gard, down for the weekend," he said morosely.

"Hi, Jas," she replied, perching herself on a stool, trying to make herself cheer up by pretending to. "A pint of . . . Royal Oak, if it's on form."

"Royal Oak it is," he said, moving to the pump. He, too, had lost weight, she suddenly noticed. It was better disguised, because of the disreputable old suit and waistcoat he affected, but the jacket was loose on his shoulders and there were flaps of flesh around his chin and cheeks.

"What's going on?" she said as he put the pint on the towel mat in front of her and took her coins. "Not just here, I mean."

"What *do* you mean?" he said off-handedly.

"In Tarburton. It's not the same." She swung her arm to indicate the pub and the rest of the village beyond its walls. "My aunt's different—like there isn't as much life inside her as there used to be. And . . . " She stopped. How can you tell someone, face to face, that they're looking bloody terrible? "And everything," she concluded limply.

"Not as I've noticed," Jas said. He was polishing his way along the optics with a torn tea-towel. "Have you noticed anything, Rupert?"

Rupert, whose job was something Joanna had never discovered but who was generally regarded as a townie because until last autumn he had commuted daily to Newton Abbot, looked up for the first time from his whisky and soda.

"Yes," he said indistinctly. "No. Young Joanna Gard, isn't it? Come to visit your aunt, have you? Fine woman, your aunt. Fine figure of a woman, too." He covered a belch with his hand. His fingers were nicotine yellow, like his moustache. "Few years ago I'd have . . . "

Joanna never found out, thank God, what Rupert'd have, because the door opened behind her. She twisted round and saw a couple of young people—people her own age—coming in. It was as if someone had opened the windows in a morgue.

At first she didn't register them as anything other than blessed interruptions, but as they came closer to the bar she began to see them as individuals rather than symbols. The woman was, on second examination, somewhat younger than Joanna—she didn't look to be more than twenty, if that. She had long hair, a glossy black, and skin of a colour that looked as if it would become a tan within days of the first arrival of summer. Her lips were full, although her mouth was small. She glanced at Joanna briefly, her dark, nearly black eyes showing no sign of interest.

The man was older—he could even be thirty. He was in jeans and a faded green Marillion T-shirt. He was quite tall, and had the same night-black hair as the woman. It was clear from stray facial resemblances—the fleshy lips, the smallness of the mouth, the cleft marking the chin—that the two were brother and sister, not a couple, as she'd at first assumed. Yet, where the woman's face seemed quintessentially feminine, his was almost defiantly masculine.

Joanna turned away and stared at her drink. She'd not been much interested in men since the abortion—not remotely interested in them, if the truth were to be told—but this stranger was something different. Things were looking up in Tarburton if they could import talent like this, she reflected wryly. She tried to tell herself that there was something lofty and romantic in that original hot flash of attraction she'd felt, but was honest enough to acknowledge there hadn't been a lot of higher emotion involved.

"Guinness, Jas." She liked his voice, as well. Not hunkish: not wimpish, either. It had an accent she couldn't for the moment place. "Tony?"

"Just a Coke."

So the girl's name was Antonia. Probably. What was *his*?

"You're new here?" Joanna said, turning towards the pair. *Oh, God, that must have sounded patronizing,* she thought. *I'm only sort of here on sufferance myself.*

"You're a strange face as well," said the man, smiling guardedly. "You must be Jill Soames's niece."

"Yes. Joanna." *News travels fast in Tarburton.*

"Jas's told us about you, hasn't he, Tony?" He was laughing at her, but not unkindly. His sister didn't join in. "Don't worry, Joanna—it *is* Joanna, isn't it?—he's given us a good report of you."

"And you?" She wished she didn't feel so much like a schoolgirl all of a sudden. She remembered when she'd been in the sixth form the school had hired a temporary assistant cook who'd looked like a sort of unraddled Mick Jagger, and how she'd always turned her face away when she passed him in the corridor in case he was telepathic and would find out what she was thinking about him. She felt like that now.

"We've been here . . . oh, four months now, I guess. Since Christmas. We moved into the big house at the other end of Ham's Lane, down by the playing fields."

"Aunt Jill told me Major Hunter had died. Was the house as much of a shambles as everyone thought it would be?"

He looked at her gravely and adopted a portentous tone. "Significantly worse." He smiled. "Oh, boy, was it bad! Mother had to call in professionals in the end, just to get all the crap out of it. There was one entire cellar filled with broken glass. Seems he couldn't face putting his bottles out with the dustbins so he just slung them down there. Enough there to keep Coventry Cathedral in replacement windows for the next thousand years, I should think."

"It's not funny, Steve," said his sister, touching his arm. "He was a poor, lonely old man, that's all. Lay off him. Let him rest in peace."

"OK, OK." He pushed his sister's hand away. "I won't even mention the heaps of girlie maga—"

"*Steve!* There were no such—"

"Sorry, sorry."

"Do you like it here in Tarburton?" said Joanna. It sounded like the kind of question someone might ask at a school prizegiving—something that indicated the asker didn't want an answer. She lifted her glass to her lips as if that would make the words sound wittier.

"As good as anywhere," said Tony. She started to say something else, but bit it back.

You were going to say, thought Joanna for her, *that, just like in all these little places around the moor, the people don't take kindly to newcomers. Aunt Jill's been here for over three years, but they still, though they're friendly enough, treat her as if she were a weekend tripper rather than someone who's come here to stay.*

"We're going to sit down," said Steve in that rich voice of his. "Join us?" He shrugged towards a table near the rear, where the loos were. Tony was already on her way across, holding her Coke out from her side theatrically, as if Jas would throw her out if she spilt any of it. Perhaps he would. Jas seemed to derive dour pleasure from throwing people out of his pub.

"Love to," Joanna said. "I don't really know anyone much around here."

She followed, amazed all over again by the contrast between these two rather beautiful people and the rest of the folk in the pub. They were bright splashes of acrylic set on the wall alongside twee, cautious watercolours. Greta, too, had had that same washed-outness about her. And Aunt Jill, of course . . .

"I can't stop long," Joanna explained as she sat down. "My aunt—I've only just arrived—something in the oven . . . "

Which is the kind of inadvertent double-entendre I could do without, she thought. *There's no longer anything in my oven. I slew it.*

"It's nice to meet you," said Steve forthrightly. He put his hand lightly on hers. "Tarburton's all right, like Tony was saying, but it's a bit—you know, dead."

Except when people like you two are around to breathe life into it. "As you said, I'm Joanna," she muttered. "And you?"

"Gilmour. Steve and Tony Gilmour. The idlest layabouts in an idle family, in case you were going to ask us what we do. Funny sort of question, that, now I come to think about it, and yet we're always asking it of each other."

For a moment Joanna was lost by him, unable to work out if "we" were Steve and his sister or the human species at large.

"As if you could tell more about a person from what they do between nine and five, by what they earn their meals from," Steve was saying, "than from whether they've just helped you out of a hole, or if they like Stockhausen better than the Black Crowes, or . . . "

Tony, who had been so indifferent to Joanna's presence when they'd met, now seemed to have decided she liked her. "You're burbling, Steve," she said. "You'll bore the poor woman before she's properly even met us."

"Tishwash, sister!" he said. "I'm sure Joanna here has long ago decided that, the sooner she can get out of this pub and never see us again, the happier she'll be. Am I right, Joanna?"

"Not at all," she said, flustered. "Quite the opposite, in fact." *And that may sound like just the sort of courtesy you'd expect from me, but it's true,* she added mentally. *Truer than you could possibly imagine.*

"But I do have to go." She gulped down half the remains of her beer—which, now she was paying attention to it, wasn't up to Jas's usual standards.

"Yes—you said." Steve's voice was sympathetic. "You have an aunt and a casserole to attend to."

"Something like that." *And quite a lot else.*

I think.

#

That night, hot although the night itself hadn't seemed to be hot, Joanna dreamed.

She was in a place where the sky was always light, a single mass of brightness that arched all the way from one horizon to the other. She knew quite a lot about her situation in this place, but not really enough altogether to explain it. There was a sun somewhere in the dome of radiance, but it was lost in the general brilliance: the sun never set, and it touched the atmosphere of this world into shining with the same unremitting vigour as itself.

There was no escape from the light. Here and there rocks stuck up out of the desert, and there were one or two scrubby-looking plants, but they cast no shadows. The radiance was not especially hot, but it was so bright that it burnt her as painfully as red-hot tongs, as if it were flaying away the cornea of the single eye that seemed to be the entirety of her body's upper surface.

She slithered. It was the only way she could move. She could extend pseudopodia—indeed, she didn't even have to think about doing so: it just happened—and then drag herself a few painful centimetres across the abrasive desert surface, looking for shadows that were not there so that she could hide in them from the light that would not permit her to hide. It was silly to go on searching, she knew that; but she was unable to take the decision just to stop where she was, to give up the hope. It was as if, wherever this hell was, she'd been condemned to spend the rest of eternity hunting for a relief that would never be granted.

It was a while before she realized she was not the only one here: although she couldn't see anything out of her single upturned eye except the lurid fire, sometimes shadows moved at the extreme periphery of her vision. Once she'd observed a few of these she realized that she'd *always* known there were others of her kind. She was of the Wardrobe Folk, as were they; and it was the doom of the Wardrobe Folk to dwell in this arid misery forever.

Unless . . .

Unless the Girl Child LoChi could come among them.

But Joanna, in her dream, didn't know who the Girl Child LoChi was, and didn't know how she could find out. Lacking that knowledge, she was sapping the strength of her people in their attempts to bring the Girl Child LoChi to their aid. She was at fault—every extra second that she and the other flat creatures like herself spent here was partly her responsibility.

Guilt. Too much of it for her mind to stay here.

She woke screaming in a tangle of bedclothes to find light pouring in through the bedroom window. She screamed at that, too, until she realized it was only the morning sunshine, and that she was in her own bedroom in Tarburton-by-the-Moor.

A few minutes later she was giggling unconvincedly. Just a nightmare. The Wardrobe Folk—next it would be the Pantry People or the Cupboard Under The Stairs Collective.

But the cold sweat all over her and the sheets and the blankets didn't go away just because her rational mind was taking over its rightful functions once more.

She pulled herself out of bed.

Later she'd tell Aunt Jill all about this, and the two of them would laugh together at the silliness.

#

Later, though, when she went to wake up Aunt Jill with a cup of tea, she discovered Aunt Jill was dead.

3

Farewells, Welcomes

There was a wind up today, coming from the sea to the south, and it was blowing away most of what the Reverend James "Call Me Jim" Daker was saying.

Which was, in Joanna's opinion, an unquestionably good thing. Her aunt had never had much time for ceremonies or for what she called "po-faced eulogies", and the Reverend Call Me Jim's utterances would have had her cringing. She was "a pillar of the community" and a "stalwart on the side of virtue" and all sorts of other things he'd never made much reference to when she'd been alive and trying to mount petitions about the Bloody Bells.

Joanna looked glumly across the open wound of the grave. She wasn't certain whether or not Aunt Jill had ever attended services at St Leonard's, and she guessed that the Reverend Daker wasn't, either. Still, these formalities had to be gone through, Joanna concluded. Viewed as formalities, they didn't seem too bad; viewed as anything else, the Reverend Daker's overblown testimonials were somehow poisonous, as if Aunt Jill's spirit were not to be allowed to ascend into the hereafter without taking with it its due quota of earthly hypocrisy.

There was a scattering of other mourners. Jas had shut the Blue Horse for the occasion, and he was standing opposite her, his eyes downcast. Out from behind the shield of his bar, he looked even less substantial than he had the other day. She willed him to look up at her, but he obstinately refused. Rupert was there, too, his eyes betraying whatever private wake he'd held for himself the night before. He, too, didn't seem to want to look at her. And there was Greta, and the woman from the post office, and even the chap who organized the Bloody Bell-ringing sessions—probably telling himself that the Christian humility he was showing in coming to the funeral of his old enemy would serve him well in the life to come, or maybe he was just here to gloat—and a dozen or so others. All of them elderly people, around Aunt

Jill's kind of age or older; Joanna was the only person there under fifty.

The fresh spring wind made their clothes flap. Joanna was reminded of a different season—of autumn trees. Come winter, would this leaping breeze be a gale, and would all of the trees be able to withstand it?

She straightened her shoulders and told herself to stop being morbid. The Reverend Daker seemed to be coming to the end of his oration—or, at least, he was pausing for breath—and she must brace herself to receive the sympathies of the others. On second thoughts, cemeteries were about the one place in the world it was perfectly permissible to be morbid. And why *should* she don a cloak of false happiness?

They took turns tossing earth down onto the coffin-lid. Joanna wiped off her hands on the sides of her skirt. Surely that was about all they had to do; surely they could all pack off home now, herself included. She'd decided against holding one of those glacial funeral teas people seemed to go in for; there weren't any relations, and the only residents of Tarburton whom Aunt Jill had known at all well were gathered here and looking about as uninterested in protracting proceedings as Joanna herself. She had a bottle of scotch back at the flat—*her* flat, now—and proposed to spend the rest of the afternoon getting as much of it into herself as possible before she passed out. From the look of Rupert, his intentions were very similar.

As if at a signal, the rest of the party moved off, leaving her alone at the graveside for a moment with the sexton.

"She was a nice woman, your aunt," he said, bending to pick up the first spadeful of earth. "She'll be missed around here."

It was a better funeral oration than the Reverend Daker had been able to compose.

#

The level of whisky in the bottle had gone down by about a third, and she'd given up bothering to mix it with water. The light coming in through the drawing-room window was a golden mellow colour, a paler variation on the liquid in the bottle: in an hour or so it would be sunset. She knew she was really quite a lot drunk, although still not drunk enough.

Something had wasted Aunt Jill away, something that had grown inside her, devouring her. In other circumstances Joanna might have guessed cancer, but there hadn't been that funny smell cancer victims usually give off, and Dr Grasmere had sworn to her that her aunt had been in perfect health.

"She just died," he'd said. "She was old, you know."

"She wasn't yet sixty-five," Joanna had said, and she said it again now, raising her tumbler to the whisky bottle in some sort of tribute. "She shouldn't have died. She wasn't old enough to die. She didn't . . . " No: saying that people didn't deserve to die was stupid, and somehow uncharitable. No one deserved to die except those who wanted to, and Aunt Jill hadn't wanted to.

Well. Maybe not. It was hard to tell what the frail old grandmother who called herself Aunt Jill had actually wanted, or not wanted. Joanna wished she'd come down here to Tarburton more often, or at least more recently. She wished she hadn't spent part of that last evening down in the Blue Horse chatting with Steve and Tony Gilmour. She wished . . .

Right at this moment, she discovered, she wished more than anything else that she didn't have to go and pee. The stairs up to the loo suddenly seemed a challenge. Maybe it was stupid of her to have got this plastered.

The irony was that she'd driven down from London intending to ask Aunt Jill if it would be possible for her to come to Tarburton to live for a while. Her redundancy money from Rolfe & Baldwin wasn't going to last forever, not at London rents; and there weren't any very appealing jobs around right now, and . . . Well, now the flat was hers. She could come and live here any time she wanted—and probably would. She'd wait a week or so, and then she'd go up to London and give in notice to her landlord. The few possessions she really wanted to keep, apart from the books, could probably all be jammed into the Mini. Mike—good-old-faithful-spaniel-Mike—Mike would bring the books down in the back of his van some time.

If she asked him nicely.

The loo, woman! Not a second more!

She was coming back down the stairs, taking them one at a time and gripping the banister so tightly that her hand would hardly slide, when the doorbell rang.

"Shit!" she muttered. "Bloody well-wishers. Bloody vultures."

But instead she found Steve and Tony at the door.

"Hi. Come in. I'm pissed."

Steve laughed, his arm round his sister's shoulders. "Then this is a fine time for us to join you." He moved forward, not exactly pushing her but at the same time giving her no opportunity to refuse admission. "We thought you might be drinking, Tony and I, and we thought you might like some company. Miserable occasions, funerals—more miserable than the deaths themselves, in some ways."

"You have a great experience of deaths, I suppose?" said Joanna, trying to put some acidity into her voice. The result sounded to her as if she were speaking through cotton wool.

"More than you might think," he said lightly. He was past her by now, standing at the bottom of the stairs, looking upwards. He wrinkled his nose. "Aunt Jill rather let things go to pieces towards the end, didn't she?"

For a moment Joanna couldn't think of anything to say. The effrontery of him! The other evening in the pub she'd found his male vitality, his assuredness, immensely attractive. That had been before she'd seen this oafish, arrogant intruder.

"Aunt Jill was *my* aunt," she said deliberately. "Not yours."

"I'm sorry," said Tony quietly beside her. "Would you really rather we went away and let you be?"

"No," said Joanna automatically. "No—no, it's kind of you to come. I'm sure I . . . "

"She told us to call her Aunt Jill," Steve was saying. "Over the last few months she and my mother were seeing a lot of each other, and so it seemed only natural we should come to call her Aunt Jill."

"She never told me anything of this," said Joanna thickly as she followed him up the stairs—*her* stairs. "I think she would have mentioned . . . "

"It's quite true," said Tony. "Steve exaggerates about a lot of things, but he's telling you the truth about this. Your aunt and our mother did seem to be . . . very *taken* with each other, is how your aunt put it. Afternoon tea the two of them would be over here, morning coffee at our house."

"And lunch every day at the Crafts Centre," boomed Steve, looking almost proprietorially around the drawing-room. He'd smuggled in another bottle of scotch somehow, and had placed it on the coffee table beside Joanna's. "That was, until your aunt's health began to get so low. Probably's Greta's wholefoods, I should imagine."

He cut another chuckle off short. "I'm sorry. I shouldn't have said that. What *did* Aunt Jill die of, by the way? Did that old quack from up the hill tell you?"

"Old age, Dr Grasmere said."

Joanna crossed and sat down in Aunt Jill's armchair. It must have been obvious to Tony that this wasn't where Joanna had been sitting before, because she said: "Look, are you *sure* you don't mind us two storming in here? We honestly won't mind if you tell us to go away again."

"You're here now," Joanna said with an effort at grandness. "Settle yourselves down. No doubt you know where the glasses are kept." She indicated the kitchen, and Tony slipped quietly out of the room.

"I'm surprised my aunt never mentioned your mother to me," said Joanna again, worrying away at the problem. "Even though I didn't see her as often as I should have, we spoke on the telephone most weekends, and she was always filling me in on events in the village. I'd have thought she would have said *something* about . . . "

"It's a mystery," said Steve with finality, landing with a thump in the chair she'd not long vacated. "That's all. You can ask mother about it when you meet her, which I hope won't be long. Oh, yes, that's right—I almost forgot. That's one of the main reasons we came across here, Tony and me. My parents would like you to come to dinner one evening soon. In fact, mother was mad keen you should come tonight, but I guess that's . . . not possible."

She saw her dishevelment reflected in his gaze and laughed. It was the first genuine laugh she'd uttered since finding Aunt Jill dead in her bed.

"I've got the glasses," said Tony.

She appeared around the wing of the armchair carrying a tray with a couple of mismatched glasses and the aluminium milk-jug. "Water," Tony explained.

Steve leapt to his feet and poured for both of them; at the same time he topped up Joanna's tumbler. She waved away his offer of water from the aluminium jug.

"I'd like to accept your parents' kind invitation to dinner," said Joanna, forming the words carefully. "Not tonight—not so soon after my aunt's funeral. But tomorrow, if that would be convenient."

"Perfect!" said Steve. "Tuesday evening it shall be. I shall call for you, ma'am, at eight o'clock precisely. We shall have drinks on the veranda beforehand and . . . "

He talked on, and Joanna let the words wash over her. She became much more conscious of Tony, sitting demurely on a chair's edge to her left. It was obvious from the way the girl—Joanna found it hard to think of anyone younger than herself as a woman—had her denimed knees so tightly pressed together that she was still nervous about being here, still wishing that her brother would shut up so the two of them could make their polite escapes. *It's funny*, thought Joanna, *the way I was so wrong about both of these two when we met. Tony seemed all haughty and aloof, as if she wouldn't wipe her feet on me, and Steve seemed like the answer to a maiden's dream. Hmmf! Some maiden: some dream.*

"How old are you?" Joanna suddenly asked the Gilmour girl, cutting Steve's witterings off mid-flow.

"I'm . . . uh . . . I'm nineteen. And Steve—Steve's twenty-four."

"I guessed you about right," Joanna said. "But I thought Steve would be older—more like thirty."

Steve brayed with good humour. "I don't know whether to be complimented or . . . " he began, but Joanna ignored him.

"And yet sometimes," she said to Tony with the slow honesty of drunkenness, "when I look at you more carefully, or when the sun catches your face just *so*, you seem much older than your brother."

Tony flushed under her pale-tea skin, and looked down to where her hands were toying with her whisky glass. "I guess that's a way of looking at it," she mumbled, glancing up suddenly at Steve.

Joanna sensed there was something here she ought to know more about, but her mind, slowed by the whisky, wasn't capable of framing the next question. Instead she said: "Where did you live before you came here?"

"Oh," answered Steve airily before his sister could say anything, "here and there, you know. The way one does."

"Here and there?" said Joanna.

"Round and about. We're sort of like gypsies, our family—we never stop in any one place too long. And you?"

"I live—used to live, I suppose I should say—in London, in a bit of London called West Hampstead. Pandora Road. Number 48. It's about seven minutes from the tube station. I rent a place. The landlord calls it a flat, but really it's just a glorified bedsit, with its own bathroom. I pay . . . "

And the words kept on tumbling out of her. To her horror she discovered she was pouring out in front of these almost total strangers every detail of her life, of her work at Rolfe & Baldwin and of how that had come to such an abrupt end, of her relationships with Mike and Peter, of the baby that never was—she remembered to call it a baby, at least, because if she called it just a fetus people might think she was a bit cold-blooded, or something—and of how it had been Mike's kid when at first she'd thought it was Peter's because she'd got mixed up with her months because being with Peter made for such a lot of turbulence in her life and . . .

All of it. Some bits she'd never properly told *herself* before, let alone other people. Once or twice during the flood of words she tried to bite her tongue, anything to stop herself blabbing her innermost secrets, but it swivelled easily out of the reach of her teeth.

There was darkness outside the window when finally she ground to a halt. She'd lost count of the number of times Steve had quietly leaned forwards and topped up her glass. There was nothing left now of the bottle she'd started on her own, and the level in the second was half-way down the label, and yet she didn't feel nearly as drunk as she had been earlier. Perhaps the adrenalin of confession had burnt away the alcohol.

"I'm sorry," she said in a low voice. "I shouldn't have burdened you with all that. I had no right."

"You had every right in the world," said Steve boisterously. "That's what friends are for, isn't it, Tony?"

Slowly Joanna turned her head to look at the girl. The frame of black hair was lost in the shadows of that corner of the room; through the gloom she could see pale smudges that were Tony's hands and face. Yet she could see enough to know that the girl was profoundly uneasy.

"I'm sorry," Joanna repeated in Tony's direction.

"No. Nothing to be sorry about. But Steve and I must leave you now. At once. Come on, Steve."

Her brother half-rose, then settled back again. "Are you sure you'll be all right?" he said with heavy solicitude. "Have you eaten anything today?"

"I'll be OK." Joanna shook her head. She felt angry with him for having been there to hear everything she'd told him, and now all she wanted was for him and his sister to be out of her sight. "Tony's right. Please do go. I don't mean to be rude, but . . . but I need some time on my own, right now. I'll see you tomorrow night. I'll be over this by then. But could you . . . ?"

"Come *on*, Steve," Tony said tightly.

"Of course, of course," said Steve, and this time, to Joanna's relief, when he got to his feet he stayed there. "Maybe it was wrong of us to come blundering in here but . . . "

"No, but . . . " said Joanna.

Somehow, in a blizzard of apologies from all of them, she got the two

33

Gilmours out the front door. Leaning against the cool wall at the foot of the stairs, she heard them whispering to each other as they tip-tapped down the steps outside. She might have been able to hear what they were saying if she'd strained her ears, but she found she wasn't interested enough.

In fact, all she really wanted was some more scotch, a hot bath and bed. Maybe it'd be wiser to alter the order of proceedings a bit: a hot bath while she was still enough in control of herself not to fall asleep or trip and bang her head, then bed with the remains of the scotch to make sure she slept soundly.

And, she hoped, for the first time this week to sleep dreamlessly.

4

Not the Munsters

Her hangover had largely ebbed by the following evening. She'd slipped guiltily down to the strangely subdued Blue Horse at lunchtime to feed it a couple of pints of Royal Oak, keeping her fingers crossed that the two Gilmours wouldn't come stumbling in and catch her in the act. She'd meant to have only the one pint, but Jas had refused to accept any payment for it, so she'd asked for another to settle up the score, as it were, but then he'd refused to take her money for *that* one, either. She'd have felt better about it if he'd shown her any signs of friendship, but instead he'd made both refusals with a sort of glum resignation that told her he was merely doing his duty.

Still, the beer had worked its magic. She'd climbed into this bath mostly cured, and she was feeling fine now that she was climbing out of it.

She looked at herself in the mirror, striking a girlie-magazine pose, grinning; then suddenly straightening up as if Aunt Jill could be watching her from out of the walls. She was just an inch or so below medium height, with shoulder-length ungroomable hair that couldn't decide whether it wanted to be dark or fair. Her nose was snub, her eyes blue-grey. Her breasts weren't large enough and her bottom was too big. It was hopeless telling herself that virtually everyone else she knew likewise thought their boobs were too small and their bums too big: *she*, Joanna Gard, was the one woman who really *was* big and small in all the wrong places. She found she was grinning again. *Well, at least I'm unique in some*thing.

She dried herself on the thick pink towel she'd given Aunt Jill for Christmas three or four years ago, enumerating her other failings as she did so. Her ankles probably in fact were—*objectively* were—a bit too thick, and they were looking worse than usual today. Maybe she was suffering a bit of water-retention because of all the stress. Her toenails badly needed cutting, but there was no one going to see them, so it didn't matter. She had a little heat-spot on her waist, still left from where the seat-belt had been chafing against her during the drive down from London—how long ago? Just over a week, wasn't it?

What to wear? She slipped into a pair of pants with pictures of the Gummi Bears on them—Peter said he'd picked them up in Disneyland the last time he'd been in California and had been waiting to find the right woman to wear them—and a plain white Marks & Spencers bra: very sensible. But as for the rest? The trouble was, she hadn't a clue what the Gilmours senior were like. She'd kept a watch from the window most of the morning—it had been something to do while waiting for her head to stop expanding and contracting—hoping to catch sight of anyone coming up Ham's Lane who might be them, but everyone she'd seen had been depressingly familiar. Rupert on his way to the Blue Horse. Greta popping in and out of the side-door of the Crafts Centre to puff at a cigarette whenever trade slackened off a bit. The Reverend James "Call Me Jim" Daker huffing officiously about his business. The reputed gay who lived up at the far end of West Street and was said to be a writer of some kind; Aunt Jill had introduced them once but Joanna couldn't remember his name. There were a few others, but no one who could have been the Gilmours.

Their children seemed casual enough: both of them seemed to live in jeans—neatly pressed designer jeans that probably cost a fortune, but jeans nevertheless. If their parents were likewise . . . But . . . Maybe . . .

Joanna swore at herself. It wasn't as if she had much choice. She'd packed a skirt for the weekend, just in case Aunt Jill had company, but it was only the kind of thing you could wear for standing around politely sipping sherry. Her own jeans weren't knife-edged like Steve's and Tony's: they could do with a wash, she realized as she put them to her face. There were some clothes in the wardrobe, left behind other times she'd been here—maybe there'd be something wearable among those.

The Wardrobe Folk.

She shook the thought away with an angry jerk of her head. Last night's booze hadn't spared her the nightmare of the world with the sky of unrelieved light. She'd been unbearably thirsty as well—though whether this had been genuinely part of her dream or her body telling her that all the whisky was dehydrating her was something she didn't know. Probably the latter: the creature who was her in that other world didn't seem to have a mouth, so presumably couldn't feel thirst. But she had discovered something new: there was a certain frisson of excitement among the other creatures who shared her predicament, because somehow they all knew—herself included—that the advent of the Girl Child LoChi would not be long, now.

Joanna hoped so. Maybe the dreams would stop pestering her then.

She found what she was looking for at last. It would have looked hideously quaint in London, but down here in Tarburton it was probably all the rage: a black jumper suit that caught her around the hips and waist so that her bum looked bigger than ever. "Good breeding stock," she said to her reflection in the wardrobe mirror. "A fine figure of a woman. You'll make someone an excellent wife, some day."

Mike had always liked her in this, so was probably the subliminal reason she'd left it down here. "A Freudian jumper suit," she said to her reflection, waving her forefinger at it like a schoolmarm.

Shoes. Ah, yes. She had some little black sandshoes that would have to do.

The end product, she decided, once she'd brushed her hair and her teeth and was back in front of the wardrobe mirror again to practise her smiling, wasn't too bad. She'd lay money she'd be able to turn Rupert's head, anyway. If ever she wanted to. Maybe even Steve's, although after his performance last night she was absolutely certain that she wasn't in any way attracted to him, would never be, and the very thought of him made her feel queasy.

Maybe even Tony's . . .

Eh? Where had *that* thought come from? It didn't seem to belong to her.

"Getting more versatile in your old age, hmm, Joanna Gard?" she said to the mirror.

She glanced at her watch. Forty minutes until Steve was due to arrive to pick her up. She could put her feet up and maybe, very cautiously, take a little scotch just to make sure the hangover didn't suddenly come back again.

She was abruptly very tired. Sitting in the armchair swilling scotch seemed like a much better idea than going out to have supper with the Munsters—or whoever Steve's and Tony's parents turned out to be.

Joanna giggled.

Oh, yeah: the Munsters in Tarburton.

#

They were charming, of course. Ronnie Gilmour was at the door when Joanna and Steve arrived. She proved to be an older version of her daughter, but with some of her son's flamboyance. She drew Joanna to her for a brief, almost contactless hug, then stood back to look at her properly.

"Steve warned me you were pretty," Ronnie remarked, clearly unaware that she was saying exactly the wrong thing, "but he obviously didn't warn me enough."

Joanna mumbled something embarrassed and allowed Steve to guide her by the arm through the heavy blackened-oak door. At least she was wearing the right sort of thing: Ronnie was in a brightly coloured gypsy dress with a line of faded-blue lace across the bosom—more or less the uniform of the middle-aged hippie. Her voice had the same fullness as Steve's.

Joanna was led into a large room with a fire blazing in an open cast-iron hearth at the far end. The furniture was characterized by its weight rather than by any apparent comfort; what a second-hand dealer might have called "much loved". The walls had been left unplastered, with whitewash over the rough-hewn stones. Here and there were pictures and hangings, an odd mixture— so far as Joanna's untrained eye could ascertain— of ancient and modern, fine and garbage. Getting up from one of the overstuffed armchairs gathered around the fire was a man of about fifty whom Joanna guessed must be Gilmour père.

"Vic Gilmour," he said, smiling, extending a massive hand towards her. "And you're Jill Soames's niece. We were so devastated to hear of her death. Ronnie took to her bed for a day to get over it."

But none of you thought to go to the funeral, Joanna thought resentfully. *She was such a good friend of you all that Steve and Tony were supposed to call her Aunt Jill, and yet you didn't walk a hundred yards to see her stuck into the ground. Too shy? Too shy of what the villagers would think? Or didn't you really know her that well? Hmm?*

"We wanted to come to the funeral," said Vic Gilmour, as if he had heard her thoughts, "but it wouldn't have been right. That was a time for the people of Tarburton to express their grief, not for outsiders like us."

"But Aunt Jill was an outsider herself," said Joanna, moving to the chair Vic had indicated. "She wouldn't have . . . minded."

"A drink?" said Ronnie, coming to the fireside. She'd got a trail of flour on the sleeve of her dress, which was more than Greta of the Crafts Centre ever allowed herself.

As the evening progressed Joanna found herself thawing to this family. She'd thought that Vic was merely giving excuses when he'd said that they'd been reluctant to trespass at her aunt's funeral, but soon she came to realize that he'd been perfectly serious: the Gilmours really did feel like interlopers, like gypsies who would naturally be resented by the community among which they'd parked their caravans for a while. Soon Joanna began to recognize that they were seeking in her a kindred spirit, just as presumably they must have sought out Aunt Jill when first they'd come here.

Over soup—which was Unidentifiable Country Vegetable or Country Unidentifiable Vegetable, she couldn't make up her mind—she wondered if Steve or Tony had told their parents anything of her drunken outpouring last night. If so, there was no trace of the knowledge in the two older people's eyes. Vic and Ronnie seemed concerned to be as frank and open with her as possible, and to make sure she knew this. She wasn't sure she much enjoyed that part of the experience—it was like a stranger who insists on standing too close to you.

The main course was a triumph, and by then the wine they'd been drinking had started to work its relaxing magic. Cutting into a slab of pork that had been marinated in cider and some herbs she didn't recognize, Joanna began to feel more at ease with the world than she had since arriving in Tarburton. The conversation had veered away from her and Aunt Jill and anything to do with current circumstances towards politics, which in a paradoxical way was safer territory. They were all good liberals, of course, as she'd known they would be—and as she was herself—and they bemoaned the difficulties of getting hold of the *Guardian* or the *Independent* regularly down here in the wilds. Yet as the discussion progressed—she held herself back any time she felt herself becoming too prescriptive—she discovered that the Gilmours' knowledge of their subject matter was oddly . . . amateurish. They were going through the motions, it seemed: they were saying most of the right words, and in general they were saying them in the right order, but there were *gaps*. Midway through a mouthful of strawberries and ice cream Ronnie said something about the former Yugoslavia that let Joanna perceive that the woman had the country positioned in the wrong continent—somewhere to the east of Moscow. And Steve described Nelson Mandela as head of the CIA rather than the ANC without any of the rest of the family seeming to notice the slip.

If Joanna had been a little more sober or a little drunker she might have been more concerned by these lapses, but she was too full of her hosts' generosity and wine to give the matter too much thought. She was reminded of a couple of right-wing *Sun* readers she'd once met in a seaside hotel who'd sombrely told her that Shirley Porter was deputy leader of the Labour Party. It was reasonable for the people at the other end of the political spectrum to be equally vague about such irritations as *facts*: no one section of society should be allowed a monopoly on ignorance.

"How long are you staying down here for?" Vic asked her once they were sitting back around the fire again. He'd poured brandies for them all except Ronnie, who'd pleaded migraine. "Now that the funeral's over, and all."

"I thought," said Joanna, shy now she was voicing the idea, "that I might come down and live here for good—well, for a few years, anyway. My aunt was—well, not wealthy exactly, but not poor either. The flat's mine, and there's enough money invested to give me three-quarters of an income. I thought I might see if I could drum up some freelance work to make the other quarter."

"Tired of London, eh?" said Vic, smiling encouragingly at her. "But obviously not tired of life."

The remark threw her. It wasn't something she'd thought about before. The truth was, now she came to confront it head-on, that perhaps she *was* tired of life, too, in a way. The past six months had given her more of "life" than she could have wanted in a decade. Maybe a large part of her urge to kick the dust and soot of London off her feet was that she wanted to leave that sort of life—what the Chinese curse calls interesting times—behind her as well.

Once again she had the disconcerting sensation that Vic could tell her thoughts.

"That's not what I meant," he said. "I meant tired of *living*. You have so much vitality locked up inside you, young Joanna Gard, and you seem just to let it out in small, carefully measured doses. Maybe you're wise. You seem to me to have more life inside you than all the rest of us put together."

Joanna laughed, embarrassed. "Not true!" she said, throwing up her hands. "Look at your children, Vic. Look at Steve. Look at Tony. Can't you feel the vitality pouring off them?"

"No," he said flatly. "Not the same way you have it."

She looked up, alarmed. Then she relaxed: at some stage while they'd been talking the two younger Gilmours must have slipped out of the room.

"I don't know what you mean by that," she said slowly.

"Haven't you noticed anything odd about this village?"

"Well—yes." She took another sip of brandy and rolled it around the inside of her teeth. "Yes. Everything seems to be sort of slowly winding down, as if the people were getting tired, or something. They're still the same people all right—I'm not talking any *Invasion of the Body Snatchers* stuff—but they seem sort of *resigned*, sort of *lethargic*. Sort of dying from the inside out, like my aunt did . . . "

What a horrible thought. She'd begun to connect up Aunt Jill's wilting with the quietness in the Blue Horse and the sense of futility she felt clinging to all of the village's foci, but that had been before Aunt Jill's death. The event had shocked her out of any temptation towards introspection; it had made her concentrate on living through the surface layers of each day, unwilling to let her thoughts paddle any more deeply than was necessary to guide her to the next place where she'd be safe from the waves. But talking with Vic was making her stop dodging the waves any longer—and as she looked up into his brown eyes, which seemed softer than before, she realized he had deliberately guided her to this state.

"You think there's something really . . . really *wrong* here, don't you?" she said. Her voice was hardly more than a whisper, barely loud enough for him to have heard it above the crackle of the logs in the hearth.

"I wouldn't like to put it as strongly as that," he said, shifting uneasily in his seat. "It just seems . . . Well, I've heard of dying villages and ghost towns before, but those have always been just metaphorical terms. Here in Tarburton it's as if the metaphors are being made real—reified, if that's a word you use."

"I'm a publisher's editor," she said archly. "Was."

He chuckled. The spell that had seemed to be settling down around them dissipated. "We've both maybe been reading too much creepy fiction," he said. "Watching the wrong sort of movies. Looking at something perfectly innocent and assuming there must be some dark secret lying at the heart of it all."

"I wish I could say I agreed with you—entirely," said Joanna, suddenly serious again. "But there *is* something creepy here, you know. Take Jas, the landlord of the Blue Horse. I never much liked the old bastard—his racism is hard to stomach, just for a start—but you always used to . . . to know when he was around, if you like: he was hail-fellow-well-met with a vengeance, telling jokes or losing his temper or *something*. But now he's like a ghost of himself. He looks like a set of articulated clothes-hangers walking around under cover of a tweed suit, and it's as if his personality were the same. He's *there*, but he's *not* there at the same time. He used to be himself: now he's rather like the bar-tender in a grotty old Western movie—there's an actor in the rôle, but he doesn't actually have to *do* anything except be the Standard-Issue Bar-Tender."

This time when she looked at Vic's eyes she saw pain in them. "We were very fond of your Aunt Jill, you know, Joanna," he said quietly.

"Are you two having a nice old heart-to-heart?" said Steve from the door. "We've been doing all the washing up and stopping Mum from whacking into the cooking sherry."

Vic grinned. "Liar," he said to his son. "You mean you've been in the kitchen getting in the women's way, more like."

"How could you be so cruel?"

This, thought Joanna as she turned in her seat, *is the man I thought was so goddam attractive when we first met? Bloody hell, but the usually 100% reliable Gard Hormonal Targeting Device sure came a cropper with this one.*

Though she smiled politely, as if Steve had said something witty, and not too long after that it was time to go home.

Alone.

5

Night Times

The squashed-flat creature who was Joanna had managed to manoeuvre herself close to a crumbling earth-column in the desert and was trying to wrap her body around it. The top of the column, less eroded by the sands than the rest, overhung just enough that it might—it *should*—cast a shallow necklace of shadow onto the ground beneath. If she could somehow lever herself up vertically, so that she could make herself like a cuff . . .

No. The rules of this place forbade it. There was nothing she could imagine that could logically stop her from achieving her aim, but she knew almost from the outset that doing so would be impossible. That was the way this particular existence was scripted. It was her lot in life to remain horizontal at all times, with her single eye turned ever towards the sky.

Her eye didn't have the capacity to weep, but she imagined it blurring with tears. Even those tears might have provided some respite from the ferocity of the sky's brilliance; doubtless that was why crying was impossible, too.

The Girl Child LoChi was coming. That prospect was her only succour. The thoughts of the other creatures like herself drifted in and out of her own, and always there was the same undercurrent: that at last, after all these uncountable millennia, the Girl Child LoChi was coming to bring shadows to the sky.

The Joanna-creature slowly, inch by agonizing inch, dragged herself away from the earth-pillar. It was better to be nowhere near it than to see it close by, enticing her with promises of blissful shadow it could not in the event grant her. Some of the others had heard rumours of water—the first open water that anyone had discovered in living memory—and they were heading in the direction the rumours dictated. The Joanna-creature knew that the expedition was a waste of time—that it was every bit as futile as her attempt had been to harvest the shadow of the earth-column—but she decided to go along with them anyway.

Every location in this nightmare place contained the same amount of pain.

#

There were more stars in the sky than was possible.

At least, that was Joanna's first thought when she looked up from the side of the tor at the velvet of the night. The moon, close to the full, had set a couple of hours ago, and the last vestiges of its milky light were gone from the horizon. The tor itself was invisible, although she could feel its bulk near her. She and the two younger Gilmours had taken her bumped red Mini on the spur of the moment, after the pubs had closed, and driven out here onto the moor. Now they were in the middle of an area that seemed of infinite extent and totally devoid of people, except for the distant whisper of the traffic on the A38 and the occasional flash of headlights, somewhere far away, as a farmer headed for home. The darkness made the world featureless. *Rather like my recurring dream,* thought Joanna as she breathed deeply of the cold air—it was as if she were inhaling cold, pure starlight. *Only there the sky is one single ceiling of fire, and here it's blackness spotted with ice crystals. How jealous my friends there would be if they could see me now.*

"They say there are ghosts out here," said Steve cheerfully at her side.

"You can see why," Tony said. She'd borrowed an old fur coat from her mother—synthetic fur, of course—and the fluffy ruff around her neck made her look like an Elizabethan portrait. "I bet the tor is haunted. And there're those funny constructions near the road back towards Tarburton—rings hollowed out of stone, and little cones. I bet our prehistoric ancestors knew a thing or two about the ghosts around here and built those megaliths to propitiate them."

"I bet our prehistoric ancestors *are* the ghosts around here," said Joanna, and the three of them laughed. She felt what Tony was feeling, though: as if millions of tiny eyes might be peering at them inquisitively from the crevices of the tor. Yet the sensation didn't repel her—rather the other way around, in fact: it was as if Tarburton were undetectably dying, so that it was preferable to be out here in the presence of the fully dead. Or something. She didn't want to dwell on it for too long. No—one other realization: there was a taint of something like malice enveloping the village, but that was completely lacking around here. The ghosts of the tor weren't friendly, but on the other

44

hand neither were they malevolent: their existence was too divorced from that of mere human beings, their mentalities too different, for them to bear their mundane counterparts either good *or* ill will.

"Werewolves as well, I should think," said Steve. "And the Beast of Dartmoor."

"I thought it was Exmoor that had the Beast," said Joanna.

"Oh, I'm sure Dartmoor has one as well," breezed Steve. "In fact, I'm sure that Dartmoor says to Exmoor, 'Huh! Anything you can do I can do better, because I'm bigger than you. You've got the Beast—well, I'll show you: I'm going to have *hundreds* of them.'"

Joanna giggled at the thought of the squabble. "Hundreds of very small, perfectly formed Beasts?" she suggested.

"No, tishwash, woman!" He patted her too roughly between the shoulder-blades. "We're not dealing with any little soft, cuddly, children's-tv-style monsters here. The Beasts of Dartmoor are bound to be enormous, ravening creatures, with their naked fangs dripping luminous goo in the moonlight—isn't that right, sis?"

"If you say so, Steve," said Tony's voice from the darkness. She sounded bored of her brother.

"They're like werewolves, only a lot viciouser and a lot less susceptible to reason. That's what I think. Can't you see them, Joanna? Can't you *hear* them?"

He threw his head back and let out a long, vibrating howl. The sound vanished into the night, echoless.

"Stop that," said Tony calmly. "You'll have the cops out here to see what's going on."

"Piffle! There aren't any plodders within twenty miles of here!" He let out another yell, even louder than before.

Joanna felt an edge of ice running up her spine. The ghosts of the tor might be real—in fact, she was perfectly willing to concede, now, that they were—but they didn't frighten her half as much as this overgrown youth imitating something much darker, something crueller, something born from the human imagination rather than from the timeless rocks.

"Yes, do shut up, Steve," she said, hearing the uncertainty in her own voice. "It's . . . "

She couldn't bring herself to admit out loud that he was scaring her, but it must have been obvious at least to Tony that this was what she'd been trying to say.

"Yes, put a fucking sock in it, Steve. We're out here to enjoy ourselves, not to watch you put on the fucking Gang Show."

But:

"Can't you imagine them, Joanna?" he whispered. She could feel the wind of his breath on her ear. "Can't you see them playing in the moonlight, dancing and fighting and spinning around each other, secure in the knowledge that no one can see them? Doesn't it make your blood sing to think of them doing that, Joanna?"

"No."

"Not even a little bit?"

"No. It just reminds me that I'm cold."

She felt him retreat from her. The night seemed to have grown even blacker, because now she could make out nothing at all of her two companions.

"Think of them," said Tony—not Steve this time. "Think of them playing so free under the stars." Tony's voice had taken on extra sibilants.

"Stop pissing about, you two." She should have left a light on in the Mini, but she hadn't wanted to spoil the starscape. Now she hadn't a clue where the car was. "Unless you want to have to find your own way home on foot."

Steve's response—she was pretty sure it was Steve—was yet another of those long ululations. The noise seemed to be travelling away from her, as if he were sprinting across the rough surface of the moor. She could envisage him with his arms thrown out to either side and his head arched back, yelling madly at the sky like an animal.

Like a werewolf.

"Tony," she said, no longer trying to conceal the nervousness in her voice. "Tony, for God's sake can't you try to get your brother under control?" She tried a good-sport laugh, but it didn't sound very convincing.

Tony said nothing, but there was an answering howl from the direction in which Joanna had last seen the girl.

"That's synthetic fur you're wearing," she bellowed. "Not the real stuff."

There were answering howls on both sides. More than two of them, it seemed. She looked directly upwards at the stars, half-expecting to see strange silhouettes occulting them; but the sky was impassive.

"This isn't funny any more!" she screamed. "Stop it! I thought you were my friends!"

There were certainly more than two people raising their voices in that long, bestial chorus. Half the moor seemed to be alive with noise. And it wasn't just the howling. Sometimes she could hear heavy, ragged panting, like big dogs make when they've run themselves to exhaustion.

The car must be down that way. I'm sure that's how we came up from the road. Just keep your senses together, lass, and you'll find your way out of here. No problem. Think of Dunkirk. Think of getting to the lavs at a rock festival. Think of how brave Aunt Jill would be, in these circumstances.

She turned her ankle on a stone and let out a yip of pain as she went down. Her body hammered against the hard, cropped ground, and for a few seconds she was incapable of breathing. The wild cacophony of the werewolves—she was certain by now they were werewolves—continued unabated.

She rolled over onto her back. Just a couple of minutes ago she'd been bathing appreciatively in the cool disinterest of the stars; now she found it loathsome.

"Stop it, you two!" she screamed. "For the love of God, just *stop* it!"

Now she could hear their paws. On the rough grass of the moor itself, cropped short by ponies and sheep, the wolves' feet made a steady swishing noise, like intermittently running water. When they crossed the road, though, their claws skittered like gravel thrown onto a sloping roof. There seemed to be hundreds of the creatures milling around her.

But she couldn't *see* anything.

And they were making no apparent move to attack her.

The agony from her ankle was subsiding quickly—she couldn't have hurt it badly. *Keep collected, Joanna,* she seemed to hear Aunt Jill's voice saying to her. *Keep collected and you'll be able to find a way out of this. Pretend it's something you're more accustomed to—imagine it's an interview for a job you don't much like but* have *to get . . . that your life depends on your getting it!* Which was just about the case, thought Joanna dourly. But Aunt Jill's voice wasn't finished with her yet. *Think!* it urged. *Use the evidence of your senses. Think, girl! Think!*

It was easy enough for Aunt Jill to say that: she was well and truly dead and out of it all. She wasn't lying on her back in the middle of Dartmoor with nothing visible but the stars overhead and just the sound of a million werewolves in her ears. And the beasts were coming closer to her now, as if earlier they'd been afraid of her human-ness but were now learning to conquer their timidity. She felt a hot gust of wind against her cheek, and smelt rotting meat.

Oh, all right then: she'd *think*, just like Aunt Jill told her to. She'd use the evidence of her senses. Sight wasn't going to do her any good, but hearing . . .

The brittle sound the werewolves made as they slid on the hard tarmac of the road.

The Mini was parked on the road.

She rolled onto her belly and started to writhe forward, serpent-like.

The pack knew what she was doing immediately. Interspersed among all the other noises there were now whimpers of doubt, as if none of them had known she could move. She tried snarling herself, just to give the creatures something to think about, but the sound came out thin and pathetic.

She pulled herself up onto her hands and knees. Her handbag tangled with her arm, and she coughed with astonishment to discover she hadn't lost the thing somewhere back in the blackness. There were cigarettes in there—ye gods, but she could do with a cigarette right now.

Silly idea.

But there was a box of matches nestling alongside the Lambert & Butler's. And wolves were supposed to be terrified of fire—werewolves maybe likewise, although she was less certain of that.

She scrabbled at the catch of the bag, bending one fingernail back, almost tearing it. Suddenly the clasp leapt open, spilling some of her stuff out onto the ground.

She patted her free hand around on the grass, feeling for the matches. No, dammit—that was the little travel box she sometimes used for Tampax. Ah—there they were.

One of the creatures came pounding past, very close to her. She kicked out at it, missed. Now that she had the matchbox in her hand she was beginning to feel more assured. She let out the most ferocious yell she could manage, and this time it was nothing like the forlorn little bleat she'd produced earlier.

There was an answering chorus from the wolves, but she persuaded herself that she could detect further signs of uncertainty in their sounds.

She fumbled the matchbox open—the tray was the right way up, for a wonder—and tugged one of the matches out. She ran her finger along the length of it, feeling for the smooth knob of the head.

Gotcha.

Letting a smile spread across her face, she deliberately ran the match-head hard along the abrasive strip.

Nothing.

She felt the match-head erupt beneath her fingertip.

She heard the little explosion.

She dropped the match as the flame seared her hand.

But there was no light.

#

She awoke to the sound of a doorbell, ringing insistently.

She sat up in bed, instinctively gathering the bedclothes around her shoulders. What time was it? She must have had a few too many at the Blue Horse last night, because she couldn't remember putting on her pyjamas and getting into bed. Yet her head wasn't nagging her, the way it had too many mornings these past ten days or so.

Whoever was at the door pressed the bell again, a long, long peal.

"I'm coming," she said crossly. "Have a bit of patience, can't you?"

She fell into her dressing-gown and made for the landing. As she passed her dressing-table she saw the time on the alarm clock there: 11:32 said the red numbers accusingly.

She *had* slept in. She must have needed the rest, that was all she could think: Aunt Jill's death and then the funeral and the way Vic Gilmour had been so amiable and intimate and in the summation so creepy the other night and then . . .

And then there'd been *last* night, out on the moor.

The wolves.

The *were*wolves.

The matches that wouldn't light.

She didn't know if she wanted to answer the door. If she was going to find Steve Gilmour standing there, his smug smile already in place . . .

On the other hand, it might *not* be Steve Gilmour, and she desperately needed some human company, someone whose words—*whatever* they were talking about—would wash away the memories of the terror she'd felt out on the moor when she'd realized that not even a burning flame would puncture the darkness.

49

She pattered down the stairs in her bare feet, feeling the friendly roughness of the old carpet.

It was Ronnie Gilmour.

"Come in," Joanna said. "I'm in a mess, the flat's in a mess, you won't believe the . . . "

Ronnie grinned. "Heard you three had quite a night of it," she said. "Steve was all for coming across here himself to find out if you were all right, but I told him this wasn't any job for a mere man. Besides, I didn't think you'd thank him for seeing you with a hangover."

"I don't have a hangover."

"Well, you *should*, if half of what my pair have told me is true. Come on, let me in and I'll make you a cup of coffee."

"Yes. I said yes. Do come in. Make yourself at home. I haven't moved things around since my aunt . . . since Aunt Jill, you know . . . so you shouldn't have any trouble finding things. I'll throw on some clothes and . . ."

"Are you *sure* you're all right? Tony said it was quite a crack you took on your skull. Maybe you should have Dr Grasmere take a look at it before you go bounding around like this."

They were in the kitchen by now, Joanna poised to dash on upstairs to her room. Ronnie did indeed seem to know her way around, filling the kettle with one hand as she reached out with the other for the coffee jar. Joanna had a brief hallucination that it was Aunt Jill standing there, not this woman whom she hardly knew, but then everything returned to normal. Maybe she *had* taken a bump on the head after all. That was the trouble with concussion: it made you forget the fact that there must have been something that concussed you.

"I'll just be a moment," she said weakly. "I'll just throw on my jeans."

"Take as long as you like." Ronnie was smiling at her, much as Aunt Jill would have done. Not the Aunt Jill who had died—the other one, the one she'd known most of her life.

"No, I'll be just a minute." It was abruptly very important to Joanna that Ronnie should realize this. "I really won't be more than a minute or two."

Ronnie turned back to the kettle.

In her bedroom, Joanna stripped out of her pyjamas, then realized she needed to go to the loo. Naked, she darted across the landing. On the way back, walking more casually, she chanced to glance downstairs, and saw Ronnie Gilmour on the lower landing, gazing emotionlessly up at her. She put on a smile and dashed back into her own room.

These Gilmours are getting to be a bit much, she thought hotly as she struggled into her blue jeans. *(If my bum weren't so big I wouldn't have so much trouble getting into my jeans. Tomorrow I start slimming. Definitely. Cross my heart.) The bloody woman comes charging in here as if she owns the place, then starts peeping-tomming at me. I've a good mind to . . .*

Downstairs, she said: "Sorry about that. I forgot to put my dressing-gown on."

"It's all right," said Ronnie easily, passing her a mugful of coffee. The mugs were Joanna's innovation since the funeral: she was collecting the naffest she could find. This one welcomed her to Paignton with a picture of a man with his willy sticking out of his y-fronts. "I shouldn't have been looking. But I was just worried about you, you see—we're *all* worried about you. All us Gilmours, you know."

"I'm not sure how much I *do* know you Gilmours," said Joanna slowly. She ought to ask Ronnie through to the drawing-room, but for some reason she didn't want to.

"Well, of course, it's only been a few days, but I'd begun to hope that . . ."

"What did Steve and Tony say happened to me last night?" Joanna interrupted.

"Can't you remember?"

"No." *Well, put it this way, I'm certainly not going to tell you what I remember. They're your children, after all.*

"The three of you went out for a drive on the moor after Jas chucked you out of the Blue Horse."

"I remember that bit." Joanna took a sip of her coffee. It could have been Coke for all she knew.

"And you parked out there by one of the tors, and Steve had a bottle of whisky with him."

"And I don't remember that bit."

Ronnie coughed. "Well, maybe it's better if you don't remember some of the next bit, either."

"No. Go on. I want to know." She tapped the rim of her Paignton mug against the tips of her lower teeth. "I want to know everything."

"Well, you all three got a bit . . . well, *tiddly,* don't you know, and—well, perhaps Steve and Tony are a bit more used to drinking than you are, or maybe they'd had less back in the Blue Horse, but you suddenly were very ill."

"Sick, you mean? I puked?" *I didn't. If I had there'd still be some of that scummy saltiness in my mouth, no matter how hard I scrubbed my teeth later.*

"No, not exactly that—or, at least, I don't know about that. Do you really want me to go on?"

"Every last bit of it."

"Well, you started . . . you know, *making up* to Steve, making up to him in a very sort of physical sort of way, if you understand my meaning. Don't get me wrong!" Ronnie Gilmour held up her palm to forestall any objection Joanna might make. "I don't make any moral judgements. You and Steve can get up to whatever you want to. But not, I don't think, in front of Tony."

Joanna found herself grinning.

"Carry on," she said.

"Well . . . "

"Do you need to start every sentence with 'well'?"

"Well, I . . . Are you *sure* you want me to carry on? I only came here to see you weren't seriously injured, you know."

"I'm sorry. It's just that what you're telling me is so radically different from my memories."

Ronnie Gilmour paused before continuing.

"After Steve had told you that your actions were . . . well, *inappropriate* . . . the two of them tried to get you back to the car. But you struggled." Ronnie Gilmour drained her coffee. It was obvious she was nearly at the end of her tale. "You slipped out of their arms and tried to run away, but you fell and hit your head on a stone."

"I did? But I don't have a cut or a bump or a bruise." Joanna felt around the back of her head to make sure this was the truth. It was. "I seem to have miraculous powers of recovery."

"Well, I'm not going to examine your head, young miss. I'm just going by what Steve and Tony told me this morning. Tony, who seems to have been the only one of the three of you sober enough to know exactly what was going on, drove you both back here and got you into bed. Then she did the same for her brother, at our place."

"Steve told you this?"

"Yes."

That didn't come as a shock, somehow.

"And Tony?"

"Just the same."

And that *was* something of a surprise. She'd assumed Tony would have more . . . integrity. But then Tony had been howling as loudly as her brother, out there in the place where even naked flames couldn't show a light.

"Word for word," added Ronnie Gilmour for emphasis.

Ah—*that* made more sense. Tony had been doing what her brother told her.

"I'm afraid that my recollections of what went on last night are still very different from those recounted by your offspring," said Joanna with straining dignity. "And now, if you will excuse me, I have things to do this morning."

"Quite," said Ronnie, coldly but without any apparent rancour—indeed, if anything, she seemed to Joanna to be relieved that she was being let off so lightly. "I have things to do as well. Perhaps we'll be seeing you around."

"Perhaps."

#

Fifteen minutes later, relaxing in her bath, Joanna felt her bruised ankle. That part of it was real, at least—only, she could just as easily have twisted it when falling out of Steve's arms. Her fingernail, the one she'd twisted back when she was trying to get her bag open—that was tender, too. But there were a hundred and one other ways she could have done that.

She couldn't prove, even to herself, that her own account of events was the true one, and that Steve and Tony Gilmour were lying.

Couldn't prove it, even though what had happened was as bizarre, as fantasticated, as any nightmare. The Gilmour children's explanation was a lot easier to accept, unless you happened to be the person who'd lived through the reality.

She was certain she was right.

It was just then, soaping her knee, that she realized last night was the first for ages that she hadn't had the dream about being in the world where the advent of the Girl Child LoChi was so desperately anticipated.

6

Alas, Poor Jas

Joanna spent the next few days smoking too much, drinking too much and trying to work out the solutions to two riddles: first, what had happened that night on the moor, and why the two young Gilmours had lied so comprehensively about it; and, second, the reason—if any—for the symmetry that existed between her experience on the moor and the recurring dream of the light-saturated world. On the moor the sky had been unrelievedly black, save for the stars' pinpoints, and even the flame of the match had shown no light; while in the world of her dreams there was no escape from the sky's radiance, no merciful shadows even in the lee of tall objects. There had been noise on the moor, the cries of large animals and the racket of their rapid movements; while in the desert the sluggish creatures of which she herself seemed to be one made no noise as they slithered from each almost identical site to the next.

Had the dreams been some kind of forewarning of the reality, skewed into oppositeness as precognitive dreams so often were? Or was it possible that the reality had, in some way she couldn't properly understand, sparked off the dreams ahead of time? A third possibility, one that she didn't much like to think about, was that in some obscure fashion the dreams might have *triggered* the reality. But if that were the case then she had to re-examine her whole notion of what the word "reality" meant. She was not prepared to accept that her recollections of events on the moor were illusory, but neither was she able to accommodate mentally the concept of solid, basic, physical reality being sculpted by something as transitory as dreaming—as soon accept the possibility that someone could dream the world was flat and wake the next morning to discover that indeed it had become so.

But, if the events of that bleak black night had been brought into being by the dreams—as a reaction to them, perhaps: a form of psychological enantiopathy—and if, at the same time, reality was some kind of tangible, inalterable substrate to the universe, then how could the two be reconciled?

Only, she mused, if there were varying *degrees* of reality, different *types* of it, different *qualities* of it. And here her mind rebelled. The whole line of speculation was beginning to lead her into territory that she regarded as mystic claptrap: today pondering the nature of reality, tomorrow signing up as a full-time Hare Krishna zombie—no sirree!

Something else puzzled her, but, because of the amount of scotch she was drinking, she couldn't bring her mind to focus on it. She was fully aware that matters had gone seriously awry in the village of Tarburton-by-the-Moor, and that in the normal way she'd be trying to call the attention of the authorities to what was going on— or, at the very least, she'd be trying to get away—but there was something stopping her from doing either of these two things. Something more than just the lethargy induced by the booze, although that was undoubtedly playing its part: when she wasn't reeling from the debilitating effects of last night's excesses she was already half- or entirely pissed from the morning's.

#

She didn't go out much during those few days, except to fetch further supplies of cigarettes, whisky and food from the International Stores down on the corner of Queen Street and Regent Street. But, even as lacking in alertness as she was, she couldn't help noticing that the little supermarket was like a haunt of its customary self rather than the real thing: the assistants behind the cheese counter and at the check-out were pale and listless, and spent most of their time playing with their nails or chatting dully because of the dearth of customers. She felt obscurely glad, once she'd signed her cheque and loaded up her carrier bags, to be scuttling out of the place and into the fresh air.

She kept these excursions as brief as possible, and made no detours: she just went straight down West Street to the junction, crossed over, into the shop, and then back home again, not looking to right or left. If she had had any courage, she kept telling herself, she'd have made a point of confronting the Gilmours rather than avoiding them; but there was always a good reason why it would be better for the moment of confrontation to be put off until tomorrow.

Life just . . . flowed on, at a very low ebb. She hoped that ghosts didn't exist, because Aunt Jill would be horrified at the kind of existence her solitary niece was leading but even the image of that erect, vital figure, with her grey hair in its neat curls and her mouth drawn into a featureless tight line of contempt, didn t have the power to drag Joanna out of her laggardly abyss. And she didn t *want* to be dragged out of it: she was honest enough to recognize this, and accept it. The longer she continued this half-existence, the longer she could delay the moment when she had to accommodate herself to reality—or reality to herself.

And so it was back to the nature of reality again, and from there into conjectures about the wolves on the moor, and from there . . .

The circle was unbroken.

#

On the Sunday night Mike phoned.

"Darling! Is that you?" His voice was distorted on the line, and for a few moments she thought someone must have rung the wrong number. She'd got out of the habit of thinking of herself as anybody's darling.

"Who's there?" she said guardedly.

"Mike. That *is* you, isn't it?"

"Mike—Joanna."

"Darling, I've been worried about you. No word for nearly a fortnight."

"You're not responsible for me any longer," she said, knowing she was being unfair. "We're not an item any longer: we're two individuals."

She hunkered down beside the telephone and put her back up against the landing wall. One of Aunt Jill's cacti served as an ashtray.

"That's easy enough to say." Mike's voice, even through the *Hitch Hikers' Guide to the Galaxy* effects, was obviously distressed. "You can't just draw a curtain over the past and pretend it never happened."

"You no longer have any claims on me," she said. *It's easier to put it that way around than to admit to him the great act of betrayal I've performed. It was his fetus as much as mine that was flushed away at the clinic. I took that fetus from him without his permission.* "If you hadn't got it into your head that you owned me, maybe we'd still be together. But we're not. That's over."

"I'm trying to be your friend, darling. One of the things that friends are *for* is to look out for each other. I'm not making any claims on you."

"Same difference."

"Oh, *shit*! We're getting into an argument again. Do *you* want an argu-

56

ment? No?"

"Of course I don't. There's nothing left between us to argue about."

There was a long enough silence on the line—if the sound-effects for an electric toaster going berserk could be called silence—that she began to wonder if he'd hung up on her. She deserved to be hung up on. She took another swig from the bottle and told herself she enjoyed being a bitch, and, anyway, Mike was such a doormat that he deserved whatever shit got wiped on him.

"You're all right?" He was there again.

"Yes."

"You're not lying, are you? Just to not worry me? If you like, I could get in the car and be with you by the morning."

"I'm fine. Everything's brilliant. Aunt Jill's died—did I tell you that?—and I've inherited the lot, although it'll be a few months before all the papers have been signed. Oh, yes, and I've decided to stay down here in Tarburton rather than live in London any longer: I'm going to be a country girl from now on, and go around with muddy boots and a straw in my mouth. Apart from that, though, it's been just another humdrum fortnight in sleepy little Tarburton-by-the-Moor." *Or should I tell him about the night when a pack of creatures that could have been werewolves stretched around me from one side of the moor to the other? Or the way that Aunt Jill's life was drawn from her, sucked out as if by a vampire's bite? Or the way that, every now and then, I catch myself fancying Tony Gilmour, which is a new and not entirely welcome development so far as I'm concerned though at least she couldn't get me pregnant the way Mike did? No, better tell him none of these things. They'd only make him pile into the car, like he threatened, and come down here to make everything even more complicated and even worse . . .*

"You're still there? Joanna?"

"I'm still here."

"Your voice sounds funny. Are you *sure* there's nothing wrong?"

"It's a fundamental impossibility that my voice should sound any funnier than yours," she said deliberately. "Impossibility" was something of a triumph. "The BBC Radiophonic Workshop would be proud of what Telecom's doing for you."

He laughed, observing the protocols. "You sound a bit newted," he said at last.

"I am. I'm allowed to be. I told you, I'm a free person, now."

"You always were."

"Sez you."

"You know you were. Don't let's get into that again. All I was trying to say was . . . "

". . . that if I ever get into any trouble or difficulties, you'll always be there to help me out. I knew that already. Your script's beginning to repeat itself rather too often, Mike."

There was another of those crackling, explosive pauses. When he spoke again his voice sounded much fainter, as if Ford Prefect were retreating across the galaxy.

"You're not a very easy person to be a friend of, Joanna."

"I never said I was."

She put the phone down, feeling in some obscure way that she'd scored a point, but almost immediately it rang again.

"Joanna? We got cut off."

This time his voice was as clear as if he'd been in the next room.

"Spose so," she said.

"Are you going to be coming up to London any time soon?"

"Maybe in a week or two. I've got to see Rinaldo about terminating the lease on the flat, and I've got to sort out how I'm going to get everything down here."

"I can help with the van," he said. She'd known he would—she'd been relying on his van—but at the same time she hated him for his predictability. *It's a good job you like being bitchy, Joanna my lass, because you do it so well and such a hell of a lot of the time.*

"If you want to," she said.

"I do." He breathed heavily. "Just don't let yourself ever forget that I'm your friend, darling. I don't ask to be anything more than that, I realize the way . . . "

"Don't," she said. "Don't go on. I'm happy you're my friend." *Now I'm sounding patronizing, which is surely way more than the poor guy deserves.* "Let's just leave it at that, hey?"

"Yeah." His voice was subdued. She knew him well enough to know that he'd been hoping for something more, telling himself not to hope for it, and was now disappointed that his non-expectations hadn't been fulfilled.

"I love you," she said out of habit, then hurried to make amends. "I mean, I love you as a friend. I'm not *in love* with you. It's different."

"Yeah. I know. Night, Joanna."

She relented a little.

"You're one of the good guys, you know, Mike? Maybe people don't tell you that often enough. Maybe *I* don't tell you that often enough."

"Yeah. Joanna, it's late: I've got to be up early in the morning. Night-night. Sweet dreams. Don't let the beasties . . . "

She slammed the phone down, and lit a cigarette fiercely. She tilted back the bottle and drank deeply, the whisky seeming to scorch the tender inside of her throat.

How do you stop *the beasties biting when there's a moorful of them and only the one of you?*

You bite them first, I guess.

But what if you have no teeth?

#

It was a couple of nights later that the dream presented itself to her in its fullest manifestation yet.

The world of the Wardrobe Folk, and the Wardrobe Folk themselves, were brought into existence at the same time as the rest of the universes of the polycosmos by the god Qinmeartha, known to the other gods as "the Insane"—for surely only an insane god would wish to create existence, and then to continue to tamper with what went on in it. Qinmeartha had initially revelled in the glories of his creation, but after a few billions of years he had come to resent the way that the other gods mocked him, and he had begun to avenge himself on his creations. In those days the world (which had never been named, even by Qinmeartha himself, who was better at making worlds than naming them) of the Wardrobe Folk was a balmy, temperate place, with forests covering much of the land and broad grey clouds often in the sky. Each of the Wardrobe Folk had been attended by their personal angel, who hovered always overhead and had voluminous black wings that could be spread wide whenever the person required greater shade. It was always summer, in the world that used to be, with the trees eternally panoplied in protective leaves; but the summer was a cool one.

The Wardrobe Folk had speech then, and music, and eyelids. They built tall houses, ascending and descending between the floors using ramps. They were not immortal: they bred in groups of three or more, imitating their god by producing offspring before they died; perhaps, in that case, they were possessed also by something of his insanity, but what is madness in a god is benign necessity in a mortal.

Pastoral days.

Soon ended.

Qinmeartha could not express his wrath against the other gods, for their retaliation would have destroyed him and then, as an afterthought, the universes he had brought into being, so that there would have been nothing at all of him left. But the mortals who dwelt within his universes were without power, and he had long ago—without knowing why he was doing so—designed them so that they could experience pain to a depth of excruciation beyond, although he did not admit this, even what a god could suffer.

Qinmeartha the Insane God, in the cosmic glory of his spite, took away the shadows from the universes. Everywhere there was unalleviated light, so that nothing could escape being seen. He drove the angels who had ever accompanied the Wardrobe Folk into invisibility and intangibility, so that, while they were still there hovering overhead—this was a matter of knowledge that transcended faith among the Wardrobe Folk—they could no longer interpose their dark wings between the lurid sky and the wide eyes of their wards. The flaring sunlight—the luminance of Qinmeartha—stripped the leaves from the trees and then the bark from the branches and at last the branches from the boles; and the rivers and seas dried away to leave a world of sands. All the myriad sounds that the world had been accustomed to enjoy were replaced by just one: that of the wind blowing dry sand over dry sand; the music and speech of the Wardrobe Folk had died along with the rest. The Insane God burnt the buildings the Wardrobe Folk had erected, so that the light of the flames ascended into the sky and added to its brightness; and in one terrible day he sent imps down into the world who with their long serrated knives cut away the eyelids of every one of the Folk, from the newest child to the dying.

And then, setting his final curse upon his creations, the Insane God Qinmeartha afflicted them with immortality.

They were condemned to eternity.

Yet he had not succeeded in entirely extinguishing hope among them. Perhaps one of the imps he had used to effect his punishments had been careless, or perhaps one of the angels had succeeded in conveying some fragment of knowledge in the instant before banishment, but there survived among the Wardrobe Folk the concept of *change*. There had been no change in the universes since close to the beginning of time, since the end of those cataclysmic days when Qinmeartha had exacted his vengeance upon his mortals, and there were no overt signs that change would ever again return to the universes; but the *concept* still existed, in the form of a fragment of rhyme that was somehow known to every individual of the Wardrobe Folk—and, they extrapolated, presumably to the mortals surviving on every other world of this god-tormented polycosmos. That rhyme was:

> see LoChi
> girl child LoChi
> her back bends not for the heaviest load
> she is
> starwatcher
> she is
> cloudrider
> she is
> she who seeks to the ends of roads.

In their slow way, the Wardrobe Folk spent the billennia attempting to interpret this fragment, but always without success—although even the attempts kept alive among them the notion of change. There was the idea of the Girl Child LoChi's back, which did not bend; yet the Wardrobe Folk did not have backs, did not know what backs actually *were*. She sought to the ends of roads, the rhyme told them; yet there were no roads in the sandy wastes, only the tracks that each individual made by creeping from one place to another. And the greatest of all mysteries was the word "starwatcher"— for what in all the universes was a star?

But it is not necessary to understand the workings of things in order to be influenced by them, and the Wardrobe Folk knew from this shard of rhyme that one day, in the future either near or far, the Girl Child LoChi would come among them, and with her she would bring the power to put curtains of clouds across the sky so that shadows would come back to the world.

All of this Joanna knew in her dream: it was the knowledge of the Joanna-creature, knowledge that had always before been hidden from her. Thus read the history of the world, the history shared by all its immortal

Wardrobe Folk.

This was the first time that the dream was not a nightmare, for now that she understood the nature of the world it could hold no terrors for her. There was the pain of the light, of course, filling everything that her huge single eye could encompass; and there was the pain of the sharp-edged sand crystals grating across her sensitive lower surface; but these were merely agonies, which could be endured.

And there was the hope to make their endurance more possible.

The hope that the Girl Child LoChi would soon, herself dark, descend from the burnished scream of the sky.

#

The following morning, noon came and went and still the Blue Horse didn't open.

Joanna first became aware that something was amiss as she was dressing after her morning bath. It was a grey-skied day, at last, and so she'd thrown open her curtains and yanked the stiff window up a few inches to let the whisky- and smoke-saturated atmosphere of her bedroom clear a little. She was climbing into the jeans which she'd *still* never gotten around to washing, wrinkling her nose at their fermentish stale-sweat smell, when she registered a noise like the humming of contented bees from the pavement outside.

The window screeched as she hauled it further up in its frame, and a couple of pale faces turned skywards to glance at her.

Greta was among the little throng, wringing her hands agitatedly in her apron.

"What's going on?" Joanna mouthed to her.

Greta shrugged lethargically and pointed a thumb towards the front of the pub.

Looking down from above, Joanna could see nothing different. She raised her eyebrows theatrically, still questioning.

Greta shrugged again, and made a gesture that told her to come down and take a look—she, Greta, wasn't going to make an exhibition of herself by yelling the information up to her.

Crossly, Joanna jabbed her feet into the tired black sandshoes that were as much in need of a respite as her jeans—they smelt like a man's socks, and there was a tear at the toe of one of them where her uncut nails had stabbed through. Half a minute later she was coming out through the concrete tunnel onto the pavement to join the rest.

"What's happening?" she said to Greta.

"The pub."

The black-painted doors were firmly closed.

"So what?"

"Do you know what time it is?"

"No." She hadn't the first idea. These days she just got up when the notion took her and staggered through her hours of wakefulness until booze or exhaustion or both sent her back to her bed again.

"It's nearly one."

"Oh." The information took a while to sink in.

"Not as it makes much difference to some of us," said Greta slyly. She'd caught a whiff of Joanna's breath.

The crowd fractured, like a puddle that's just been stamped in, as a police car pulled up by the side of the road and then turned to park in Ham's Lane. Two young policemen climbed out and ambled across the road. While one of them began to ask the villagers what was going on, the other, absent-mindedly scratching his beard, turned the handle of the doors.

They opened.

Shrugging, the policeman pushed his way in, and without pausing to think Joanna followed him.

The first thing that struck her was the smell: the redolence of smoke and alcohol was even stronger than in her bedroom upstairs, but it was also overlain by the stink of feces.

The policeman glanced at her, and made a face. "I think you'd best stay outside, young lady," he said.

"I know what to expect." She did. Aunt Jill's bedroom, that morning only a fortnight ago, had taught her.

"I mean it," he said.

"So do I." She managed a grim smile. "If I go straight back out now, people will start to think things are even worse than they are."

He nodded. "Come on then."

They found Jas right at the back of the bar, lying half in and half out of the door that led to the lavatories. For a second Joanna had a picture of him dashing through to try to reach them before his bowels loosened, but then she saw that his body was lying the wrong way around: he'd been coming out when death had struck him.

The policeman knelt down beside Jas's head. He put his hand briefly inside Jas's waistcoat, then stripped back one of the body's sleeves to feel for the pulse at the wrist.

"I really think you ought to go, ma'am." There was no command in his voice. Whatever had ensnared the rest of Tarburton seemed to have acted on him as well.

"I can help you," she said.

"You can't help *him*. He's dead."

"Still."

He pulled the arm of the suit back down, covering up Jas's white flesh. "You a journalist or something?"

"Yes," she lied, then added: "Or no. Whichever you'd prefer."

"Figures." He cracked his knuckles. "Could you nip outside, Joanna, and fetch my partner?"

She was at the door before she realized he'd used her name. She turned back, staring at him.

"Didn't recognize me under my beard, eh?" said the policeman, face splitting into a grin. "You didn't know I'd taken on a day job, did you? We do a little bit of everything, you see."

She was pushing through the noisy knot of villagers, all of them tugging at her, demanding that she answer their questions. Her mouth tightly closed, her face set in rigid lines, she just shook her head and burrowed with her shoulders.

She eased a little as she got into the concrete passage, which echoed to the sounds of her hurrying footsteps. Luckily she'd left the flat door open, so she didn't have to stop for the ritual struggle with the lock.

Upstairs, in the kitchen, she tugged a fresh bottle of whisky from the cupboard where Aunt Jill had kept her cornflakes and raised it to her mouth. It was only as the liquid clug-clugged in the bottle's neck that she began to have coherent thoughts once more.

No! I don't believe it. I can't believe it.

But it was him.

It was Steve Gilmour.

#

Ronnie Gilmour phoned to tell Joanna they were burying Jas that afternoon. Joanna had some difficulty keeping track of the conversation, because she'd been belting into the bottle in the kitchen ever since she'd got back, and Ronnie had to repeat the information two or three times before it registered properly on her. What she really wanted to do was yell, *You're the mother of a shapeshifter, you stupid cunt! And you know you are, but you don't seem to realize just how desperately, desperately important it is that you* denounce *him, denounce him to the world!*

Or would denunciation be enough? The telephone conversation had finished some while ago without Joanna having been aware of the fact, and she was now sitting in the drawing-room, hauling deeply on a cigarette. Her throat hurt, and she knew smoking was making it worse in the long term; but in the short term each inhalation brought a few moments of blessed relief from the pain.

The quality that had initially attracted her to Steve Gilmour—what she'd at first interpreted as his elemental vitality, his unabashed masculinity—had not been an illusion. What had been at fault was the gloss she'd put on her perception. He was indeed something elemental, and he was indeed rippling with the raw stuff and potency of life; but he was more powerful than any human being should rightly be. She hadn't any proper idea of where he might be drawing his energies from, but she suspected that he had some kind of direct connection with the earth itself: no mere animal could be as stuffed full of the *élan vital* as he was. When she'd been thinking of him just now as a shapeshifter she'd been grossly undervaluing him: yes, he was a shapeshifter, but that was only one small fraction of the whole of him. He had transformed himself—she now fully credited this—into not just a single wolf but a whole, huge host of them. Dracula, according to the stories, had been able to transmute at will into a plague of rats; but rats were small creatures, not powerful carnivores that weighed each as much as a grown man.

And now Steve had manifested himself to her as a bearded policeman. She hadn't looked closely at the man's face as he'd preceded her into the Blue Horse and peered around the gloomy bar, but she was sure he hadn't been Steve then—not at first. Even while he'd been kneeling beside Jas's lifeless form he'd still been just another bobby on patrol. But at some time immediately after that the spirit of Steve—did Steve have a spirit, or *was* he a spirit?—had come into him, transforming him, overwhelming him.

She had three more bottles left untouched in the kitchen, and was worried that wouldn't be enough to see her through until the morning.

Oh, shit, she'd just remembered: Jas's funeral. That was what, ostensibly, Ronnie had been phoning her about. There seemed something vaguely wrong with the fact that he was being bundled into the ground so very rapidly after his death, but for the moment Joanna couldn't work out what it was. Her mind probed once or twice at its own unease, but each time retreated almost immediately. It made sense to bury him as fast as possible, she rationalized wretchedly, before the body began to decompose; that must be why.

She couldn't remember what time Ronnie had said the service was going to be—if indeed Ronnie had given her a time at all—but she gaped at her watch and saw that it was four o'clock already. Four pm sounded like a respectable sort of a time to be holding a funeral; and as if she'd cued them the Bloody Bells started up their doleful chorus in the steeple of St Leonard's across the way. Getting to her unsteady legs, Joanna slowly moved to the window and pulled back the curtain. There was already a double line of mourners moving slowly up the path towards the church door.

She ought to be among them. Jas had known her aunt, hadn't he? And he'd been kind to Joanna herself after Aunt Jill's death, refusing to accept any money for those two pints of Royal Oak, to symbolize his sympathies. There were few enough in Tarburton who would sincerely grieve for the Blue Horse's landlord that she should allow herself to be absent.

Her jeans. They were filthy. You couldn't go to a funeral in jeans like these. But what else was there? Some time in the past few days—she couldn't remember when—she'd got mud all over the black jumper suit, and one night, drunkenly, she'd taken a pair of kitchen scissors to all her skirts. It was the jeans or nothing.

Upstairs in the loo she spent a few explosive minutes. The smell made her want to be sick, but she wouldn't allow herself to go to Jas's interment with vomit on her breath, so she fought down the nausea, forcing herself to take long, deep, controlled breaths through her nose. Standing, she wiped her bottom on the front page of a fortnight-old *Guardian*—toilet paper was something she kept forgetting to buy during her furtive trips to the International Stores—and tried to flush the foul-smelling mixture of newsprint and pale yellow shit down the pan.

She lurched to her room, fastening her jeans. They sagged to her hips, and without thinking she scrabbled along the rail inside her wardrobe door to get a belt. It was crimson, with a gaudy buckle done in fake gold and glass diamonds, but at least it would hold her goddam trousers up. In front of the mirror she dragged a brush through her hair and slashed a thick line of lipstick across her mouth; the waxy colour caught the ends of her front teeth, but there was no time to salvage that now—she'd just have to make sure she kept her mouth shut throughout the proceedings.

That was everything, that was everything, surely that must be everything. She stood in the middle of her bedroom's devastation and stared around her in a series of jerky, hopeless glances, as if anything she'd forgotten might suddenly volunteer itself from the midst of the shambles. Her knickers were climbing into the crack of her bottom, which felt moist and sticky, and she tugged vexedly at the sides of her jeans.

Downstairs again, she took a slug of whisky from the drawing-room bottle, just to steady her nerves, then grabbed up her handbag (No, it wasn't *her* handbag: it was Aunt Jill's handbag. Joanna had lost her own handbag somewhere on Dartmoor while the wolves had been filling the skies with their song. But *in a way* it was her handbag, because when Aunt Jill had died the kind old bird had left her everything, and it wasn't unreasonable to assume that "everything" included this handbag. So Joanna didn't feel like a thief or anything using it.) (Besides, Aunt Jill would have wanted her handbag to be at Jas's funeral, wouldn't she?) and made for the door.

The bells had stopped. She could hear voices joined in a hymn—"Be Thou My Vision"—as she scurried up the path that wound from the churchyard gate to the church itself. She'd been wrong to think that there'd be a small turn-out to say a last farewell to Jas: from the sound of it there must be forty or fifty, quite an assembly for a little place like Tarburton. She wondered if she should turn back, since her absence would hardly be noticed, but then the thought of Aunt Jill and those two pints of Royal Oak drove her on. She pushed her fingers through her hair, yelping as she tugged on a knot, and wished that she'd thought to bring a hip-flask or something in case the Reverend James "Call Me Jim" Daker guffed on for ages at the grave-side.

The church doors seemed to be locked, like those of a theatre once the play's started and the auditorium's full. She knew that St Leonard's had another entrance round the back somewhere, because she'd seen it from the vicarage garden once when Mrs Daker, during a weekend when her husband was away at a conference, had invited Aunt Jill and her visiting niece across for tea. But her recollections of it were vague, and she wasn't about to start stumbling through the rose-bushes looking for it.

Thwarted, she stood back from the doors and looked upwards at the sheer sandstone façade of the church.

There was someone on the roof, leaning over and peering straight back down at her.

She flinched, then recovered herself. It was only a gargoyle, its hideous face twisted into a malicious sneer. *Qinmeartha, the Insane God*, she thought. She was panting rapidly, unsteadily, and she could feel her heart echoing her breath. *Get a grip on yourself, Joanna lass. The Insane God Qinmeartha belongs in that other world, the irrational one he created: not here, not here in good old Tarburton-by-the-Moor, prettiest village in South Devon, winner of seven major tourist-industry awards and blah-de-blah-de-blah-blah. That's just a gargoyle that the good Christian souls of the parish of St Leonard's clubbed together five hundred years ago to erect as a symbol of their . . . Of their what? Hardly as an image of their god, surely. The Judaeo-Christian Jahweh was a benign face with a long white beard, a sort of poor man's Santa Claus, not a malevolent sadist like the Insane God who tormented the Wardrobe Folk's world.*

Wasn't he?

In front of her the church doors suddenly opened, so that she was hit by a burst of song. The hymn seemed to have been going on for a very long time. Perhaps the Reverend Call Me Jim had decided that a single rendition was insufficient to express the respect in which old Jas was held in the community, or perhaps the organist had brought only the one piece of sheet music with him. It was still "Abide with Me", which Joanna had always regarded as one of her favourites; but surely it wasn't right that it should be repeated over and over, like this week's hit on a pub juke-box.

She stepped forwards, hoping she'd be able to slip in quietly among the congregation without being noticed. A flutter of movement behind her made her turn her head, and she saw that a single crow had come down to walk towards her along the path, parodying a human being as it rocked its shoulders from side to side. *Is that what I looked like to anyone who was watching me?* she thought.

She dragged her eyes away from the creature, and inched forwards into the church's gloom.

At first she couldn't see anything at all, although she was aware of the presence of a mass of people. Instinctively she looked in the direction of the altar, expecting to see at least a few candles, but once again there was only darkness. This was coming to remind her too much of the night on Dartmoor, but she kept her nerves curbed: it was just a coincidence, that was all; these old country churches had been built with thick walls and narrow windows, so it was often gloomy inside them. She hummed along with a few bars of "Jerusalem", wondering how long the choir had been singing it before she'd heard them from her window.

Windows. Yes, the windows of St Leonard's were quite narrow, which no doubt accounted for the lack of light in the church. There was some fine stained glass in those windows.

The doors silently fell shut behind her, closing off the rectangle of sunlight that had failed to spill over the threshold.

The windows weren't all *that* narrow. There should be a matrix of glowing colour falling across the congregation.

There should be candles at the altar.

And suddenly the whole of the interior was flooded with light, brighter even than her recollections of the sky of the Wardrobe Folk's world. She reeled back against the unyielding doors, holding her arms up to cover her face, dropping her handbag and hearing, despite the lusty hymn, the echoes as her possessions flew away in all directions across the cold stone floor. She knew she'd feel better if she screamed, but some misplaced remnant of decorum forbade her to do so: she was in a church, after all.

The light pulsed, impossibly, even brighter, and then dwindled.

Cautiously, Joanna lowered her arms. The church was illuminated as if by spring daylight. She could see that the glass of the two windows in the long wall opposite her had been blasted out of the frames; strips of lead hung twisted in place.

St Leonard's was empty, except for herself.

No, there was somebody else there, standing alone among the pews, hands clasped reverentially across her chest.

Tony Gilmour looked blankly at her for a moment, then opened her mouth to launch into the next verse of "When the Saints Come Marching In".

7

Friendly Pariahs

Joanna opened her eyes again. The church was full of people, one or two of whom were smiling kindly in her direction. The windows opposite were intact. Candles flickered merrily in their holders around the altar. In the gilt pulpit the Reverend James "Call Me Jim" Daker was holding forth about his namesake Jas, who'd run the pub across the road.

Joanna looked for Tony Gilmour's face, and saw the girl standing where she'd seen her only a moment ago, but this time surrounded by the rest of her family and much of the rest of the village.

Tony smiled at her shyly, as if uncertain of how Joanna would react.

No one was singing.

Joanna took a step forward to grip the end of the nearest pew. She imagined that the Reverend Call Me Jim paused momentarily in his homily, as if he disapproved of her late arrival—which he quite probably did. She needed to sit down, urgently, but all the pews seemed to be full.

She looked towards the Reverend Call Me Jim, and he smiled at her.

This time there was no imagining that he hesitated. The beefy man stopped entirely, and beckoned her forward towards him. Obediently she moved along the aisle, aware that every eye was on her. She became aware, too, of the rich gamey smell that hung on her: the sweaty jeans, the unwashed bottom, the socks that she'd been wearing awake and asleep for more days than she could remember. She put a hand to her face and found a little crust of dried food at the corner of her mouth.

"Come on, dear friend," said the Reverend Call Me Jim, kind but firm. "We can't wait all day for you."

There was a solitary chair placed in a space of its own directly in front of the altar. It was to this that he was pointing. Gratefully Joanna tiptoed towards it, knowing that it would make just as much sense to walk normally, since everyone was anyway watching her progress, but wanting to go through the pantomime of courtesy.

Once seated, she lit up a cigarette and began to relax.

The Reverend Call Me Jim continued his flow mid-sentence, as if there had been no interruption. Jas Paisley—it was the first time Joanna had known the landlord's name, although it must have been staring her in the face over the lintel every time she went into the Blue Horse—had shared many of the same fine qualities as her Aunt Jill, if the vicar was to be believed: he had been sober and upstanding—rare qualities in a publican, remarked the vicar with a condescending smile—and the community had been fortunate to have such an outstanding person in its midst.

There was much more of the same, and Joanna fished out a second cigarette. Yet again she wished she'd had the foresight to equip herself with a hip-flask. The little chair on which she'd perched herself was not overly comfortable, as if it had been designed for the use of penitents, and she shifted around in it, trying not to make it creak. She ground the butt of her first cigarette out beneath her heel, and put its replacement in her mouth, sucking on the unlit tobacco while she burrowed in her pockets for her matches.

". . . and now," the Reverend Call Me Jim was saying, "we have here before us our old friend Jas for one final time . . . "

The man seemed incapable of saying anything briefly. Joanna toyed with the idea of getting to her feet and interrupting him, of reeling off a far terser oration that she knew would much better summarize the character of Jas Paisley, the intolerant old bastard, than any of the vicar's kind words could do, but she restrained herself.

There was no coffin.

It wasn't the sort of thing you expected to notice at a funeral—the fact that one of the most vital pieces of the whole rigmarole had been forgotten—but it was the case. She was closest to the front of the church so she had the best view, and it was a certainty that the coffin was missing. She twisted right around to try to see over the heads of the congregation in case the box had been put somewhere at the back, but it didn't appear to have been. She felt her cheeks twitch, and wondered if she'd started grinning like an imbecile. *This is going to be something to laugh about later,* she thought, *over a couple of drinks in the Blue Horse.*

Near the rear of the church sat Rupert, the longest-serving of all the pub's regulars and possibly the closest friend the dead man had possessed. Tears were flowing down the wrinkled cheeks; the eyes were like a pair of stagnant ponds. Rupert, too, had begun to lose a lot of weight. *You're going to be the next,* Joanna thought. *First there was Aunt Jill, and then came the landlord, and the third on the list is going to be you, old man.* Unless, of course, there had been others before Aunt Jill. It was something she had never thought to ask, and no one—certainly not Dr Grasmere—had volunteered the information.

"... I'm sure our good comrade Jas wouldn't be averse to giving us a final song, if we all asked him," concluded the Reverend Call Me Jim above her.

She turned to the front again. This was the most bizarre funeral service she could remember attending, but at last it seemed to be wending its way towards its close. She realized she hadn't got a hymn-book, and hoped that the concluding psalm would be one of the few she knew well. She peeked into her crumpled cigarette packet and discovered she'd got only three left: enough to get her through the rest of the service, certainly, and with luck also the ceremonies at the grave-side. If need be she could always cadge a couple from one of the other mourners.

"Please, a song, Jas," said the Reverend Call Me Jim insistently.

Joanna, glancing around, suddenly realized that he was looking directly at her.

There was a rustle of voices from elsewhere in the church. "Yes, Jas—come on—just one more song for old times' sake—buy you a pint afterwards, har har."

"Please don't keep us waiting all day," said the Reverend Call Me Jim, a hint of annoyance coming into his voice. He was not a man who took kindly to having his wishes ignored, as Aunt Jill had discovered during her disputes with him over the Bloody Bells. "It's the least you can offer us in return for this splendid service we've been holding for you."

Now the man's stare was certainly fixed on her.

"But," Joanna piped, "there must be some mistake. I'm not Jas. I'm Joanna."

Several of the villagers chuckled, but the Reverend Call Me Jim's face became severe.

"This is surely neither the time nor the place for jest, Jas," he said. "All of us here can recognize you. Even the newcomers, like the Gilmours, know you well enough not to mistake you for that bitch Jill Soames's tart of a niece. Sing us a song, if you please—and preferably a respectable one, such as befits the occasion."

She could hear her voice winding higher. "But I'm *not* Jas Paisley!" she protested. "I'm Joanna Gard, I tell you. I'm nothing like old Jas at all. I'm a *woman*, for God's sake!"

"God moves in mysterious ways," murmured Rupert from the back. "His bleeding wonders should bleeding perform when He bleeding asks them to."

"Stop this!" she yelled, standing up, so that the cigarette packet shot out from her lap and slid under the step in front of the altar. "The joke isn't funny! Leave me alone, won't you! Stop doing this to me!"

"It seems," said the Reverend Call Me Jim with heavy irony, "that our dear, deceased friend declines to give us this last little pleasure. Well, that must remain a matter to be settled between himself and his Maker; it is not for us to be his judges. So in the mean time there's nothing left for the rest of us to do but bury him."

Pews screeched and squawked on the floor as they were pushed back. Joanna could hear the clumsy crowd movements of the congregation getting to its collective feet.

"Wait!" she cried. "There's a mistake! You're making a dreadful mistake!"

"The grave's already *dug*, Jas. Surely you're not saying we should let all the sexton's hard work just go to waste?"

"But *I'm not Jas!* Can't you understand that?"

The Reverend Call Me Jim looked exasperated. He shut the book in front of him with a loud slam, and turned away from her, raising his hands as if to appeal directly to the Almighty. "Jas, I'm certain you've told more lies to your God in your lifetime than all the rest of the village put together, but surely you must realize that *now*, of all times, there's no point in keeping up the pretence any longer. Maybe you'd be able to get away with this sort of nonsense in one of the big cities, like Newton, but not among a small, close-knit community like ours. I *appeal* to you to abandon your lies at this turning point in your existence."

The words that came out of Joanna's mouth weren't the ones she'd intended to say. They tasted strange, as if they belonged to someone else.

"You're quite right," she said. "I'm Jas. And I'll sing you a song."

"Glory be!" cried the Reverend Call Me Jim sarcastically. "The man's come to his senses at last! And what's your song going to be, Jas? 'Three German Officers Crossed the Rhine'? 'The Ball of Kirriemuir'? ''Twas on the Good Ship *Venus*? Something in keeping with the way you lived? Or are you going to honour us with a testament to your new, repentant soul?"

His concluding shout died away in echoes.

"The Lord is my shepherd," Joanna sang, "I shall not want . . . "

As she continued, other voices raised themselves in chorus alongside hers, so that, in later verses where she grew less certain of the words, her stumbles were able to pass unnoticed. The organist, unseen somewhere among the rafters, joined in with both his instrument and his voice—a booming bass, hitting each note to perfection. Up in the pulpit, the Reverend Call Me Jim rocked his shoulders from side to side, moving his body in time to the music. His red face beamed at her.

The psalm ended in a triumphant peal from the organ, and hush crept slowly across the space. Joanna stood with her head bowed, trying to look contrite, portraying—she hoped—the image that Jas would have wished to project.

"And now," whispered the Reverend Call Me Jim at last, "it is time to proceed with the burial."

There was a buzz of excitement from the congregation.

This can't be happening, thought Joanna. It seemed to be the leitmotif of her stay here. *Singing a song was one thing, but surely they can't really be intending to bury me, for Christ's sake?*

The Reverend Call Me Jim descended the pulpit steps in stately fashion, his hands folded across his belly—no longer so ample, Joanna noticed distractedly, as it had used to be—and crossed the floor of the church towards her. "Come along with me, my child," he said amiably, "for we are all children in the eyes of the Lord."

"Hallelujah!" someone shouted, and others took up the cry.

"I am only a child," Joanna responded dutifully.

"We are *all* only children," stressed the Reverend Call Me Jim.

"Yes!" She recognized Rupert's voice again. "Let's scrag him, lads!"

She tugged herself away from the vicar and threw herself towards the side of the church.

"All those years," bellowed Rupert, tears choking his voice, "all those years he was pretending to be my friend he was short-pinting me, the bastard! Every effing pint! And he knew I'd never say anything about it, because I'm not that sort, so he just kept on doing it."

"*And,*" said someone different, "he was always cheating in the cricket. That time he gave me out lbw, I knew it was just because the . . . "

74

"He told all his customers I put poisonous love philtres into my flap-jacks so that they'd die if they dared to eat in the Crafts Centre . . . "

"He ran over my dog in 1972 . . . "

"*Please!*" roared the Reverend Call Me Jim, lifting up his hands to quell the mob. "Please, my friends. This is the house of the Lord. Let us not permit anything unseemly to occur between these walls! One at a time, for the mercy of Christ! Rupert—you were the closest to him, so you must have suffered his evils the most. You can lead the way to the cemetery. Put a rope around Jas's neck so that he does not stray from the path."

There was already a rope around Joanna's neck, she discovered—a rope made of plaited seaweed. She couldn't remember putting it on in her bed-room, but then she'd been in such a rush to try to get here on time.

The organist struck up a new tune, and it took her a moment to identify it. It was the grotesque *Dies Irae* from the fifth movement of Berlioz's *Symphonie Fantastique*, but played in the style of Scott Joplin. Some of the vil-lagers were linking arms and beginning to dance together. Rupert, implaca-ble, was stalking towards her, his face twisting furiously, spittle dribbling from the corners of his lips. The heavy arm of the Reverend Call Me Jim fell across her shoulders, pinning her in position.

Rupert grabbed the free end of the seaweed rope. "Every effing pint," he grunted at her, and then he spat at her, the thin spittle spattering across her lips.

She broke.

Her hand clawed across Rupert's face, the long nails digging deeply into his flesh. She felt the edge of his eye tear. She knew she was screaming something, but they weren't words and they weren't under her control. She kicked Rupert hard in the knee, breaking something of her own—a toe—in the process, but she didn't feel any pain. The old man was crumpling up in front of her, his face a curtain of blood.

"Unseemliness in the house of the Lord," thundered the Reverend Call Me Jim. "Is our esteemed old friend possessed by demons? Drive out the de-mons, my friends! Drive out the implements of evil!"

And now the whole congregation was upon her, hurling her to the stone floor and kicking at her, jabbing at her with their walking-sticks and umbrellas, beating down on her with weighty handbags.

"*Stop!*" came a voice, louder than even the Reverend Call Me Jim's. "Stop that! Leave her alone."

A last few kicks, and then the people were pulling back from her.

"Are you wild animals?" said the unidentified voice. "Have you gone mad? Leave the child be!"

"That's no child," said the Reverend Call Me Jim. "That's Jas. Dead Jas. We all know him as Jas."

"Are you nuts, fat boy? That's Jill Soames's niece, Joanna. She's only a slip of a girl."

"He's right. The abomination's right," someone said, sounding puzzled.

A hand reached down to help her up. She clutched gratefully at the strong arm, then released it almost at once, tipping back towards the floor. *This must only be Steve, in another of his incarnations.* The hand grabbed her by the elbow and hauled her to her feet.

He wasn't Steve. His face was sombre as he looked her over. She guessed he was about her own age. Sand-coloured hair, just too long and just too short to be fashionable, fell over his forehead. He was wearing black-rimmed glasses.

"Are you all right?" said her rescuer.

"Joanna," Greta from the Crafts Centre whined from behind him, "has something been going on?"

You were within seconds of pulling me to pieces, that's what was going on.

"Take me out of here," she said to the sand-haired man. "I need fresh air. Help me."

His side felt reassuringly strong against hers as she hugged him to her.

"Help me," she said again.

#

"I know you," she said twenty minutes later. They were walking among the ancient gravestones that surrounded St Leonard's. No one had been buried here in the church's original plot for over two hundred years; nowadays the graves were dug in the New Cemetery, as it was called, on the far side of the Ham's Lane playing fields. "I've seen you before somewhere."

"I've seen you before, too," he said. "You used to come and visit Jill Soames every now and then. She introduced us once, in the street. I'm Ian Piper."

"I'm sorry," she said. "I don't . . . "

"It's all right. Lots of people don't."

"I'll remember you now, though," she said after a pause. "I'll remember you for the rest of my life. Which I think you've just saved, back in there."

She gestured towards the silent church building. No one had followed them out, yet now the edifice seemed deserted. Perhaps they'd all slunk away shamefacedly through the exit by the vicarage garden.

"A small labour." He looked embarrassed. "I was passing, and heard the noise. I thought a rat must have attacked the Bloody Bell-ringers, or something."

"The Bloody Bell-ringers," said Joanna. "That's what my aunt used to call them. The Bloody Bell-ringers."

"I liked Jill. She and I felt the same way about the bell-ringers." He grinned suddenly. "The same *robust* way."

"Forthright," she countered.

"Unsubtle."

"Candid."

"Direct."

"Unembroidered."

She giggled. It was a game Aunt Jill had played, the Jolly Roget Game, but only when she was secure in her company. This man must indeed have known her well. Unlike Ronnie Gilmour, for example, who had claimed so much.

"You need to get cleaned up," he said. "I don't like to be the one to say it, but . . . "

"I smell a lot."

"I was thinking more of the blood on your clothes. And the dust on your face. For all the Reverend James Daker's holiness, he's never shown very much interest in keeping St Leonard's clean. You do look a shambles."

"I guess I must." She looked down at her hands. The right was covered in blood from where she'd torn Rupert's face open. "I'd best get back to the flat."

"I'm worried about leaving you alone."

"I'll be OK."

"They might come for you again."

She considered this. She didn't think it was likely—the people seemed to have been caught up in some blinding spell, which Ian had broken by his arrival among them. But it was possible.

"I can't let you come back to the flat with me," she said at length. "If you think that I look a mess . . . " The attack in the church had made her sober, and now the memories of what the flat looked like—and smelt like—were becoming oppressively clear.

"I understand," he said, and in a strange way she thought that he probably did. "Well, my house probably isn't all that much better, but the towels are clean and the water's hot."

She looked at his eyes. They seemed guileless. "You won't . . . ?" she began.

"You'll be safe," he said. "I'm just offering you my bath, and maybe a meal, after. I haven't got any clandestine motives, if that's what you're concerned about."

She trusted him.

"Apart from anything else," he said, "I just happen to be gay."

She stopped in her tracks. "You're the writer," she said. "I do remember you now."

"Not much of a writer," he said. "I'm basically just long-term unemployed. I write things sometimes, but I don't often finish them."

"I thought you were only *reputedly* gay, rather than the real thing? I thought you were enigmatic about it. Aunt Jill never seemed to be quite certain."

She took his arm and walked beside him out through the churchyard gate.

"I don't make a habit of telling people about it—especially not here in Tarburton." He put his hand over hers, as if they were an elderly couple promenading along the front at Margate. "But with you it doesn't matter if you know or not."

She smiled. "I don't matter, hmm?"

"I didn't mean it that way," he said hurriedly. "It's just that . . . Well, the reason I keep quiet about my sexuality in Tarburton is because, to a lot of the locals, it makes me some kind of pariah. That's why you've never seen me in the Blue Horse, for example. I don't know if it was Jas who barred me from the place first or if it was just that I got fed up with all the abuse he used to yell at me every time I went in there. It's the same at the Customs House: the bikers would beat me to a pulp without a second thought, and most of the other regulars would applaud them for it."

"They're a bunch of real bastards down there," Joanna agreed. "But what makes you think I'm any better than they are?"

"Don't you see?" He stopped on the pavement half-way up West Street and came around in front of her. The eyes looking earnestly into hers were sky blue. "I feel safe to tell you anything about myself because you're just like me."

"I'm not gay," she said, hoping she wasn't sounding defensive. *With the possible exception of Tony Gilmour,* she thought guiltily.

"I didn't mean that!" He took both of her hands in his and placed them flat against his chest. "It was what I was saying about being a pariah. We're two of a kind."

"You mean, I'm a pariah, too?"

"Well, aren't you?"

She thought for a moment. "I suppose I am," she said.

"Join the club, then. Be a Charter Member of the Pariahs Club."

8

Qinmeartha the Insane God

If she'd been at her own flat she'd probably have hit the whisky as soon as she got inside the door. Instead, after she'd bathed, Ian fed her cocoa. She sat wrapped in an old towelling dressing-gown he'd lent her and looked at the flames jumping in the hearth.

"Thank you," she said. "And I don't just mean for pulling me away from the mob in the church. I think this—the fire, the cocoa—is you saving my life for the second time in a day. Thank you."

"Next time maybe it'll be your turn," he said. He'd poured himself a glass of beer and was sitting to one side of the fireplace. He looked embarrassed.

"I mean it . . ." she started.

"I really wish you'd stop," he said. "You'd have done the same for me."

I hope I would have, she thought, *but I'm not sure I'd have had the courage. They were wilder than the wolves . . .*

"What's it like, being gay?"

He laughed. "What's it like being straight?" he said.

"I meant, what's it like being gay in a little dump like Tarburton-by-the-Moor? You said you were a pariah. Can it really be like that?"

"Oh—easily. It's not just my imagination. I got on well with your aunt, and Greta's always been all right with me. But most of the rest . . . " He let the words hang, then added: "Well, you saw them for yourself, today."

"Yes, but that wasn't *really* them. They were . . . "

"Oh, it was really them, all right." He stood up and looked for something on the mantelpiece. "Just pray to the gods of your choice that you don't see them as they really are ever again. They're bad enough, a few of them, when they're just the way they hope everybody thinks they are. Ah—got it."

He was holding a joint. "You don't mind, I hope?" he said, suddenly unsure.

"No—go ahead. I don't, myself, much. Dope usually just makes me feel a bit sick."

She finished her cocoa and put the empty mug down by the edge of the hearth, then wrapped her arms around her knees. She was naked under the dressing-gown, and she felt the warmth of the fire directly against the undersides of her thighs. She couldn't recall having felt as contented as this—not since before Aunt Jill's death, at any rate. She wanted to stretch herself out in front of the grate like a cat, and purr.

"Do you have a lover?" she said.

"Not at the moment. There's not much of a choice, locally, is there?"

"No one in Newton? Or Plymouth?"

"No one at all, for a while. There was someone out at Dartington, but he moved to France and I was left behind."

His voice was unhappy.

"No one in Tarburton you sort of fancy?" she said. "I could do with a lover myself. Maybe you've got better taste in men than I have. We could hunt as a pair—you taking the gays and me the straights." She cackled. She liked the idea of this man being a close friend of hers; and she wanted, too, to be *his* close friend, his sister almost.

"There's one, but he's not interested."

"Who?"

He dragged on the joint, making little sparks in the air.

"I promise I won't tell," she said.

He grinned. "Like being out behind the bike-sheds at the back of the school playground?" he said.

"Exactly. Cross my heart."

"OK, I trust you, Joanna Gard." He leaned forward. "It's Tony Gilmour."

She couldn't say anything for a moment.

He misinterpreted her silence. "Yes, I know he's not even gay, but I can't help the fact that I've fallen in love with him. I saw him one night coming out of the Blue Horse, and we just said 'good evening' to each other, the way you do, and that was it for me. I've told myself that . . . "

"B-but . . . "

"Don't say you fancy him too." Ian was obviously trying to banter, but he wasn't completely able to conceal the bitterness.

"Well, yes. No—I mean, no. It's just that . . . "

"Just what?"

"Tony's not . . . not male. Not a man. He's—she's a girl, a woman. She's Steve's younger sister. You haven't got the two siblings mixed up, have you?"

He was shaking his head. She put her hand anxiously on his knee, removed it quickly, replaced it.

"Tony's as male as I am," he said. "Yes, he's the younger one. I mean, whatever made you think he was a girl? Tony's a boy's name, not a girl's."

"Antonia. I thought it was short for Antonia."

He took another long toke. "Just like Steve's short for Stephanie," he said.

"Or Stephen."

"But Stephanie in this instance."

"Steve. Tony's older brother?"

"Older sister."

Now Joanna was shaking her head. "There's something terribly wrong here," she said. "There's something wrong with this whole fucking village, and whatever it is has been stopping me from thinking about it too hard. Steve's a man. He's a pompous, self-satisfied, over-bumptious, not terribly bright man. I *know*! I bumped into him once and felt his balls!"

She gulped.

"By accident," she added quickly.

Ian shrugged. "And I've seen her sunbathing in a bikini. There wasn't much bikini. Not enough to . . . "

Joanna's mind was racing. If Tony were in fact a man, even though the evidence of her five senses had told her otherwise, then maybe this explained why she'd found herself drawn to . . . him. But not entirely. Because her first sight of Steve had likewise made her short of breath. And it was impossible to think of Steve as being a Stephanie—even more impossible than it was to accept that Tony might be an Anthony. *All right, let's not take this seriously for a while. Let's just pretend that it's a silly parlour game, with rules that don't make a whole lot of sense, and keep going along with it until we see what we come out with at the end.*

"Maybe they swap sexes backwards and forwards between them," she said slowly.

"I wouldn't be at all surprised," said Ian, so casually that for a moment she thought she'd misheard him.

"What makes you say that?"

"The fact that Tony isn't remotely interested in me is only one of the reasons why my falling in love with him was such a dumb thing to do."

"What else is there?" she said. "Oh, and I think I would like a bit of that joint, please, after all."

"You said it yourself, Joanna Gard." Ian passed her the spliff, holding it neatly between his fingers and thumb. "Something's been going drastically wrong in this village for months now—and nobody's been able to do anything about it. Nobody's even *wanted* to do anything about it. Except me, and I don't count—because I'm a pariah. They've just watched as the people have, one by one, begun to shrink away until finally they die, all watched over by the benign eye of the Reverend James 'Call Me Jim' Daker, vicar of St Leonard's, his parish."

"Are you trying to say that the bloody vicar's knocking off his parishioners?"

She began to laugh. Maybe it was the joint getting to her.

Ian smiled, too, but wanly. "No—no, of course I'm not. He's an evil old bastard, but I don't think he's a serial killer. Not a polite sort of a thing to be, if you take my meaning." His mimicry was good enough that she started laughing again. "But he's been watching it happen, and I think that, early on, he could have stopped it if he'd wanted to."

"What started it all off?" Joanna said.

Ian drew a deep breath and reached for the joint. "It started when the Gilmours got here," he said. "They're what began it."

"I . . . believe you," said Joanna after a long silence. "There's something . . . odd about them."

He hooted. "That's the understatement of the year!"

"What have they done to you?" she said. And then she began to tell him about what had happened with the pack of wolves up on Dartmoor. It all seemed very silly to her, sitting here in front of this chuckling fire, warm in a sensible towelling dressing-gown, and she half-expected him to begin to look at her askance or just to start poking fun at her. But he remained entirely serious throughout her account, listening to her intently. She told him, too, about the conversation she'd had with Steve and Tony when she'd told them all the rotten things that had happened to her—and that she'd done—since Christmas; which meant that she told Ian some of them as well, although she glossed over the fact that the fetus ("The child," he interposed) had really been Mike's, not Peter's. Then she moved on to what had happened at the church this afternoon, before Ian had intervened to save her from the mob.

And finally, before she'd quite realized what she was doing, she told him about the dreams she'd had of the world created by Qinmeartha the Insane God, and of the hopes of the Wardrobe Folk for the coming of the Girl Child LoChi. And as she told him these last pieces, which had seemed to her totally disassociated from the rest, she began to wonder if in fact the dreams actually fitted in with what the Gilmours had been doing to her, if they were all part and parcel of the same thing: the completion of the picture. There was a symmetry she'd noted before between the darkness on the moor and the unending light of the Insane God's world; and that symmetry had been extended during her experiences at St Leonard's, when the false darkness had given way to the pulse of searing light. And had events here in Tarburton, since her arrival, been any less insane than those in the world under Qinmeartha's rule?

"That's quite a tale," said Ian when she'd finally come to a halt. The joint had long ago burnt out; he chucked the roach onto the fire, then added some coal on top of it. "It's more than I had in mind. No insane gods or other worlds in my hypothesis."

"Which was?"

"That the Gilmours are vampires. Not tall old men from Transylvanian castles flitting around the countryside in Batman outfits sucking blood from virgins' throats—not Hollywood vampires. I was thinking more of psychic vampires, preying on people's life-forces, sucking them dry of their souls so that they can live themselves forever, eternally young."

"Anyone listening in on this would think we were both equally nuts," said Joanna. The fire didn't seem to be warming her as effectively as before. There were shadows in the corners of the room that she hadn't noticed earlier.

"I don't think we're nuts," said Ian. "I don't think we *can* be nuts, in this situation. It's the circumstances that have gone nuts, and we're very sanely trying to find the least absurd way of explaining them."

"Or, anyway, you are," she corrected. "I don't have any theories, remember?"

"You think that all the rest of the weird things around here tie in with the dreams you've been having," he pointed out. "You were talking about Qinmeartha the Insane God and the Wardrobe Folk as if they were as real as you and me."

"But they *are* as . . . " She stopped. "I think they are. Ian, do you think, maybe, that I actually have gone off my trolley?"

"No," he said immediately.

"That's gallant. But . . . " She thought for a moment. "This past fortnight, I haven't been acting too rationally. Apart from the fact I've spent most of the time pissed out of my skull, I've been letting everything else go. I mean you didn't see those knickers I had on: I had to flush them away down your loo. (Hope I haven't blocked it.) And . . . hell, a lot of the things that've been happening to me, maybe they've *not* been happening, as it were. Maybe it's just been that I've gone not-so-quietly bananas. I've been imagining it all."

"You weren't imagining being attacked by a mob of church-goers," he said. "That is, not unless you're imagining sitting here talking about it with me now."

"That," said Joanna, "is a horrible thought."

"I'm *real*," he said, laughing. He stretched out his hand to her. "Go on—feel it."

She felt the hand, but only because it was there. "I wasn't just making conversation when I was asking you if you think I'm crazy," she said. "I believe that's what the Gilmours have been trying to do with me. I don't know why they'd want to—perhaps they haven't got any real reason, but have just been doing it for fun, or maybe using me as a scapegoat, like the Insane God Qinmeartha is using the Wardrobe Folk as his scapegoat. I can't tell you their motives: all I can say is that maybe that's what's been happening to me."

She paused, expecting him to say something, but he just stared at her in the firelight.

"It's been like trying to walk through glue," she suddenly burst out. "I haven't known what's been really happening to me, and what hasn't! Sometimes I've been certain I really was beset by werewolves, other times I've thought it was all just a load of garbage, or maybe a dream that I've somehow drunkenly remembered as if it actually happened. I haven't known, one way or the other."

She was crying. In front of anyone else, apart from Aunt Jill—except that Aunt Jill was dead, of course—she'd have felt ashamed of breaking down like this. But Ian just put his hand softly on the back of her neck, comforting her by his touch.

"It may not be much consolation to you to know this," he said, "but I really did see you being assaulted by the mob this afternoon. And I heard what sounded like wolves howling the other night. Faint and distant they were, but that's what it sounded like to me. Coming from the direction of the moor. I think all those things did happen to you, Joanna Gard. I believe you."

He continued to massage her neck.

The phone rang, breaking the spell.

Ian rose, removing his hand gently, and moved off into another room. She could hear him talking urgently to someone, but couldn't make out the words.

"That was Ronnie Gilmour," he said when he came back. His face was white, and he looked as if he were freezing. "He knows that you're up here with me. He was ringing for both of us. He says he's got something to show us—something he says might interest us. Now. Down at the playing fields at the end of Ham's Lane."

"I'm game," Joanna said. "Are you?"

"Better get dressed," Ian said.

Dressing in his bedroom, trying to ignore the clammy feel of her jeans against her thighs, she let her eyes run along the spines of the books on his shelves. There was a lot of stuff by Colin Wilson—that was where he must have picked up the notion of psychic vampires—as well as books by other authors with whose names she was less familiar: Stan Gooch, John Gribbin, Jenny Randles . . .

She leant down to tie her laces, and saw a small piece of torn-edged paper, like something he might have been using for a book-mark, sticking out from under the bed. She didn't know what made her pull it towards her for a look, but she did.

There was a piece of rhyme on it:

see LoChi
girl child LoChi
her back bends not for the heaviest load
she is
starwatcher
she is

86

cloudrider
she is
she who seeks to the ends of roads.

"Are you ready yet?" called Ian from below.

#

All along the railings on the West Street side of the St Leonard's church-yard someone had stuck up bills advertising a

> **GRAND START-OF-SEASON DANCE**
> **ALL WELCOME**
> **COME AND BE REELY KRAZEEE!!**

"That's for us," said Joanna, nodding as they passed the first one. She'd said nothing to Ian about the piece of paper she'd found. Now that she knew he was one of them—one of the same league as the Gilmours, whatever that was—she was guarded by the knowledge almost as well as if he'd been her knight in white armour, the way he'd pretended to be. She'd brought the paper with her, but now she crumpled it up and threw it away, letting the wind catch it.

He noticed nothing.

"You're not crazy, Joanna," he said coldly. "You're not crazy at all."

They passed the end of the railings and turned right into Ham's Lane. The windows of the Crafts Centre were blank darkness, but there was a light on behind a plain blind upstairs. Greta was still up and about, or perhaps she was reading in bed. Somehow Joanna couldn't imagine Greta reading in bed. Couldn't imagine her reading at all, unless it was something on the mystic power of crystals.

On impulse, she turned to look towards the vicarage. There was an up-stairs light on there as well. In the bright frame she could see the bulky sil-houette of the Reverend Call Me Jim, looking out. Watching them as they went by.

Ronnie Gilmour must have told him they'd be coming. Young Joanna Gard and the gay from up the street who's putting the trimmings on the in-sanity we've all spent so much time creating for her. *But the trouble with your*

87

schemes is this, my beloved enemies: I found that rhyme under Ian's bed, and it told me that all his talk about you lot being the wrong sexes was just so much bullshit. I know a set of balls when I bump into one: Steve's never a Stephanie. And all the illusions you've been creating for me, using whatever magic it is you have access to—they all fell tumbling down like a card-house as soon as the breath of Ian's duplicity touched them.

It was dark down Ham's Lane, darker than it should have been. Acting her part, Joanna clutched Ian's arm tightly. She was expecting an owl to hoot, just like in the movies, but the night air was silent. Above her she could see the stars, almost as clear and many as there had been on Dartmoor.

As they came out of the end of Ham's Lane onto the playing-fields, the full moon emerged in sudden splendour in the middle of the night sky, casting silver shadows everywhere. The naked goal-posts were like geometrical diagrams; the trees in the distance seemed to have been lightly touched by a mist of mercury.

And in the centre of the playing fields, about fifty yards away, stood a group of people.

Or wolves.

They were standing upright, like human beings, but the moonlight picked out the silver of their shaggy fur.

"The Gilmours," Joanna said. "They're letting me see them at last."

The wolves remained motionless for a few seconds, long enough to ensure that Joanna could be looking at nothing else but them, and then they began to dance.

No human being could have reproduced the shapes these creatures made with their bodies and the air. Time and again Joanna had the illusion that there were no animals there at all, merely some slowly boiling mass of metallic liquid. Their bodies seemed to blend into each other, fusing and separating and fusing again, all in time to some stately, silent rhythm.

Beside her, Ian began to hum. It was a tune she'd never heard before, but she recognized it immediately: it was the melody which had been written by the angels of blessed shade billennia ago, adopted as the melody for the Wardrobe Folk's song about the Girl Child LoChi.

She began to sing it, amazed by the clarity of her own voice in the stillness of the night air. But the words she sang weren't the ones she'd discovered in the fiery world ruled by the Insane God Qinmeartha and later read on the scrap of paper in Ian's bedroom. Not quite.

see LoChi
girl child LoChi
her back bends not for the lightest load
she is
cloudshredder
she is
shapeshifter
she is she who forbids the ends of roads.

"That's wrong," she said, when the short song was done. "Those aren't the true words, not the words the Wardrobe Folk have."

"The song isn't theirs," said Ian, equally quietly. "It reached them only by mistake, and it was corrupted by them. The version you sang is the real one, the one sung by Qinmeartha the Insane God."

"Him!" she hissed. "You are *his* creatures?"

"We *are* him," said Ian. "We are almost the whole of him. We are all that there has been of him since the universes were very young. What the Wardrobe Folk tell each other is not a lie, for they do not know its falsity: but it is an incompleteness."

"You've been tormenting them for billions of years—Qinmeartha the Insane God has! Is it any fucking wonder they slip up on a few things?"

"No, not at all. And we, Qinmeartha, do not blame them for their imperfection."

"*Blame* them!" She twisted her arm away from his. "And I was the one thinking I was going crazy! Either you people think you're an insane god, or you actually *are* an insane god! Either way sounds pretty fucking fruitcake to me!"

"We *are* insane," he said, grabbing after her. "We are the god. But we are not forever insane. And we are not insane *here*."

She halted. "What do you mean by that?" she said. "'Here'?"

"In this facet. Your near facet."

Still the wolves—no, now that she had become more accustomed to the moonlight she saw that they didn't really look much like wolves at all—still the silver-grey creatures danced. They, if there was more than one of them, had picked up the song from Joanna's lips, and slowly chanted it, over and over, as they moved among each other's bodies.

"I don't know what the bloody hell you're talking about," she said tiredly. "What new line are you going to try to feed me, Piper? That you're the Second Coming? Or is that too tame for you?"

"You see only the one facet of reality," he said urgently, pulling her towards him; this time she didn't resist. "There are two. Each mortal being exists in both of them, the near and the far, always, although the two segments of every individual mortal are each unaware of the other's existence. That is what happened when the rival gods drove me mad: the fragile balance I'd built up between the two facets was destroyed. It had been my intention, in creating the universes and those who dwell therein, that the two facets should become united in my mortals, so they would experience the entirety of the reality I had also created for them. It is a glorious reality—wonderful!"

"You remind me of a small boy crowing about how clever he's been with his Lego," she said acerbically. "It's all so really great, Mummy, only it keeps falling down."

"This is not something to be mocked!" cried Ian. The noise was enormous. The stars seemed to tremble in their paths. "We are the god Qinmeartha, and we shall not be mocked by our creations."

"You're mad."

"Am I? What do you see over there in the moonlight?"

"I'm not certain what I see. German Shepherd dogs out late, playing on the grass."

"If we did not need you so badly . . . "

"Need me?" Joanna laughed in derision. "You're going a bloody funny way about getting me, buster."

"Need you for our completeness. To restore our sanity. Haven't you started to wonder about the meaning of the song the god Qinmeartha composed about the Girl Child LoChi? What type of human song does it remind you of?"

They were walking slowly together towards the dancing shapes. Joanna hadn't noticed this until now. A tiny part of her wanted to turn and run, but its voice was very faint and she ignored it.

"A love song, I guess," she said. "It's more like a love song than anything else I can think of."

"The rival gods were not content with ridiculing Qinmeartha for his insanity in creating the universes of mortals, and the dual reality with which he had blessed those mortals. They also seized a part of him, and hid it away from him, so that without it he would truly lose his sanity. This was the portion of him that encompassed his moderation and his humility: lacking it, he became like the other gods, fierce and merciless and absolute. In his insanity he perpetrated terrible crimes against his own creations, but ever he sought the missing portion of himself so that he could become once again the fecund and benevolent god of creation, as he had been."

They were very close to the wolves—to the Gilmours—to the creature(s) that formed the lusts of the god proud to be called Insane until he became indeed so. Ian—Ian?—was intoning the words as if they were a well learnt ritual.

"The sundering of his wholeness was greater than any agony a mortal can feel, and the lack of his stolen fragment was intolerable beyond even that. The pain drove him—not his requirement for wholeness. Everywhere he went through the far facet of his creation he could find no trace of his shard—except for its name, the Girl Child LoChi. His disappointment was greater than skies and seas, and he wrote it between the stars, turning all to fire.

"And then, after too many cycles of the universes had gone by, he turned his thoughts to the *other* facet he had made.

"And he found you there."

They were close enough to the dancers that Joanna could feel the tiny disturbance they made in the air.

"He killed my aunt," she said. "He killed old Jas. He killed others before them."

"Those people are not dead," said the Insane God's voice. "I drew their entirety into your far facet. They are alive there."

Horrified, Joanna pushed the being from her.

"You condemned them to that?" she screamed. "You threw Aunt Jill into the cauldron of the Wardrobe Folk's world?"

The splinter of the god held its hands up to her.

"Only for a short time," he said. "Only until you are rejoined with us, Girl Child LoChi, so that you can put curtains of clouds across the sky and thereby bring shadows back to their world."

"A short time!" she spat. "A short time in that place is an eternity. You want me to help you, so you go about torturing the people I know?"

"It was the only way I knew to draw you to me. I borrowed the nightmares of my creations in your near facet, and I used the vitalities of the beings in your far to spark those nightmares into form. I controlled my insanity as best I could—I had to if I were to persuade you of the truth of my need."

"Then I reject you!"

The dancers froze.

"I reject you for your cruelty, Qinmeartha."

"But it is not *my* cruelty. It is the cruelty of my insanity, brought upon me by my rival gods."

"As you worked to bring insanity upon me."

"It will not seem like insanity when we are whole once more."

"You shall never be whole. I shall never consent to rejoin you."

"Girl Child LoChi . . ."

"I am not the Girl Child LoChi now! I am Joanna Gard. I am the niece of Jill Soames—that same Jill Soames whom you have condemned to everlasting hell. I am not a god: I am a mortal. I am greater than any god."

"Then we must take you," said the voice of Qinmeartha the Insane God.

The sea of hot fur engulfed her.

9

She Who Seeks to the Ends of Roads

So they found Joanna Gard on the Ham's Lane playing fields the following morning.

Emptied.

The Tomb of The Old Ones
Colin Wilson

Intending to test the theories of Charles Hapgood, a team travels to Antarctica equipped with a new super-laser capable of tunnelling into the ice at speed. For some while before, one of their number, Willoughby, has been having dreams linking the Antarctic site to the Old Ones, the aliens described in H.P. Lovecraft's fictions as having colonized the earth in remote prehistory. Guided by Willoughby's dreams, and assisted by the psychic Inga Vassilievski, with whom he is falling in love, the team uncovers at last a mass tomb of shoggoths . . . who are alarmingly undead. This is a glorious neo-Lovecraftian tale, packed with fizzing ideas and told with all Colin Wilson's customary speed and panache.

The Tomb of the Old Ones

Colin Wilson

It is a strange thought that most human beings imagine they possess free will, and yet that the most important events in their lives may be determined long before they were born. My own story is a case in point, for the genesis of the most important event in my life occurred fifty years before my birth, even to falling on the date of my birthday.

On April 19, 1930, my great-grandfather, Daniel Willoughby, at that time President of the Geographical Society of Winchester, Virginia, introduced as guest speaker the famous polar explorer Admiral Richard E. Byrd. In the previous November, Admiral Byrd and his three companions were the first men to fly over the South Pole—Byrd had already been the first man to fly over the North Pole, in May 1926.

Winchester, where I was born, was also the birthplace of Admiral Byrd, who often returned there to see his family. Before the lecture, my great-grandfather took him to dinner, and later they went back to his house for a late-night drink. It was then that my great-grandfather, fortified by a large glass of bootleg brandy imported from Canada, summoned the courage to ask the great explorer about a rumour that had been confided to him by the last guest speaker: whether it was true that Byrd had flown over an immense hollow where the South Pole should be, in which he had seen green hills and lakes.

According to my great-grandfather, Byrd looked grave, stared into his glass for a long time, then said: "To be honest, Dan, I'm not in a position to confirm it or deny it."

And at that moment they were joined by my great-grandmother, who brought in the coffee; whether Byrd would have said any more is a matter for conjecture, but in any case they now changed the subject.

Understandably, my great-grandfather took the comment as an admission that Byrd had seen something that he was not allowed to talk about—after all, if he had seen nothing but snow and ice, he would simply have said so.

Byrd was a good natured, kindly man, full of consideration for others, and this was undoubtedly why he answered my great-grandfather as he did instead of just refusing to comment.

When my great-grandfather told his wife about this at breakfast the following morning, my grandfather—also called Daniel—happened to be next door, in the kitchen, and heard every word. He went off to school in a state of wild excitement. As he understood it, Admiral Byrd had confirmed that there was a vast hollow at the South Pole, full of mountains, green vegetation, lakes and rivers. That could mean only one thing: that the earth was hollow.

At school that day, he told several schoolfriends. And, as soon as he got home, he asked his mother about it. To his astonishment and disappointment, she made light of it, claiming that the admiral had simply meant he had been unable to see the Pole through the clouds. Yet she obviously told his father, for later that evening Dan senior reprimanded his son for eavesdropping, then told him not to repeat what he had heard. To my grandfather, this only confirmed that there was some tremendous secret.

That night he had an exceptionally vivid dream. (He was to tell me years later that he had always been subject to unusual dreams.) He was in an aeroplane with Admiral Byrd, and they were flying over a snow-covered landscape. Then, suddenly, they were looking into a kind of immense volcano, in the centre of which there was a deep blue lake. Then my grandfather was alone, standing on the rim of the caldera, looking down at the magically brilliant landscape, in which the grass and trees were greener than any in the real world. The odd thing was that he knew he was lying in bed in his own bedroom, but that, as long as he kept his eyes closed, he could go on looking at the land inside the volcano. He could actually feel the solidified lava under his feet, and see a flock of strange yellow birds that rose from the trees. Then he opened his eyes and was back in his own room.

He had experienced what is now called a lucid dream. When he woke up, he could still recall the landscape as if he had actually seen it.

Naturally, he was filled with feverish curiosity, and he read all he could find on the subject of Antarctica. In fact, over the years he became something of an expert on the continent, even delivering a lecture on its history to the Winchester Geographical Society while he was still a college student. Admiral Byrd's son attended this lecture, but my grandfather was too shy to raise the subject of the "hole" in the South Pole.

In 1949, my grandfather—now a married man and a lecturer in applied mathematics at the University of New Hampshire—was excited by a piece of news that he read in the *New York Times*. In that year, an Antarctic expedition mounted by Norway, Sweden and Britain had taken sonar soundings through the ice—in places a mile thick—around the coast of Queen Maud Land, and had discovered bays that had been frozen over for thousands of years. And, although my grandfather had long ago ceased to believe in the great hole at the South Pole, he was thrilled to realize that modern science could now look below the ice. As he later explained to me, some instinct told him there was something important buried beneath the ice, and that it would be one day uncovered. He went to the trouble of obtaining copies of all the reports of the exploration team and having them bound.

My grandfather entered into correspondence with Dr G.H. Silbye, the American team's sonar expert, as a result of which he was invited to write an article for the *National Geographic Magazine*, and then for a number of other journals. He became known as an expert on the Antarctic.

There is an amusing story of how my grandfather came to marry. At a faculty cocktail party, he met a shy, brown-haired girl, and in the course of the conversation asked her whether she would prefer to spend her honeymoon at Niagara Falls or the South Pole. He was surprised and delighted when she answered promptly: "At the South Pole." Less than a year later, this is precisely where they did spend their honeymoon. The pair were subsequently to visit Antarctica many times, treating it as a holiday destination in much the same way that other families treat the Adirondacks or Atlantic City.

#

In 1954 my grandfather was appointed to a committee to coordinate planning for the International Geophysical Year, which would take place in 1957-58. It was to have a twofold emphasis: on the study of outer space, and on the continent of Antarctica. My grandfather was on the committee for Antarctica, and a fellow committee member was George Silbye.

And now came what is, I suppose, one of the major turning points in this story. In August 1956, my grandfather was asked to take part in a radio discussion of a controversial new discovery: the so-called Piri Re'is map.

Most of my readers will know about the map, so I shall offer only a brief summary.

Earlier that year, a Turkish naval officer had presented the US Navy Hydrographic Office with a copy of a map whose original had been found in the Topkapi Palace in Istanbul in 1929. It was painted on parchment and dated 1513, and showed the Atlantic Ocean, with a small part of the coast of Africa on the right, and the whole coast of South America on the left. And, at the bottom of the map, what looked like Antarctica.

The map was passed on to the Hydrographic Office's cartographic expert, W.I. Walters, who in turn showed it to a friend named Captain Arlington H. Mallery, who studied old Viking maps. It was after he had studied the map at home that Mallery made the astonishing statement that he believed it showed the coast of Antarctica as it had been before it was covered by thick ice. It appeared to show certain bays in Queen Maud Land as they had been before they were frozen over.

Now, a few days before the broadcast, my grandfather had received a copy of the Piri Re'is map from the producer of the programme. He compared it with the reports of the 1949 expedition, and was thrilled to discover that the bays corresponded exactly.

It was amazing enough that a 16th-century map should show Antarctica, which had not been discovered until 1820, but that it should show Antarctica as it had been in prehistoric times seemed preposterous. In the discussion, which took place at Georgetown University, in Washington DC, indignant scholars had said as much, but my grandfather assured them that, as far as he could see, the bays on the Piri Re'is map seemed to correspond to bays discovered under the ice in 1949. I must be honest and admit that my grandfather did not press the point—he was an academic and had no wish to be thought a crank. But he certainly threw his authority on the side of the map and Captain Mallery. The discussion was lively, and was widely reported in the newspapers.

My grandfather liked Mallery, who was a scholarly and friendly man. They had dinner together after the broadcast, and my grandfather told Mallery his story about Admiral Byrd, and how this had stimulated his interest in Antarctica. And Mallery told my grandfather that maps in the style of the Piri Re'is map, although not with its sensational content, were by no means uncommon. They were called portolans—which means "from port to port"—and they were used by mariners in the Middle Ages; the Library of Congress apparently had dozens of them.

A few months later, Mallery contacted my grandfather to tell him that he had been in touch with another academic who was interested in the Piri Re'is map—a professor of the history of science called Charles Hapgood, who taught at Keene State College, fifty miles or so from the University of New Hampshire in Durham. He gave my grandfather Hapgood's phone number, and the two of them spoke on the telephone the same evening. They agreed to keep in touch and share their results.

It was some time later that Hapgood rang my grandfather in a state of great excitement. He had spent several days at the Library of Congress, where he had been to study portolans. He expected to see half a dozen or so; instead, he found that the librarian had laid out a whole room full of them. There were dozens, probably hundreds. And they appeared to show that these medieval mariners knew far more about the geography of the world than is generally supposed. Moreover, said Hapgood, he had discovered a map that undoubtedly showed the whole of Antarctica, as if photographed from the air. The map had been drawn by a mapmaker called Oronteus Finaeus in 1531, and showed ranges of coastal mountains that are now deep under the ice. Although Hapgood was still in the process of studying this map, his preliminary findings indicated that the rivers on it followed natural drainage patterns, which meant that the coasts were then ice-free. Inland, there were no rivers or mountains, suggesting they were, as now, covered with ice.

We know that at the end of the last ice age—from around 11,000BC—Antarctica spent thousands of years free of ice. Then, about 4000BC, the ice sheets began to return. That seemed to date the map—or the original map on which it was based—to around 4000BC . . .

Then why, asked my grandfather, were these amazing maps not better known—at least among scholars?

That, said Hapgood, was precisely the question he had asked. And the answer appeared to be that no one really cared. They were just a lot of old maps, drawn in the days when one mapmaker showed England looking like a teapot . . .

A few days later, Hapgood and my grandfather met for dinner, choosing Manchester as a convenient mid-point. They took an immediate liking to one another, and spent the whole evening talking about portolans. Why, asked my grandfather, did Hapgood not organize his students to make the first complete study of portolans? "That," said Hapgood, "is just what I intend to do."

On that evening, Hapgood told my grandfather more exciting news. In the *Atlas* of 1569 by Gerard Kremer—better known as Mercator—there were several maps that showed Antarctica, including many features that had been "discovered" in recent years, such as Cape Dart and Cape Herlacher, the Amundsen Sea, Thurston Island, the Fletcher Islands, the Weddell Sea, and the Regula Range in Queen Maud Land, which was shown as a series of islands. All this left no doubt whatever that Mercator had based his maps on several older maps, not just those of Piri Re'is and Oronteus Finaeus.

My grandfather told me later that, although he drank no wine that evening, he felt as light-headed as if he were drunk. It seemed to these two respectable academics that they were discussing ideas that would change the history of the world. After all, this proved, beyond all possible doubt, that Antarctica had been known for centuries—perhaps thousands of years—before it was "discovered" by Edward Bransfield and others in 1820.

All this obviously had tremendous implications. According to the historians, civilization began in the Middle East about 9000BC, with the first farmers and the earliest cities. It took over 5000 years more to develop into the great cities of Sumer and Akkad, where writing was invented. Yet according to Hapgood Antarctica was inhabited, more than 6000 years ago, by men who sailed the seven seas and made maps. And a map would be no use without writing. Hapgood was saying that civilization is far, far older than we think.

My grandfather noted in his diary that, when he left Hapgood that night, he could not sleep. If Hapgood was correct, it would change the history of civilization. The sensation would be tremendous. And Hapgood would certainly become one of the most famous academics of his generation . . .

Not long after that first meeting, when Hapgood spent a weekend with my grandfather at his home in Durham, he brought the most exciting news so far. He had discovered yet another map, this time by a Frenchman called Philippe Buache, and dated 1737. This showed Antarctica divided into two islands, as it was before the ice came. And inland there were rivers and mountains. This map seemed to have been made in the days when the whole of Antarctica was free of ice. And this must surely mean that the original mapmakers lived in Antarctica—for why should sailors bother to go a thousand miles inland to map the interior, even if they could in those days sail clear through to the South Pole?

There could be no possible doubt: the maps demonstrated that, in the time before civilization "began" in the Middle East, there was a worldwide seagoing civilization that sailed as far as Russia and China—which were shown on other ancient maps.

This also meant, of course, that there must be evidence of ancient cities beneath the ice. Imagine, for example, what would have happened if ancient Athens, or Rome, or Ephesus had been buried under a blanket of snow and ice. Two thousand years later, their major monuments would still be perfectly preserved; the Parthenon and the Colosseum and the Arcadian Way would look exactly as they did when the ice came. And, even under a mile of ice, sonar would still show traces of their outlines.

This is why my grandfather decided to persuade the Committee for the Geophysical Year to authorize sonar soundings all over Antarctica—inland as well as the coastal regions.

#

A week later he attended a meeting of his committee in Rome; he flew there with George Silbye. Before he left, my grandfather had come to a decision. If Silbye raised the subject of the broadcast, or the Piri Re'is controversy, my grandfather would take him into his confidence about Hapgood and the "ancient maritime civilization", and ask his help in persuading the committee to authorize sonar soundings. But, if Silbye knew nothing about the broadcast or the map, my grandfather would keep silent. After all, Silbye was a scientist, not a historian. He might well feel pangs of conscience about trying to persuade the committee to spend money on an idea that could turn out to be nothing more than wild speculation. My grandfather liked him too much to want to embarrass him.

Of course, there was no question of telling the committee about the real reason. To begin with, they might think him hopelessly eccentric and unreliable. But there was also the fact that he had to right to talk about Hapgood's ideas before Hapgood was ready to publish them. It would only undermine their impact when they were finally made public.

In fact, it turned out that Silbye knew nothing of the broadcast and the Piri Re'is controversy. But his help was unnecessary in persuading the committee. After all, ninety-five per cent of Antarctica is under a thick sheet of ice; it was only commonsense to take sonar soundings to learn about the underlying geographical features. The proposal was passed without a dissenting voice.

#

The International Geophysical Year—IGY—began in July 1957; but, since this was midwinter in the southern hemisphere, the physical surveys in the Antarctic began after the September equinox (when, of course, it becomes perpetual daylight in Antarctica). This time the Russians and the Japanese conducted surveys in Queen Maud Land; the American team organized by my grandfather and Silbye was in the south, based at Byrd, while a second American team was based at Siple in West Antarctica, near the Ronne Ice Shelf.

My grandfather told me that those first two months in Antarctica were the happiest of his life. And in fact his journals show that he felt as if he were on the brink of a great discovery that would astonish the world. This was because of something he had learned only hours before he left, in late September, 1957.

He had spent the previous weekend with Hapgood at Keene State, and had looked at his latest findings. The more Hapgood studied the old portolans, the more convinced he became that the original maps proved the existence of a great civilization long before the beginnings of Middle Eastern civilization in the Land of the Two Rivers. And his students had found one piece of evidence whose implications were staggering.

A map is, of course, a distortion of what it represents, because the earth is a sphere and a map is flat. It was Mercator who found the most convenient solution to that problem when he divided the earth's surface into latitude and longitude, and then "projected" it onto a flat surface. The old mapmakers used a simpler method. They chose some town as a convenient "centre", then drew a circle around it, and subdivided this into sixteen segments, like cutting a cake into sixteen slices. Along the outer edge of every "slice", they drew various squares, and went on like this for as far as they needed to go.

It was easy to see that the original centre of the Piri Re'is map was off the map. A friend of Hapgood's, a mathematician at MIT, had calculated that this centre had to be in Egypt. This seemed to make sense, for the great library of Alexandria was in Egypt, and Hapgood had already decided that many of the original maps must have been in the library of Alexandria in the days before it was destroyed.

But more calculation revealed that the "centre" of the Piri Re'is map was not Alexandria, but a spot five hundred miles further south—a small town called Syene, which is modern Aswan. Why should the old mapmakers choose Syene as the centre of their maps?

Hapgood thought he knew the answer. About 240BC, a Greek called Eratosthenes had used a well in Syene to work out the size of the earth. He knew that at midday on June 21 the sun was reflected in the water of the well, and so must be directly overhead. This meant that objects in Syene cast no shadow at that moment. All Eratosthenes had to do was to measure the length of the shadow of a tower in Alexandria at midday on June 21, and calculate the angle of the sun's rays, which proved to be 7½ degrees. And, since he knew Syene was five hundred miles from Alexandria, he was able to work out the size of the earth by multiplying 500 by 48—the number of times 7½ degrees goes into 360. He came up with the amazingly accurate figure of 24,000 miles, which is very nearly the correct length of the equator.

But my grandfather pointed out an error in Hapgood's reasoning. If the original maps had been made thousands of years before Eratosthenes, then it was unlikely that the mapmakers had Eratosthenes in mind. Just before he left for the Antarctic, my grandfather spent an hour in the university library and learned that Syene had another significance. It was at the same location as the island of Elephantine, on the Nile, and the ancient Egyptians regarded it as the southern limit of their country. And, since they measured Egypt upside-down, regarding the south as "Upper Egypt" and the north as "Lower Egypt", Syene had the same significance for ancient Egyptian geographers that Greenwich has for modern ones—it was, in a sense, the most important place in Egypt.

My grandfather had tried to telephone Hapgood before he left, but had been unable to reach him. Throughout the plane journey to the Antarctic he brooded on the significance of what he had discovered. If the ancient Egyptians regarded Elephantine as one of the most important places in Egypt, and the ancient mapmakers had used it as their "centre", it argued that there must be some connection between ancient Egypt and the "maritime civilization" of Antarctica.

Of course, that was mere common sense if Antarctica was the home of a worldwide maritime civilization. You would expect its sailors to know ancient Egypt . . . Except, of course, that Egyptian civilization is supposed to have started about 3000BC, when Antarctica was already covered with an ice sheet. If there was a connection between ancient Egypt and the Antarctic civilization, then Egyptian civilization, too, must be far older than historians believed.

As he sat on the plane and reflected on these incredible speculations, my grandfather felt almost physically dizzy. As far as he could see, Hapgood had proved that Antarctica was the home of a civilization thousands of years older than anything known to historians or archaeologists. And now it looked as if he had also proved, quite unintentionally, that the civilization of ancient Egypt was also thousands of years older than anyone thought. This theory was going to explode like a bomb in the academic world. And if he, by some incredible piece of luck, could find evidence of an ancient civilization under the Antarctic ice, the theory would be virtually proved.

They had flown through a day and a night, and it was an hour after dawn when they sighted the coast of Queen Maud Land. This was the seventh time my grandfather had visited Antarctica, but now he saw it in a new way. Now he was looking at it as the home of a lost civilization, whose bays, invisible under the ice, had once been crowded with sailing ships. As he gazed down at the ice that reflected the morning sun like a mirror, he told me he experienced such an agony of curiosity that he said aloud: "If only I knew . . . "

Then, exhausted by excitement (and also by the sheer length of the plane journey in a propeller-driven transport plane) he fell into an uneasy sleep.

Sometime during those last few hours of the journey, he had another lucid dream. It was, he wrote, as if some invisible agency had decided to answer his prayer. In his dream, the plane was flying over an immense green continent, with lakes and forests and mountains. The dream was so clear that he was able to focus on the unfolding scenery. And, as in all lucid dreams, he was aware that this was a dream, and that he would soon be awake. What he now longed for was to see some sign of life—or, better still, some kind of human settlement. With desperate urgency, he wanted to know what kind of people had lived in this lost continent nine thousand years earlier.

And at this point his dream turned into a kind of phantasmagoria. He was no longer in the air but on the ground, surrounded by forest. The trees were conifers, and they were immense, like the columns of some Egyptian temple. Underfoot, the ground was wet, covered with some bright green moss that squelched as he walked. The air was oddly warm—unpleasantly warm, like a steam bath—and it smelt of sulphur. He had a very strong and clear sense that he was about to meet the inhabitants of this strange land. Just then one of those dreamlike transformations took place. He had become one of the inhabitants he was searching for. But it was not human. It was a kind of mass of tentacles, like an octopus, swaying as slowly and gently as seaweed in a current, or the tentacles around the mouth of a sea anemone. Yet he knew he was not under water. He was in a warm, stifling atmosphere that smelt of sulphur and decaying vegetation.

This was not a nightmare. He told me that he experienced no sense of fear. He felt he was being given the answer to his question. The only trouble was that the answer was incomprehensible.

Now, as in his childhood dream of Antarctica, he became aware that he was asleep; he could hear the engines of the plane, and feel the pressure of his seat. There was a sense in which he was wide awake. Yet, as he continued to keep his eyes closed, he continued to feel identified with the swaying tentacles. And he told me that he sat there for perhaps five minutes, absorbed in this strange sensation of being another creature, a timeless creature that had existed for thousands, perhaps millions, of years.

As soon as he opened his eyes, the "octopus" disappeared, and he was "himself" again.

#

For the remaining hour of the flight he reflected on what had happened. He was certain that it could not be dismissed as a dream. Yet what did it mean? Was it some curious hallucination, conjured up by his unconscious mind in response to the urgency of his question? If so, why did it seem so oddly real? And, if it was Antarctica that he had seen, why was it covered in enormous trees—trees the size of the giant redwoods of North America?

He was still as puzzled as ever when the plane landed at the Byrd airstrip.

Although the sun was dazzling on the snow, the pilot warned them that the temperature outside was well below zero. Silbye was there to meet him, dressed in furs that made him look like a polar bear. And as they shook hands my grandfather knew that he had to take Silbye into his confidence about Hapgood and the portolans. That same evening, over dinner, my grandfather told him the whole story, beginning with the Washington broadcast—and confessed his real reason for wanting to take sonar soundings through the inland ice sheet.

To his relief, Silbye found it all as fascinating as he did. But he pointed out that their chance of finding ancient cities under the ice was remote. If they existed they would be more likely to be in the coastal regions, particularly in bays and inlets, where harbours could be constructed.

So they got out their huge map of Antarctica, provided by the US Government, and spread it out over the tabletop. Where would an ancient civilization build a major port? The most obvious place was at the foot of the Beardmore Glacier, for that was the point where a great river had once flowed into the sea. But this area was already being covered by the New Zealand team. Their own team would be working mainly inland.

My grandfather pointed out that the Philippe Buache map suggested the civilization of Antarctica also extended inland—otherwise, why bother to map it? If the Ice Age took a thousand years to arrive, the inhabitants of Antarctica would have chosen sheltered places. You would not expect to find the remains of a city on the Rockefeller Plateau or the Holick-Kenyon Plateau. Since the prevailing winds blow from the west, you might expect to find a city under the brow of a mountain or in the shelter of a plateau.

They marked out on the map the area assigned to their team. It covered about thirty thousand square miles between the Byrd Research Station and the Ross Ice Sheet. In those days, most of this area was unmapped. But Silbye had already decided that the best place to set up a base camp would be about two hundred miles southeast of Byrd, in the area now called the Robertson Plain, sheltered from the prevailing west winds (which have been known to reach more than a hundred miles an hour) by Holyoake Peak.

As my grandfather studied the map, he saw that Silbye had also, unwittingly, chosen the best place to search for signs of a lost civilization. Between Holyoake Peak and Mount Jerome there is a valley that runs southwest towards the Dotson Ice Shelf—clearly a river valley. It is a place to avoid because of the winds that are funnelled down from the Amundsen Sea—the team would christen it Windy Gap. But in the days before the ice it would have been an obvious place to choose for an inland city. The width of the valley suggested it had once held a river that was both wide and deep, ideal transport for a nation of seafarers.

They saw the actual site for the first time a week later, on October 9, when their seven-man team arrived with dog sleds. Silbye was waiting for them—he had gone ahead by helicopter with the team that had constructed their living quarters. That afternoon, while the technicians tested their equipment, Silbye and my grandfather trudged two miles through the hard-packed snow until Mount Holyoake ceased to protect them and they were struck by the icy wind from the southwest. Behind them stretched the Robertson Plain, with Faure Peak visible in the distance. It certainly seemed an unlikely place to look for a lost city. But Silbye pointed out that it was less unlikely than it looked. At present Mount Holyoake ends in a forty-five degree slope, and as soon as they were beyond its protection they were almost blown off their feet by the wind. But in the days when Antarctica was green the valley floor was perhaps half a mile below their feet, and the mountains probably descended into foothills that would have afforded shelter.

Their first sonar soundings showed that Silbye was correct. There were indeed foothills at the base of the southern slope of Mount Holyoake, and the main one stretched like the foot of some gigantic three-toed saurian towards the river; its southern lee would have been ideal for a settlement. But the sonar revealed no traces that might have represented the remains of buildings.

I have said that my grandfather regarded those first two months in Antarctica as the happiest of his life. His journal describes how he woke every morning with a wonderful sense of excitement and optimism—the feeling: "This is going to be the day!" Yet when he climbed into his sleeping bag in the evening, after sixteen hours of utterly routine surveying, he felt no disappointment—only the same curious sense of euphoria, the feeling that something wonderful and exciting lay in store the next day.

In fact, from the point of view of topography, the Robertson Plain was disappointing. They had hoped to find interesting geographical features that could be mapped, but the land below the ice seemed as flat as its surface. (It has now been established that the ice in Antarctica follows the contours of the underlying land; in 1957 this was unknown.) But there would have been no time to feel discouraged. They were busy from morning till night. On some days they travelled as much as fifty miles with the dog teams, then set up camp overnight—in tents whose design was basically the same as those used by Scott and Amundsen—moving on again the next day.

I have a photograph of my grandfather and George Silbye outside the hut they shared below Mount Holyoake. The photographer is standing with his back to the mountains, and behind the men stretches an endless flat expanse of snow, looking as bleak and dreary as the midwest on a dull winter day.

My grandfather would tell me—forty years later—that when the photograph was taken he was reflecting on the fact that the secrets of an unknown civilization lay under more than half a mile of ice. He said he often found himself thinking how wonderful it would be if a sudden change in the earth's climate melted away the ice—until he remembered that ninety per cent of the world's ice is locked up in Antarctica, and that, if it should melt, the sea level would rise by 200 feet, enough to submerge half the populated areas and drown most of the great coastal cities, including New York, London, Tokyo and Amsterdam.

The journal records that the team spent that Christmas in the "township" of Little America, on the Ross Ice Shelf, and ate turkey and Christmas pudding and drank rum punch. On Christmas morning they were all invited to make telephone calls to their homes at the expense of the US Government. After exchanging greetings with his wife and children, my grandfather rang Hapgood.

"Merry Christmas, Charles. Anything new?"

"Not a lot. We make steady progress. How about you? Have you found anything interesting?"

"Afraid not." He summarized the result of their sonar findings. "My own feeling is that, if there was a pre-Ice Age civilization, it's probably left very few traces behind."

Hapgood said: "Oh, I don't know. Look at those descriptions in Plato—huge palaces built from stone blocks. They wouldn't disappear in a hurry."

My grandfather had lost the thread of the conversation. "Plato? What has Plato to do with it?"

"Don't you remember the description of Atlantis in the *Critias*? That's supposed to be before 9000BC."

My grandfather had never read Plato, but he had read about Atlantis as a child.

"But wasn't that supposed to be in the north Atlantic?"

"Plato just says it was beyond the Pillars of Hercules—Gibraltar."

"That's a long way from Antarctica."

"Of course. But there was a time when Antarctica was closer to the equator. In fact, there's evidence that it was once on the equator."

"Are you sure?"

"Haven't you read my book *Earth's Shifting Crust*?"

"No."

"I'll send you a copy. It has an introduction by Einstein. I argue that the surface of the earth is like the skin on gravy—it can be pulled around. There's evidence that seventeen thousand years ago Antarctica was thousands of miles further north."

My grandfather asked incredulously: "You're not suggesting . . . "

Hapgood said quickly: "I'm not suggesting anything. Look, it's too complicated to discuss over the phone. We'll talk about it later."

Then it was time to end the conversation—there were still a dozen people waiting to use the phone. As he hung up my grandfather felt utterly baffled and frustrated. For the first time since he had been in Antarctica, he wished he were back home— back in Hapgood's study at Keene State, where he could ask him what on earth he was talking about.

Outside, he met Silbye. "Do you know anything about Atlantis?"

"Only what everybody knows. Why?"

"Oh, I think Hapgood's gone mad. He seems to think Antarctica was once at the equator."

"So it was. But that was millions of years ago—when there was only a single continent, Pangaea. But what has that to do with Atlantis?"

"I'm damned if I know. Do you know if there's a library in this place?"

"A small one. It's in the hut next to the quartermaster's. You won't find much there."

Silbye was right—the library consisted mainly of detective fiction. But there was a college paperback called *Ten Dialogues of Plato*, and it contained the dialogue my grandfather was looking for, the *Critias*. He took it back to his quarters and read it in less than an hour—it is only a fragment. Critias describes to Socrates how there was a great war nine thousand years earlier, between "those who dwelt within the Pillars of Hercules, and those who dwelt without". Those who dwelt without were the inhabitants of the island of Atlantis, "bigger than Libya and Asia put together". Critias explains that his grandfather heard the story from the statesman Solon, who had heard it from the priests in Egypt. And his description of the city and harbour of Atlantis is incredibly detailed—Plato makes it sound as massive as the Acropolis of

Athens.

But when my grandfather had finished reading he was as confused as ever. Why had Hapgood mentioned Atlantis? Was he suggesting that the inhabitants of Atlantis—whose homeland had, according to the *Critias*, been destroyed by earthquakes and engulfed by the ocean—had fled to Antarctica?

He felt he had to speak of it to someone—otherwise he thought his head would explode. Yet, as he was about to sit up and leave the room, he was overcome by unexpected drowsiness. He closed his eyes, and fell asleep.

Once again, he experienced a curiously vivid and realistic dream. He was back at the base camp below Mount Holyoake; but there was no ice, and the atmosphere was almost tropically warm. The Robertson Plain was covered in lush grass, and he could see many trees. He turned north and began walking in the direction of Windy Gap, as he and Silbye had on their first afternoon there. On his left he could see the three outcrops of rock that looked like the foot of a three-toed saurian. Then, suddenly, he was aware that he was looking at the Robertson Plain as it had been in the remote past. At this point it became a lucid dream, in which he was aware he was dreaming. He began to walk faster, anxious to see as much as he could before waking up. He noted that there were no birds in the sky, no animals visible on the plain, and that a broad river flowed northwest towards the sea. Now he emerged past the outcrops of rock and looked along Windy Gap. The mountains on either side looked taller. And about a mile away, on both sides of the river, he could see dark grey angular masses that looked like the buildings of a city. He stared at them, wondering if they were some kind of natural formation. But when he raised his field glasses to his eyes there could be no doubt about it; these were buildings, massive buildings, with sloping sides and flat tops. To remove all possible doubt, many of them had tall openings, like doors, with curved tops—although as far as he could see there were no windows.

What puzzled him was that this did not look in the least like the city Plato had described in the *Critias*. That sounded more like ancient Athens; this looked like something out of a science-fiction story.

In spite of his efforts, the dream dissolved and he found himself back in his room. As he lay there on the bed, he said aloud: "Of course!"

For what he had forgotten was that Antarctica had not always been a land of icy winds. Exploration of some of the five per cent of the land that was free of ice had revealed coal deposits, which meant that it had once been covered with forests. And, surely, the natural place to choose for a city would have been a river valley . . . ? They had been looking in the wrong direction.

His first impulse was to hurry off and find Silbye. Yet the thought of describing his dream aroused in him an odd feeling of reluctance. He rationalized this by telling himself that, after all, Silbye was a scientist. What would he say to the suggestion that they should take soundings in Windy Gap simply because of a dream? Finally, my grandfather decided to keep it to himself.

#

The next day, December 26, they returned to the base camp. There was no time for a Christmas holiday; they had only twelve weeks before the Spring equinox, when Antarctica would return to darkness.

As the helicopter descended towards the foot of Mount Holyoake, my grandfather pointed to Windy Gap and shouted above the noise of the engine: "Why don't we take some soundings there?"

Silbye shrugged. "Why not?"

That "night" there was a storm. But when they woke up the next day the sky was clear and bright and the wind had dropped. By ten o'clock they were taking their first sounding in Windy Gap. By midday they had established that the river at this point had once been about two hundred yards wide, and about twice that in depth.

At five o'clock that afternoon they were taking their eighth sounding, about a mile down the valley. This, my grandfather was convinced, was roughly where the "city" of his dream was situated. He describes in the journal how he found it hard to maintain his air of casualness as Jim Peavey, the technician in charge of the sonar equipment, took another sounding. He watched intently as the pen traced a graph line on the paper tape.

My grandfather said: "Anything interesting?"

Peavey—a phlegmatic southerner—did not even bother to reply; he merely shook his head.

"Let's try further on."

They loaded the equipment on to the dog sled, and moved on. Silbye said: "I think we'll make this the last of the day."

My grandfather said nothing. He had no doubt that they were now above the city of his dream.

Half an hour later, Peavey again activated the echo, then rotated the equipment to cover an area of a few hundred yards. As he studied the paper tape, his face remained impassive.

My grandfather experienced a leaden sense of disappointment. "Nothing?"

"Nope."

And then my grandfather was struck by a sudden thought. A river cuts down into the earth, deepening its valley. Suppose the city of his dream was very old—more than ten thousand years old? If the ice returned to Antarctica five thousand years later, the river would have had a chance to cut far deeper than when the city was built. In that case, the remains of the city would now be above the floor of the valley, against the side of the mountain.

"Can you direct it over there?" He pointed towards the slope of the mountain.

"OK."

My grandfather was aware that Silbye was looking at him curiously. He went across to Peavey, and watched as the tape came out of the side of the equipment. As he looked at the graph's curve his heart began to beat painfully. The sonar pulse was being reflected back off large and irregular objects. Peavey said with sudden excitement:

"Yeah, there's somethin' there all right."

Silbye studied the tape for a long time, then looked up at the mountain.

"It's debris from a landslide. Look."

My grandfather could see what he meant. In the side of the mountain, a path about a quarter of a mile wide had been scooped in the grey rock. It was so smooth that no snow had settled on it.

He pointed to the steep curves on the tape.

"These are big rocks. Do you mind of we take a closer look?"

They moved five hundred yards closer to the mountainside. Five minutes later, Peavey said again: "Yeah, there's somethin' there."

Silbye was studying the tape. "Big rocks, some of them bigger than houses."

Peavey looked doubtful.

My grandfather said: "What do you think, Jim?"

Peavey said: "I'd say it's some kind of natural formation—like weathered volcanic lava."

My grandfather knew what he had in mind—he had seen photographs of the forty-foot hexagonal columns of basalt in Fingal's Cave. "But I think it's too big to be basaltic lava."

Silbye said: "You could be right. We'll come back tomorrow."

"Why can't we do a few more soundings now?"

"Because the wind's springing up again. Besides, we'll be late for dinner."

They were back again early the next morning—Silbye admitted that he had unable to sleep, wondering about the massive shapes. This time the sonar was set up close to the mountain face. During the next few hours it was moved a dozen times to try to achieve greater definition—at a depth of more than half a mile, the outline of the "rocks" was blurred.

While my grandfather was pinning the paper tapes on a sheet of hardboard, Silbye said casually: "Let's go and get some coffee."

They went to the sled, and poured coffee from a flask. When Silbye was sure Peavey was out of earshot, he said: "How did you know there was something there?"

"Educated guesswork."

Silbye said: "And what else?"

My grandfather decided to tell the truth. "All right, but you'll think I'm mad. I had a dream."

"A dream of what?"

"A city. Here in Windy Gap."

"What kind of a city?"

My grandfather did his best to describe it. When he had finished, Silbye said: "Will you do me a favour?"

"What?"

"Don't mention this to anyone else."

"My dream? Of course I wouldn't. They might want to lock me up."

"Not just your dream. Don't mention the city."

My grandfather was astonished. "Why not?"

Silbye said patiently: "Because it doesn't look like the remains of a city. It looks like the remains of a landslide." He pointed up at the mountain. "And the evidence is there."

My grandfather said: "There's an easy way to find out. Move the sonar to the other side of the valley. The city was on both sides of the river. What do you bet that we find the same thing on the other side?"

Silbye said urgently: "Keep your voice down." He glanced towards

Peavey, who was looking across at them.

My grandfather was baffled, and beginning to feel rather indignant. "I simply don't understand. If I'm right, it could be the greatest discovery of the century."

Silbye said patiently: "You're not thinking this through, Dan. Think what will happen if we go back to Byrd and say we've found the remains of a city. It will be on the front page of the *New York Times* the next day, and in every newspaper in the world the day after that. And if you even breathed the name Atlantis you'd be a laughing stock."

"For heaven's sake, I'm not that crazy. But you've got to look at the evidence. All right, there was a landslide, and it's covered some of the evidence. But look at those tapes. There's more than a landslide there. And all we have to do to prove it is move the sonar to the other side of the valley."

"That's just what we shouldn't do. For the moment, we've got to keep this to ourselves. Look out . . . "

Peavey came and joined them. He was carrying the hardboard under his arm.

"I don't understand this. If it's a landslide, it's not like any I've ever seen. Just look at the size of this." He pointed to a curve. "That must be a fifty-foot block." He looked up at the mountain. "And I just can't see where it came from."

Silbye said: "We'd have to climb Mount Holyoake to find out."

Peavey was obviously intrigued by the problem. He walked away across the valley, taking the binoculars, so he could get a view of the higher reaches of the mountain.

When they were alone again my grandfather said: "I agree with you about scientific caution. But this is suppressing information."

Silbye said: "Have you ever heard of Don Marcelino de Sautuola?"

"No."

"He was a Spanish nobleman who found an underground cave on his property. When he looked inside it, he found pictures of bulls on the walls—bulls drawn by Cro-Magnon men. But the pigment was still wet, and when he announced his discovery, the experts denounced him as a fraud. He fought for years to clear his name—he pointed out that he had no reason to forge the paintings, but no one believed him. Then they began to discover more paintings, in caves in the Vezere Valley, with the pigment still wet, and they realized that Don Marcelino had been telling the truth all along. But it was too late to apologize—he was already dead. The experts had made the rest of his life a misery with their accusations. So Don Marcelino never lived to see Altamira become one of the most famous caves in the world. Now tell me—if he'd been able to foresee what would happen, do you think he would have announced his discovery?"

My grandfather had to admit that this was unanswerable. He knew enough about the academic world to know that a professor who becomes an object of ridicule is a liability to his university.

He said: "But suppose we had evidence—evidence of massive structures that couldn't be natural features?"

"If we had real evidence, we'd be obliged to announce it. But we don't have evidence yet."

"Then let's look on the other side of the valley!"

"All right. But not now. Let's wait for an opportunity when there's just the two of us."

That evening, when they were alone, they renewed the conversation. This is what my grandfather said in his journal:

I have to admire Silbye's cool head. Without him, I would have told Peavey that I think it's the remains of a city, and Peavey would have told the rest of the team (in fact, they're away mapping Erebus at the moment), and someone would have passed it back to Byrd, and it would be unstoppable. But Silbye's obviously right. With something as big as this, it's best not to go off at half-cock.

Now we have to wait for an opportunity to try the north side of the valley.

#

Four days later, after a New Year's Eve celebration, Peavey stayed behind with an upset stomach, and the conspirators had their opportunity. It was an icy cold day, with the temperature well below zero and a strong wind blowing down the valley; but this did not deter them. By ten in the morning they were back at the site of their previous soundings; then they turned across the valley at ninety degrees—they were so anxious to get it right that they preferred to do this rather than travel down the far side of the valley and risk missing the spot by a hundred yards.

My grandfather told me that, as they unloaded and set up the sonar, he felt like a burglar, afraid they'd be interrupted. For this first probe they set up within a few hundred yards of the side of the valley, which was less steep than on the south. As the paper tape came out of its slot, Silbye glanced at it and said: "It looks as if you could be right."

My grandfather's hands were shaking as he reached out for the tape. The shape of the graph curve left no doubt that there was something down there under the ice—something big.

My grandfather pointed up the mountain.

"You see—no sign of a landslide here."

Silbye studied the tape. "True. But this doesn't look like buildings either. It's not regular enough."

"For God's sake George. Neither are the ruins of ancient Rome."

Over the next two hours they moved the sonar a dozen times. The results were exciting and at the same time frustrating. The "ruins" extended along a slope several hundred yards above the valley floor. To my grandfather, what had happened was obvious. The city he had seen had been undermined by erosion, so that most of it had collapsed into the deepening valley carved by the river. What remained clung to the hillsides on either side of the valley. But the ice in the valley was, in effect, a gigantic, slow-moving river, and the remnants of the city had been ground like rocks into the bed of a torrent. The clear, rectangular shapes that my grandfather had glimpsed in his dream had been eroded into irregular masses that could be mistaken for gigantic boulders. It was true that many of these "boulders" looked oddly like the work of man. But to the eye of the sceptic they were merely impressive natural features.

By one o'clock, when they broke off for a lunch of sandwiches and coffee—huddled under blankets in the sled—my grandfather knew that Silbye had been right. With evidence as ambiguous as this, it would have been a disaster even to hint at man-made structures.

Which is why, when reports of their findings appeared in the publications of the International Geophysical Year, the "ruins" were described as "puzzling and undetermined natural features under the ice, which spread along both sides of the valley for a distance of perhaps a quarter of a mile".

#

When my grandfather returned home in the third week of March he could hardly wait to tell Hapgood what he had found. Yet their meeting also turned out to be something of a disappointment. Hapgood was deeply interested, of course, but my grandfather's hints over the telephone had led him to expect something more definite than huge blocks that might be natural features—he later told my father he had been hoping for evidence of a port, or some similar discovery, where the ice shelf joined the land.

And, when my grandfather asked him what he had meant about Atlantis, Hapgood explained he had merely intended to point out that, if Plato was right, a pre-Ice Age civilization could have created buildings as massive as the temples of Egypt. But then, he added, Atlantis was probably a myth created by Plato . . . My grandfather felt that Hapgood was being less than candid—after all, why bother to mention Atlantis at all if he felt it to be a myth? So the afternoon he spent with Hapgood, although friendly enough, lacked the warmth and excitement of their previous meetings. Between March 1958 and the publication of Hapgood's *Maps of the Ancient Sea Kings: Evidence of Advanced Civilization in the Ice Age* in 1966 they met on only three occasions. The third of these was at the book's launching party in Philadelphia—it was brought out by a Philadelphia publisher—when my grandfather and grandmother drank to Hapgood's future fame and success.

Of course, nothing of the sort happened. The reviews were mostly favourable, and Hapgood made a number of appearances on radio and television. Naturally, the academics ignored it completely. And within six months the book had been more or less forgotten.

How could this happen to a work as important as *Maps of the Ancient Sea Kings*? The answer, unfortunately, is that Hapgood had been anticipated. In 1960 a book called *Le Matin des Magiciens* (translated into English as *The Morning of the Magicians*) had been published in Paris; the authors were a journalist called Louis Pauwels and a student of alchemy named Jacques Bergier. It is a strange mishmash of occultism, prophecy, flying saucers, the Great Pyramid and Hitler's astrologers, and it became an immediate bestseller. Translated into a dozen languages, it launched the "occult revival" of the late 20th century.

And, in the midst of a discussion of lost civilizations, it explains that "in the middle of the 19th century, a Turkish naval officer, Piri Re'is, presented the Library of Congress with a set of maps he had discovered in the East". All this is, of course, absurdly inaccurate. The authors ask: "Had [these maps] been traced from observations made on board a flying machine or space ship of some kind? Notes taken by visitors from Beyond?" And so the medieval portolans achieved worldwide notoriety as proof that earth had been visited in the remote past by creatures from outer space. *The Morning of the Magicians* appeared in America in 1963 and became a bestseller there too. So the critics can hardly be blamed for failing to distinguish between Hapgood's sober and serious study of ancient maps and this lurid "occult" journalism.

Worse was to come. In 1968 a Swiss writer named Erich von Däniken produced a book called *Chariots of the Gods?*, which was advertised under the rubric: "Did God drive a flying saucer?" It sold a million copies and, since it contained even more absurdities and inaccuracies than *The Morning of the Magicians*, aroused the same fury in serious reviewers. "The latest studies of Professor Charles H. Hapgood," declares von Däniken, "give us some more shattering information. Comparison with modern photographs of our globe taken from satellites showed that the originals of Piri Re'is's maps must have been aerial photographs taken from a very great height. How can that be explained?"

It can be explained, of course, by recognizing that von Däniken is talking nonsense. Hapgood never mentioned aerial photographs taken from a very great height. But everyone who read *Chariots of the Gods?* assumed that Hapgood believed Antarctica had been photographed from a flying saucer in the days before it was covered with ice. There was no way he could escape being tarred with the same brush as von Däniken and the authors of *The Morning of the Magicians*. Hapgood succeeded in getting his book republished in 1979, not long before his death, but by then the damage had been done. A book that should have been as epoch-making as Darwin's *Origin of Species* continued to be ignored.

#

And how did I, Matthew Willoughby, come to be involved in this bizarre and complicated story?

It started when I was thirteen, and was spending the weekend in Rye Beach, a small sea town in New Hampshire where my grandfather had retired when he left the university.

My father, Richard Willoughby, had inherited none of my grandfather's interest in science and mathematics—in fact, he hated them both. As a teenager, he came upon a book by Jung and decided he wanted to be a psychiatrist. He studied medicine at Johns Hopkins, became a consultant psychiatrist in the mid-1980s, and achieved celebrity with his book *Shadows in the Mind* in 1989. We lived in Riverside Drive, New York, and I went to school in Morris Heights.

My grandfather said very little about his son's chosen profession, but I had a feeling that he regarded psychology as a pseudoscience.

I took after my grandfather, and from the time he gave me a kind of cartoon picturebook called *Frontiers of Science* when I was ten, dreamed of becoming a scientist. Our family often went to visit with my grandfather at weekends. In the year that I was thirteen I spent most of the summer holidays at Rye Beach.

My grandfather was at that time seventy-three, a tall man with a nose like an eagle's beak and a pointed chin. We used to take long walks, and he first introduced me to the ideas of Einstein, Planck and Gödel. Both his sons had been something of a disappointment to him, for neither showed any aptitude for mathematics—my Uncle Carl became an actor. So he was delighted to find that I wanted to follow in his footsteps.

I was given a free run of his library, and it was there that I discovered his signed copy of *Maps of the Ancient Sea Kings*. It seemed an unusual kind of book to find on his shelf, among volumes on bridge-building and chaos theory, and I took it off to the beach. As soon as I read the opening sentence, "This book is the story of the discovery of the first evidence that advanced peoples preceded all the peoples now known to history", I was hooked. All this talk about the sea kings of ancient Crete and the great library of Alexandria made my hair tingle with excitement. I found it so exciting that, before the afternoon was over, I had turned to the last chapter, "A Civilization that Vanished", and read it while I was still only halfway through the book proper.

As soon as I got back I asked my grandfather about it all, and about why Hapgood had inscribed the book, "To my old friend and supporter." My grandfather was drinking the martini he always poured himself at half-past five, and was feeling relaxed and expansive. He told me to sit down in the other armchair, poured me a glass of sweet sherry, and then recounted to me the whole story, from the time he went on the radio with Mallery to the fiasco of the publication of Hapgood's book.

By the time we went out to dinner at the seafood restaurant across the road I was as excited as my grandfather had been when he overheard his father talking about the great hole in the South Pole. It seemed to me incredible that Hapgood had proved an ancient civilization existed in Antarctica thousands of years before ancient Egypt, and that this findings had been ignored. I was also excited by his hint about Atlantis. My grandfather told me that, when he pressed Hapgood to tell him whether he thought these inhabitants of the South Pole came from Atlantis, Hapgood privately admitted he thought it highly probable. I wanted to know why Hapgood had not said so in his book, and my grandfather explained that this would have been disastrous for his academic reputation.

But I still found it impossible to understand why my grandfather himself had not continued to pursue this fascinating question; after all, if an ancient civilization did exist under the ice of the Antarctic, it would change our whole vision of human history. And the man who first proved it was true would achieve everlasting fame.

My grandfather smiled ironically, and said he had once thought the same thing.

At this point, my grandmother intervened. She was a quiet woman who seldom spoke, but now she said she had often wished he had pursued the question of the lost civilization. He had frequently talked of writing a book about it. Why not start now?

He shook his head. "Silbye was right. There's just not enough evidence. I fed those paper tapes into a computer, and they show immense blocks. But, if there was a city down there, it's been pulverized by the glacier."

I didn't understand this. "But you told me that there were huge blocks of stone on either side of Windy Gap."

"And if there was some easy way of getting down to them I'd be trying to form an expedition myself, Matthew. But there's no conceivable way of cutting down through three thousand feet of ice."

"How about an oil drill?"

"That would do it, of course. But what would we do then? Send someone down in a bucket with a candle?"

"But there must be some way? Isn't there any drill that could make a wide tunnel—the kind of drills they use to make railway tunnels under mountains?"

"I've thought that too. It would cost millions of dollars to transport such a drill to the Antarctic. And what would happen when you got down there?

You'd find yourself looking at a rock as big as a house. What do you do then? Take a pick and shovel?"

My grandmother said: "But perhaps it wouldn't be a rock. Perhaps it would be a house."

"True. That would settle it once and for all. But it wouldn't be worth spending a million dollars unless you were fairly certain it was going to be a house. You see, the truth is that what we really need is for all the ice in that valley to melt away, so we could see exactly what's underneath it. Then, I'm sure, we'd find all the evidence we need about a city—if it exists."

I asked: "Do you think it exists?"

"I honestly can't say. I believe there's evidence of an ancient civilization somewhere under that ice. But whether it's in Windy Gap I don't know. I just had a dream, that's all."

My grandmother said: "And your dreams often come true. You remember about Mary Dexter's wedding . . . "

My grandfather began to laugh. "You're the kind of wife who ruins her husband's reputation . . . "

And at that point the food arrived and the subject was abandoned. But the conversation—aided possibly by the lobster claws—had inflamed my imagination to such an extent that I spent half the night dreaming about Atlantis and vast underground cities.

Back at home, I told the whole story to my father, and was gratified when he seemed fascinated. Intellectually speaking, he and my grandfather had never been close, since my father's interests had always been literary rather than scientific. But this strange tale of a lost civilization touched his imagination, and he borrowed *Maps of the Ancient Sea Kings* from the New York Public Library. He was as impressed as I was, and next time my grandfather came to visit I listened in while they had a discussion about how the ice could be penetrated. Like me, he suggested tunnelling equipment; my grandfather pointed out that, when a tunnel is driven through a mountain, they build a railway track to remove the earth in trucks. Such a track would have to be built in Windy Gap to remove millions of tons of ice. The cost would be prohibitive.

I asked: "What about some machine that breathed fire, like that thing you have for burning weeds in the garden?"

My grandfather laughed. "It would fill the shaft with water."

"But you could pump it out."

"Yes . . . I suppose you could."

I had an idea. "Couldn't you make some kind of machine like a rocket, with a red hot point, that would cut down through the ice? Then you could travel down through the ice as if you were in a diving bell."

My grandfather nodded. "Yes, that might work."

During the next weeks I devoted a great deal of intellectual energy to the problem of how to penetrate half a mile of ice. It seemed amazing that such a simple-looking problem could be so baffling.

It goes without saying that I told everybody who would listen—all my friends, the science master, the bosomy lady who taught us literature, two uncles and, on one occasion, a total stranger who was sitting next to me on the subway and reading an article about Antarctica in *Scientific American*. All of them were interested. But they all admitted they had no idea of how to solve the problem of how to tunnel down through half a mile of ice.

As far as I could see, the simplest and most obvious solution was to use an oil drill, which would have no difficulty in sinking a well into the ice. I suggested this to Dr Silbye, the first time I met him at my grandfather's house, and he pointed out that the cost of transporting a drilling rig four hundred miles inland from the Ross Sea (where Shell were then making some test drills) would be enormous.

I refused to give up. During the next year or so, I suggested at least six more ideas that had real possibilities. The most practical of these, I believe, was using superheated steam to vaporize the ice, which would rise into the air and descend elsewhere as rain. My grandfather objected that this would merely convert most of the ice into water, and leave us with a vast lake that would freeze up again the same night. I didn't agree, but had no way of proving my point without putting it to the practical test.

#

The solution came through a series of chance events. The first was my meeting with Gordon Trask.

At that time, no one had heard of Trask. In spite of the fact that he had almost as many patents to his name as Edison or Tesla, he had never aroused the interest of the popular press. So when, in my second year at Columbia, I heard that he was lecturing to the Science Club on the future of science, I had to ask my room mate who he was. "Oh, I don't know—some kind of inventor." Even that failed to arouse my interest—I planned to take a girl named Coral to a meeting of the European Film Society. I had known her a week and was convinced I was in love. So when, at the last moment, she told me she had to go to dinner with a visiting relative, I suspected infidelity and thought of going out to get drunk. Then I realized I had only five dollars in my wallet, and decided to go home instead. Yet, just as I was about to walk to the bus stop, I felt an odd compulsion to go back on campus. I went to the notice board to see what was happening that evening, decided against the meeting of the Charles Ives Society, and somehow found myself in Trask's lecture.

There were not more than twenty people in the room, and Trask had already started when I arrived. He was talking about the psychology of invention, and some of his examples were—to put it mildly—rather abstruse, so that half the audience looked baffled.

Trask was not a good speaker—a small, thin man with a high, domed forehead, piercing blue eyes, a big, curved nose and a slightly nasal voice. He had an odd habit of abruptly ceasing to speak, and staring intently at the table as if he had seen some amazing and rare beetle. Then he would open and close the fingers of his right hand in an abrupt, jerky way, and launch into some explanation about computers that seemed to have no relation to what he had been saying earlier. Occasionally, his face would break into a sudden bright smile, as if he had just said something astounding; but what followed was as incomprehensible as the rest. His intellectual enthusiasm would have been infectious if we had been able to understand what he was talking about. He made me think of a kind of disconnected Sherlock Holmes.

In a sense, what he was saying was quite simple—that there is a fundamental difference between computers and the human brain—and he was criticizing computer experts who one day hoped to create a "living" computer. The problem was that he assumed we knew as much as he did, so that most of what he said was above our heads.

At the end of his talk, Bob Scarsby, the chairman, made a short speech about the "fascinating lecture", and most of the audience stampeded for the bar.

I was about to do the same thing when, for the second time that evening, I found myself doing something I had not intended—I went forward to the podium speak to him.

Our visiting celebrities usually ended up with a crowd around them, but on this occasion I was the only one. Which is how, half an hour later, I found myself sitting in a cheap Italian restaurant with Bob and Trask, eating pasta at the expense of the Science Club.

When Bob had invited me to join them I had been a little worried at the prospect of dining with someone whose mind seemed to operate on such an incredible level of abstraction. But, once I noticed the way that Trask spilt tomato puree on his bow tie and started to put salt in his coffee before Bob stopped him, I began to feel more at ease. He was obviously a genuine example of the absent-minded genius.

While we were waiting for the food, Bob made the mistake of asking him about pesticides, which led to a baffling discourse on molecular biology. I decided to try to get some sense out of him by asking my favourite question.

"If you were an archaeologist, and you had to penetrate half a mile of ice, how would you do it?"

He thought for a moment then said: "With a giant mechanical digger—the kind they use in open-cast mines."

"And suppose it was in the middle of the Antarctic, so the cost would be prohibitive?"

"I'd begin to think in terms of laser technology."

I experienced a bubble of rising excitement.

"Could you explain, sir?"

I saw Bob wince, preparing for another barrage of impenetrable computerese. Instead, Trask smiled and said:

"And what would be the purpose of this exercise?"

"Have you heard of Charles Hapgood?"

"No. Who is he?"

I launched into my well prepared presentation of the theory of pre-Ice Age civilization. Within a few minutes I could see I had them both hooked. Whenever I felt ashamed of monopolizing the conversation, they both begged me to go on. I told them about my grandfather's visit to Antarctica during the IGY and about the great stone blocks buried under the glacier.

Trask interrupted me: "Has he had the data analysed by computer?"

"I think so."

"With what result?"

"I couldn't tell you. But it wasn't as exciting as he expected. Don't forget their sonar was an early model—1957."

"Then what makes him so certain that it wasn't merely a landslide?"

"The fact that it was on both sides of the valley, just as he expected."

Bob said: "Haven't they been back since?"

"No. My grandfather apparently lost heart. Nobody seemed interested." And I explained how Hapgood had suffered from ancient-astronaut "theorists" like von Däniken.

Trask said: "If you'd like to ask him to send his data to my laboratory, we'll do a computer analysis."

I did my best not to show just how delighted I felt by asking: "Could a laser cut through half a mile of ice?"

"Oh, certainly. But that isn't the problem. A laser can cut through anything by focusing its energy down to a point. But, of course, that would cut a hole the width of a needle, which wouldn't be of much use. The real problem is that the most powerful lasers are about ninety-five per cent inefficient. Chemical lasers are about twelve per cent efficient. Even my new zirconium laser is only fifteen per cent. The best solution would be a free-electron laser—they can be tuned to microwave frequencies."

I knew enough about microwaves to know that they produce heat.

"You mean you could create a kind of heat ray—like Wells's Martians?"

"In theory, yes." And once again he launched into explanations that went way above our heads. But this time I was determined to understand, so I interrupted him with questions. It soon dawned on me that, after all, he wasn't really an absent-minded professor, incapable of explaining himself in simple words. The trouble was he knew so much that he couldn't really grasp that other people knew so little. But, once he knew what you didn't know, he could explain something with amazing simplicity.

I knew a little about lasers, but Bob—whose subject was sociology—knew nothing at all. So Trask began from the beginning. I was so fascinated that I can repeat it virtually word for word.

When a poker is heated, he explained, its atoms and molecules become more and more excited—like a lot of people jumping up and down—until the poker gets red-hot and gives off light. But the light it gives off is of many different wavelengths—and therefore colours. When a poker is white-hot, it is giving off all the colours of the spectrum. At this point, the "people" are running about all over the place.

Now there is a way of influencing the excited molecule or atom so it gives off energy—by firing energy of a certain wavelength at it. For example, if you fire a microwave pulse at an ammonia molecule, the molecule gives off another microwave pulse. Then those two microwave pulses hit two more molecules, and they give off two more pulses. In a short time you've got an avalanche of pulses—as in a microwave oven. The principle is fundamental to the maser.

You can do the same thing with light energy. If you fire a pulse of light at a certain kind of atom, it gives off light of the same wavelength. And if this light hits another excited atom, that one does the same. By manipulation, you can get all these identical waves of light to move in phase—so that all their peaks and troughs line up with each other. Now, instead of a crowd running madly all over the place, you have them marching in step, like an army.

A laser beam is made of light waves of precisely the same colour all marching in step. Because the crowd is acting together rather than all at cross-purposes, the concentration of energy in such a light beam—a "coherent" light beam—is immense. So, when the beam is focused and aimed at a piece of material—ice, for example—it can punch a hole straight through it.

The problem, as Trask said, is that the process is so inefficient. It takes a vast amount of energy to make a laser work, and ninety-five per cent of this is wasted. In principle, a laser or maser should give off an explosion of energy comparable to an atom bomb.

The free-electron laser that Trask mentioned is more efficient. This takes a beam of electrons produced by a particle accelerator and bends them into a spiral using an array of electromagnets. This is the type of laser that President Reagan had in mind to knock out IBMs in his Star Wars proposal.

Which explains why Trask thought that laser beams might be the answer to the problem of Windy Gap. Most scientists would have considered such an approach a waste of time—like using a surgical scalpel to cut down a tree. But Trask was convinced the free-electron laser could be made to generate the same kind of power as a chainsaw. His laboratory had been working on the idea for the past year.

I asked: "And how far have you got?"

"Quite a way. But I have to admit there's still a long way to go."

I was so excited by all this that, as soon as I got home, I telephoned my grandfather. He was in bed at the time, but not yet asleep. When I mentioned Trask, he was impressed.

"There was an article about him in *Science Monthly*. They compared him to Edison."

"He wants you to send him your sonar data, and he'll try computer enhancement."

"We've already tried that."

"But that was years ago. His equipment is state-of-the-art."

"All right. It can't do any harm to see what happens."

#

As I climbed into bed that night, I was fairly certain I was not going to sleep; it made me wish I'd had more to drink in the restaurant—since Trask was a teetotaller, Bob and I had confined ourselves to a single glass of the house wine. I could not have been more mistaken. As soon as my head touched the pillow, I fell into a deep and peaceful sleep. When I woke up in the early hours of the morning, I had a curious sense of contentment and wellbeing. And then, towards dawn, I had a marvellous dream of Antarctica. I was in Windy Gap, with a crew of scientists and technicians, and we were about to start blasting a hole in the ice with a laser that looked like a giant telescope. It was all so clear and real that I believed I was actually there. I was wearing fur-lined boots and, when I stamped my feet, I could feel the snow crunching underfoot.

At this point, one of the team got down on all fours and peered through the ice. He seemed so excited that I did the same, brushing aside the snow with my gloved hand. I was astonished to find that the ice was as clear as glass, and that I could see down through it. Far below, at a depth of about a hundred feet, I could see people walking around. Then one of them looked up and pointed. They all stared up towards us, and one of them waved.

I felt myself waking up, and struggled against it. I wanted to see what happened next. Finally I gave up the struggle, and opened my eyes. The sky was turning light, and I felt that I had been through a strange and wonderful experience. I lay there for perhaps five minutes, feeling oddly contented, as if it were Christmas morning and I was a child again.

From then on, I had an odd feeling of certainty that I was destined to play a central role in solving this problem of Hapgood's "pre-Ice Age civilization". Whenever I thought about Antarctica, I experienced a sense of warmth around the heart, as if I had entered into some kind of agreement with fate.

And from that point onward everything seemed to go right. Up to then I had been like any normal teenager—expecting things to go wrong, to miss buses, to say the wrong thing, to trip as I left the room. Now I would flip open a telephone directory and find I was looking at the right page for the number I wanted. I would arrive in a full car park just as someone was vacating a space. I would stumble upon some important piece of information just before it was raised in class, giving me a spurious air of being well informed.

Just as a test, I began trying to guess what bus would be along next, and found I had an amazingly high score. Even my love life suddenly improved. I had become accustomed to a fairly high level of frustration and failure—often due to clumsiness or tactlessness. Now I seemed incapable of saying or doing the wrong thing. It turned out, for example, that I had been correct in suspecting that Coral had been lying when she'd said she had to go out with visiting relatives; she was actually going to the theatre with a football player named Josh Rubin. But two days later they quarrelled, and when she bumped into me in Washington Square she invited me to dinner in the flat she shared with two other girls. I spent the evening telling them about Hapgood and my grandfather, and had the satisfaction of seeing them hang on every word I spoke. As she walked me to the subway, Coral was already hinting about getting engaged.

That following weekend, my grandparents came to stay, and Trask was invited to dinner. He arrived an hour late, looking untidier than ever, and with the tomato puree stains still on his bow tie. At first, he seemed shy and absent-minded—I discovered later that he hated social engagements. But when my grandfather produced copies of the sonar tapes from his briefcase his abstraction disappeared. He seemed to be able to read them as a musician can read music.

He asked: "Can I use your fax machine? I'd like to send these to my laboratory."

My mother asked: "Will there be anybody there at this time?"

"Of course. My chief assistant Bill Ruggles usually stays till midnight."

Within two hours—while we were still sitting at the dinner table—there was a ring at the doorbell. It was Bill Ruggles—a chunkily built man only a few years older than myself—with the computer enhancements. As soon as I looked at the first one, my heart began to pound. It looked, quite simply, like a giant building block. And I knew, from the earlier computer enhancement, that it had to be as at least as big as the room we were sitting in.

There were about two dozen of these enhancements, and—unlike the earlier set, which were merely line-drawings—the computer had turned these into something like black-and-white photographs. Those from the south side of the valley were particularly clear. There could be no reasonable doubt that what we were looking at were the remains of collapsed buildings—buildings that, at a guess, had originally been a hundred feet tall.

We all felt stunned. My mother was the only one to behave normally—she offered Bill Ruggles some food, which he accepted enthusiastically, and went off to carve the remains of the roast beef.

Trask handed my grandfather the sonar reproductions.

"Well, it seems we have to congratulate you."

My grandfather shook his head as if dazed. "I find it hard to take in—after forty years."

My father said: "It looks as if you were right about Atlantis."

Trask echoed: "Atlantis?"

My grandfather looked as if somebody had stepped on his corn. "Oh, for heaven's sake, Dick!"

My father said: "Why not tell them? Somebody's going to have to."

My grandfather said desperately: "Because it's just a crazy idea."

Trask said: "I enjoy crazy ideas. Please go ahead."

In the end I had to explain—my grandfather's academic caution reduced him to incoherence. I described how Hapgood had been the first to mention Atlantis, and how he'd refused to elaborate. But the evidence of the blocks made it look as if he'd been right after all. If Antarctica had been inhabited, the people had to have come from somewhere. And Plato's Atlantis seemed as good a guess as any—after all, where else was there around 7000BC?

Bill Ruggles—who had by now cleared his plate—interrupted to say that he'd seen a television programme that argued that ancient Egypt was peopled by survivors from Atlantis, and that the Egyptians also built their early temples with gigantic building blocks—some of them weighing two hundred tons. And, when Trask said he'd also heard something about the theory, my grandfather looked relieved to realise they didn't think he was mad after all.

The following day I paid my first visit to Trask's laboratory, a few blocks from Columbia, near Marcus Garvey Park. Although it was a Sunday, the place was as active as a beehive—Bill Ruggles, who showed me around, explained that nobody had to work Sundays, but that most of them couldn't be kept away. The place was enormous—a whole floor of the building—and the number of projects staggering. Bill Ruggles, working on the free-electron laser, had a whole room to himself, but in the main lab there were at least a dozen major projects, including "permanent paper" that would never deteriorate, the instant freezer (which could reduce a glass of water to ice in thirty seconds), a portable voice computer for translating instantaneously from one language to another, a glue that would seal broken glass without a sign of a crack, a hearing aid so tiny it could be implanted below the skin of the inner ear, and a long-life atomic battery that would last for twenty-five years. (Trask had already patented his own two-year atomic battery.) In the drugs research unit they were investigating the properties of the "butterfly flower" from central New Guinea, which has now been developed into the most powerful anti-schizophrenia drug so far, while in the general medical unit the "limbless genius" Brian Zworkin (who had lost both arms and legs as a result of an auto crash) was synthesizing zworkonin, which—as everyone now knows—will knit broken bones in less than an hour.

I suspect that most of the people I met assumed that Trask had selected me as a future recruit, and they treated me as a colleague. A week earlier, I would have found it overwhelming to be given free access to the secrets of Trask's "creation factory" (as one journalist labelled it). Now I took it in my stride. After all, I had been responsible for bringing Trask and my grandfather together. And if Hapgood's "lost civilization" was discovered beneath the Antarctic ice, I felt I would deserve a great deal of the credit.

What happened next confirmed my feeling that I was somehow onto a winning streak.

Bill Ruggles knocked on a glass-plated door at the end of the corridor. When someone called "Come in" he opened it, then said: "I'm sorry Anton. I thought you were alone."

"That's OK. I'd finished. Come on in."

I was introduced to Anton Voronski, a psychologist from the Manhattan Psychiatric Clinic, who in turn introduced us to a young, dark-haired girl who looked about fifteen, and whose name was Inga—I didn't catch her surname. She said "How do you do?" with a charming foreign accent. Voronski—a slight, greying man with rimless glasses—explained that he had just been testing her for extra-sensory perception and that her score had been just below a hundred per cent. He was obviously delighted, and insisted on demonstrating her prowess. He made her turn her back, then asked us to give him something out of our pockets. Ruggles produced a ball-bearing and I produced an india rubber. Voronski went to a series of inverted plastic cups on the table, and placed the bearing and the eraser below two of them chosen at random. Inga was standing in a corner with a hat-stand in front of her.

Voronsky said: "All right, Inga."

She crossed to the table, stared intently at the row of cups—twelve of them—then unhesitatingly reached out and pointed to the two that Voronski had chosen.

He said: "Any idea what they are?"

She said: "This is a steel ball. The other . . . " She hesitated and frowned. "It is some kind of cube . . . but it is made of rubber."

Voronski lifted the cups with an air of triumph. "She's been doing that all morning. And when I threw a dice, she got twelve out of twelve. In the second test I threw the dice while taking care not to see the result—in case she was reading my mind. And she still got twelve out of twelve."

Even I knew that was impressive. I looked with awe at this slender girl—who looked as if she weighed less than a hundred pounds—and wondered what my father would say when I told him I had met a witch. She even looked a little like a witch—her face would have been pretty if her lips had not been so pale and her eyes so large.

Bill and I had finished our tour, and he had to get back to work. I had seen the free-electron laser in operation, and watched it drill a two-inch hole in a sheet of copper—he explained that this was an important advance, since most lasers had to be focused down to a point. But it struck me that it would take a lot of two-inch holes to make a sizeable tunnel down through the ice.

His last words to me at the door were: "In six months, I'm hoping to make it a six-inch hole!"

#

On the pavement at 125th Street I saw Inga waiting for the light to change. I said hello and asked her which way she was walking. When she said she was headed to 138th Street, I offered to walk with her, since it was on my way home. It was a beautiful day, just cool enough to make it comfortable walking. We walked two blocks to Roosevelt Square, then north up Convent.

When I asked her if she was at school, she amazed me by telling me she was twenty-two, and that she worked with her brothers and sisters in a group called the Vassilievskies. In Russia they had been a circus act, and she had trained as a tightrope walker and a bareback rider. Her elder brother Pavel was the greatest juggler in the world. But they all had "psychic powers". An impresario called Boris Belmont had brought them to America, but he was a crook, and now they were on their own.

She asked me about myself, and, when I mentioned that my father was a psychiatrist named Richard Willoughby, she looked interested.

"Is he not a friend of Professor Hallam?"—naming one of my father's colleagues. It seemed that Hallam had suggested my father ought to meet the Vassilievskies.

"Why don't you come home and meet him now? We'll just be in time for lunch."

She thought about it for a moment, then gave a wonderful, bright smile that made my heart turn a somersault.

"All right."

In fact, my father had already asked Hallam to arrange an introduction, and was delighted to meet her. It seemed that she—and her two brothers and younger sister—were the rising stars of paranormal research. On Hallam's advice, they had turned down an offer to appear on a popular television programme; he wanted them to go through rigorous scientific tests before they exposed themselves to the media circus. As a Jungian, my father was sympathetic to the claims of paranormal research—although he had never been involved in testing "psychics"—and Hallam felt he would be the ideal person to make a preliminary assessment.

At lunch, Inga confined herself to vegetables and bottled water. As soon as she overcame her shyness, she talked freely about her life in Russia, her early years in Smolensk, her training as an acrobat, and her years in a circus.

I described how she had located the ball-bearing and the india rubber under the cups, and my father asked: "Can you do it now?" My mother started to protest, but Inga said promptly and without hesitation: "Of course."

She went and leaned out of the open window, and my father inverted six coffee cups on the table. My grandfather took from his coat pocket a tiny portable toothbrush, of the kind they issue on airlines. I knew what it was, because I had one myself, but to anyone who had never seen one it looked like just a green plastic tube.

My grandfather placed this under one of the cups. Then Inga was told she could turn round.

She glanced at the cups, and without hesitation placed her finger on the right one.

My father asked: "Can you tell what it is?"

"A little brush." She had not only seen through the cup, but through the plastic tube that held the brush.

We were all astonished. After that, no one had any doubt of her paranormal powers.

Pleased with our admiration, she said: "Would you like me to do something else?"

We nodded enthusiastically.

She said: "I will try to make that cloud go away." She pointed out of the open window. It was a clear, still day, with hardly any breeze, and a small white cloud was hanging over the river in the blue sky.

She said: "I am not quite sure I can do it. Usually my brothers and sister help me. But I will try."

We all stood up to watch her. She crossed to the window and stared at the cloud. For perhaps half a minute nothing happened; then the cloud seemed to drift apart. In less than a minute, it was gone.

We all applauded. There was simply no possibility of trickery.

Inga came and sat down. I noticed that there was a film of sweat on her forehead, and that she was breathing deeply, as if the effort had wearied her.

I said: "Was it tiring?"

She wrinkled her nose and shook her head. "Not very, but I was nervous."

I saw my father glance out of the corner of his eye at my grandfather. One of their main points of disagreement, dating back many years, was Jung's interest in the paranormal. My grandfather thought Jung was an old fraud, and that ghosts, poltergeists, extra-sensory perception and the rest were simply a silly superstition. Yet he had just seen Inga perform two "supernatural" feats that were self-evidently genuine. A sceptic might cavil: "Are you sure she wasn't peering while you put the toothbrush under the cup? Are you sure the cloud wouldn't have dissolved anyway?" But no one who was in that room could doubt for a moment that there was no trickery.

When we had finished eating, she performed several more impressive feats. She asked me to take a book off the shelf, open it, and read a page. The book was one of a set of Lafcadio Hearn, and I opened it at random—as she told me to—and read a page. She was sitting opposite me in an armchair. Before I had finished the page she said: "I see three men—Chinamen—sitting on cane chairs and drinking tea. Now they are . . . looking at something . . . looking at bowls. And another man has come in to join them."

I read the page aloud—describing a visit to a Zen temple, in which Hearn sits drinking green tea with two priests. One of them offers to show him some rare bowls, and, as they go in to see these, they are joined by another priest. Inga was exactly right—except for mistaking the Japanese priests for Chinamen.

She went on to read everyone's mind in turn. My grandmother simply tried envisaging a scene from her childhood, with her sister in a red swing under a lilac tree, and Inga described everything, including the lilac tree.

Finally, she demonstrated her ability to snap metal. My mother sealed a darning needle in a tube used for effervescent Vitamin C tablets. Inga took the tube, held it in her hands for a moment, then handed it back. When my mother unsealed the cap, the needle was snapped into two pieces.

My grandmother said nervously: "Can you read our minds all the time?"

"Oh, no. You have to create an image in your mind, and hold it like a picture. Then I can tune into your picture."

It was after four o'clock, and Inga said she had to get back. I was suddenly stricken with guilt.

"Of course! Your family doesn't know where you are."

She said: "Oh, I told my brother Rodion."

"You rang him?"

"No, I sent him a message."

My father was fascinated. "How?"

"I can't explain how. My mind spoke to his."

My father—being a scientist—wanted to check. Inga gave him the number of her hotel. My father rang and asked if he could speak to Rodion Vassilievsky. A moment later, I heard him ask: "Do you know where your sister is?" Then he smiled at us and said: "He said she is standing right at the side of me." Which was true.

#

I walked her back to the hotel, only four blocks away, and she invited me up to meet her family. It was a fairly inexpensive hotel, and all four were sharing a single large room with two double beds. Apparently they were quite used to this kind of overcrowding.

Pavel was big, powerfully built, with a very Russian face and short cropped hair. Rodion, who was eighteen, was slim, with dark hair and dark eyes, and a quiet manner. Natalia, the youngest, had short cropped blond hair, blue eyes, and a kind of bubbling vitality and charm that instantly made her the centre of attention. If she had been ten years older, I would have fallen in love with her.

They gave me tea and a cookie the size of a saucer with a cherry on top, then listened while Inga described the afternoon. Rodion verified that they had not been anxious about Inga because they had been "in touch" while Inga was eating lunch. After this, the boys announced that they were hungry, and wanted to go out for a cheeseburger. (They loved American food, particularly junk food.) I walked downstairs with them, and across St Nicholas Park. In the park, Pavel surprised me by asking if I wanted to see some of their act. Wondering what I was letting myself in for, I said yes. At this, Rodion bent down, and Natalia ran at him, sailed over his back, and was caught by Pavel, who tossed her into the air and made her turn a double somersault. She landed on her hands in Inga's hands, and the two stood upright, with Natalia upside-down in the air.

Then they did the most amazing thing I have ever seen. Inga leapt as Natalia fell, Natalia sprang upright, and somehow they were reversed, with Natalia holding Inga above her in the air as straight and still as a ramrod. They seemed to defy the force of gravity.

For the next five minutes I stood and gaped at the amazing flying bodies, hardly able to believe that human beings could be so graceful. At one point, Pavel acted as a kind of ringmaster, standing with his feet apart and one arm outstretched while Natalia, bent into a circle, whirled around his hand like a hula hoop.

By this time a crowd had gathered, and we moved on—to the obvious disappointment of the students from City College.

The Russians were in high spirits, and we walked down 135th Street towards the river. Inga pointed to a cloud and said: "Now we show you." All four stood and focused on it—and in a matter of seconds it was gone.

I said: "But how do you do it?"

Pavel said: "Easy. Anybody can do it. You can do it too." He pointed to another cloud, like a little fluffy ball of cotton wool. "Make that disappear."

"How?"

"You just look at it and do this." He twisted up his face as if scowling.

Infected by their high spirits, I did as he said. I stared at the cloud, concentrated hard—and watched it dissolve. I looked at them accusingly.

"Did you help me?"

"No. It wasn't necessary. You can do it. Look, try that one." He pointed at a bigger cloud.

This time I took my time. I stared at it, and as I focused my attention, experienced an odd feeling that I can only describe as "strength behind the eyes". I felt as if I were launching a javelin at it. After a few seconds—perhaps half a minute—it began to break apart, then dissolved.

Now I knew that *I* was doing it, without any help. I could feel a kind of momentary resistance from the cloud before it dissolved.

Pavel said: "You see, anybody can do it."

We walked on to a MacDonalds on the corner of Broadway. When they asked me to join them I refused, saying I had to get back. They were obviously disappointed—and so, in a sense, was I. But I had to be alone to think about what had happened. And as I said goodbye to Inga—shaking hands in a formal European manner—I knew she understood precisely why I was going. She could read my mind. And I didn't care in the least. It was pleasant to feel that someone understood what was going on inside me.

There were not all that many clouds around that day, but on the way home I dissolved two more. After the second, I began to feel a kind of tiredness behind the eyes, which convinced me more than anything that this was real.

Then it suddenly struck me: I was using my mind like a laser. I was focusing its powers down to a point, like focusing sunlight through a magnifying glass, then using that point to dissolve clouds, just as I could use a magnifying glass to light a match or cause a piece of wood to smoulder. At that moment I realized that I knew something that the rest of the human race didn't know. Even the Vassilievskies didn't know it, for they did this without seeing its implications—it came as naturally to them as breathing. But I could see the implications. Perception isn't just looking, like seeing things reflected in a mirror. It is more like directing a firehose at what you are looking at, and seeing the water bounce off it in a spray. This spray is what we call perception.

Another point struck me. Trask had said that a laser was only about five per cent efficient. The same was true of the human mind. Human beings had simply not learned to focus the powers inside their own heads. And I was just beginning to learn.

It was a strange evening. I watched television and did some preparation for my classes the next day. But, inside, there was the certainty that everything had changed. No matter what happened, no matter whether we uncovered the pre-Ice Age civilization of Antarctica or not, nothing would ever be the same again.

#

That night I made an equally important discovery. I was very tired when I went to bed, yet too excited to fall asleep immediately. So I lay there, deeply relaxed, feeling as I used to feel as a child—that marvellous, comfortable sensation of pure happiness, as if setting out on a voyage to wonderland. Some time during the night I woke up having an absurd dream. I was standing near a hedge, talking to another man, perhaps a farmer. There were some tall weeds around us, and they seemed to have pods on them. The other man was eating something, and, as the crumbs fell, the weeds were trying to catch them in their mouths—I seem to recall the pods opened like beaks. This didn't worry me—it seemed quite natural. As I walked a few steps onwards one of the weeds followed me, pressing against my leg, almost tripping me up, hoping for food. I remember being mildly surprised that it could walk. I returned to the place where I had been standing, and the weed subsided.

I woke up, and thought: Of course, plants are alive, just like us. And it struck me that I ought to suggest to my father that he should test Inga to see whether she could communicate with plants.

I continued to feel oddly relaxed and happy, as it struck me that the dream had been trying to tell me something. It was an interesting thought: that my dreams were not merely the confused leftovers of consciousness but had a life of their own, like the walking plant. They were trying to instruct and entertain me. And if I trusted them, and allowed them to speak, they had a great deal to communicate to me. I drifted back into sleep as if plunging into a warm sea. Strange and pleasant dreams continued all night.

As I woke up in the morning, the phrase "dream force" floated into my head.

In its way, this was just as interesting as the discovery that I could make clouds disintegrate.

#

My father liked the idea of testing Inga for ESP with plants; indeed, when he started his tests with her this was the first thing he tried. The results (published in the *American Journal for Psychical Research*) are impressive—on one occasion, she caused a tulip to grow from a bulb in less than nineteen hours—and leave no doubt that she could communicate with plants as easily as with her brothers.

These tests took place in Trask's laboratory—at his invitation—between 8 and 10 in the morning, when her powers were still fresh. From the beginning, the results were even more remarkable than those obtained by Voronski. This was because he had restricted himself to the standard tests for ESP—Zener cards and so on. My father wanted to find out what else she could do. One day, after reading about a Russian psychic who could make a matchbox hang suspended in the air, he got her to try it; she succeeded in making a glass of water hang suspended between her open palms for more than a minute before it fell to the floor.

The next day, when my father was late getting to the laboratory, he found her handling a large ruby crystal—a foot-long cylinder of ruby weighing about five hundred grams. She seemed to be fascinated by it, and asked him what it was. He explained that it was probably the ruby used in a laser.

"What is a laser?"

Since he was no expert, he tried to explain in non-technical language. She listened carefully, without taking her eyes off the crystal. When my father had finished, she held it between her palms, then carefully separated them. The ruby remained hanging suspended in the air. My father watched with increasing amazement as Inga continued to stare at the crystal, as if ordering it to stay where it was. Drops of perspiration ran down her forehead. My father had glanced at his watch when she separated her hands. Five minutes later, the ruby was still hanging there in the air. Then she gave a gasp, as if she had been holding her breath, and the ruby fell to the floor.

My father was furious with himself for failing to record the episode on videotape, and asked her if she could do it again.

She shook her head.

"Not today. I am too tired."

"Can you do that with other things—for example, this umbrella?"

"No. It was something about that ruby. I felt it as soon as I touched it. It is on the same wavelength as my mind."

At that moment Bill Ruggles came in and asked if he could have his ruby.

Ten minutes later, he was back.

"What did she do to that ruby?"

"Why? Is there something wrong?"

"Not wrong! Come and look."

They followed him into his own room, where the laser was standing on a bench. It was a big metal cylinder, six inches in diameter and four feet long, rather like a large electric torch. The ruby crystal was inside it.

Ruggles said: "Watch this."

He placed a six-inch cube of some copper alloy on a pad of asbestos at the far end of the bench, and another heavy sheet of metal-bound asbestos behind it. Then he switched on the laser. The pure red beam appeared across the bench, striking the alloy. It should have bitten into it slowly, like a drill. Instead, there was a blinding shower of sparks that made them all jump, and the beam shot out of the other side of the block. There was another searing noise as it penetrated the asbestos shield. When Ruggles leapt forward and switched it off the beam was already cutting a hole in the wall at the end of the bench.

Ruggles said: "What in hell did you do to it?"

Inga shook her head. "I don't know. But as soon as I touched it, I knew I could do something."

Ruggles went and fetched Trask, who examined the block of alloy. The hole through it was an inch wide. Then he watched as Ruggles repeated the experiment—with the same astonishing results. This time Ruggles switched off the laser before it started blasting a hole in the wall.

Trask removed the ruby from the laser and examined it carefully. When he in turn asked Inga if she knew what she had done to it, she again shook her head.

Trask handed it to Ruggles. "Do a spectroscopic analysis and see if you can find what she's done."

Inga asked: "Could I take it home with me?"

Trask looked surprised. "Why?"

"I'd like my brothers to see what they can do with it."

"I doubt whether they can do any more. I'd guess that, whatever you did, it's now operating at a hundred per cent efficiency."

In the event, Inga took home a different ruby crystal—Trask was anxious not to let go of this one until they knew what had happened to it.

The next day, when she returned the crystal, she was wearing an odd smile.

Trask asked her: "What happened?"

Instead of replying, she took it back from him, suspended it between her hands, and then—without any kind of effort—opened her palms and left it suspended in the air. Trask and my father observed this for perhaps five minutes. My father noticed that she showed no sign of effort, none of the strain of the previous day. Then, instead of allowing the crystal to fall to the floor, Inga closed both hands on it, and placed it on the bench.

She said: "You see. I knew I could do more with it."

My father asked: "But what did you do?"

She smiled. "I don't know. But this time it is very strong. You must be careful with it."

So Trask and Bill Ruggles spent half an hour setting up the experiment. They procured an even larger cube of copper alloy—I am told it cost a fortune—and clamped it so it could not move. Behind it there was almost two feet of soft asbestos—soft because a laser cuts into the material by causing the atoms to vibrate, and a softer material is more resistant, on the same principle as firing a bullet into cotton wool.

This time, the cube exploded into sparks, and again the laser punched its way through the asbestos and the wall behind it. If Bill Ruggles had not been poised to switch off the current, it would have knocked a hole in the outer wall of the building.

When they had recovered from the shock, Trask told my father: "You can tell Matthew we've solved the problem of cutting through half a mile of ice."

But it proved not to be as simple as that. When they looked at the ruby crystal, it had shattered into a dozen fragments.

In spite of which, Trask was sufficiently confident to phone me that evening and ask me if I would like to accompany an expedition to Antarctica in three months' time.

#

What exactly did the Vassilievskies do to the ruby crystal? I have to admit that we are still not certain. Trask believed they were somehow able to affect its molecular structure. In the 1970s, Trask had been present at the Inserm Telemetry Laboratories in the Foch Hospital in Suresnes, France, when they were testing the "psychic" Uri Geller. One of the experiments involved a strange alloy called nitinol, which has a "molecular memory". A nitinol wire can be squashed into any shape, but if subjected to heat or cold, will instantly straighten out again. Trask held a piece of nitinol wire stretched tight between both hands while Geller stroked it. When Geller removed his hand, the wire now had a kink in it. Trask then dropped the wire into boiling water—expecting it to spring back into shape. In fact, it bent at a right angle, and all Trask's later efforts failed to straighten it out. Geller had somehow affected its molecular memory. Even melting the wire in a furnace failed to straighten it out.

Trask believed that the Vassilievskies had done something of the sort to the ruby. His own explanation went roughly like this.

The colour of precious stones—like ruby, sapphire, emerald—is due to impurities in the crystal.

Ruby is made from a crystal of aluminium oxide, or corundum, which is as transparent as water. But it has an impurity—a few chromium atoms—which absorb all colours but red.

It is these impurities which enable rubies to act as lasers. When a ruby is bathed in ultraviolet light (which is invisible), it soon begins to glow as the chromium atoms store up energy, which they quickly release in the form of red light—rather like a compressed spring being released. The waves of this red light are all "marching in step", so when the beam is amplified by repeated reflection from mirrors at either end of the cylinder, and then focused to a small spot, it is a million times as strong as ordinary light, and has the power to cut through metal.

Whatever Inga had done had somehow altered the structure of the molecules in the crystal, causing its atoms to store far more energy than usual. So instead of operating at five per cent efficiency, it operated at something closer to one hundred per cent.

I lacked the scientific knowledge to dispute this view. But even then it seemed to me too simple. To begin with, even if the laser now operated at one hundred per cent efficiency, it would be only twenty times as powerful as when it operated at five per cent. And I knew—from having seen it in action—that the Vassilievskies had amplified the power of the laser more than twenty times.

So what is my own view? It is based on the simple fact that, if you keep on doubling a number, it soon reaches an astronomical size. There is the story of a Chinese emperor who wished to persuade a philosopher to take up residence in his court, and asked him to name his own price. The philosopher replied: "Please pay me in corn. Ask your treasurer to take a chessboard and place on its first square one grain of corn, on the second two grains, on the third four grains, on the fourth eight grains, and so on, doubling the number of grains each time." The emperor's first reaction was to say: "But surely you deserve more than that!"—until he began to work it out and realized that, by the time he had doubled one grain of corn sixty-four times, the total would be more than all the grain in his kingdom.

Now the simplest maser is based on ammonia gas; every time a microwave hits a molecule, it gives off another microwave. Then the two microwaves hit two more molecules, and produce four microwaves. And so it goes on, doubling each time. In theory, an ordinary maser ought to produce more power than a hydrogen bomb. Of course, this does not happen, due to the inefficiency of the process.

In my view, whatever the Vassilievskies did to the ruby crystal changed its structure so that it began to double its power output over and over again. They may have changed the structure of the chromium atoms so that the photon was deflected from one to another, thereby creating a "doubling effect".

Or they may, of course, have introduced some new principle into the process, perhaps some vital energy that science so far fails to recognize.

All this was another example of the extraordinary synchronicities that had been pursuing me since I met Trask at the Science Club. It was my chance meeting with Inga in Trask's laboratory that had led to the solution of the laser problem— my father admitted to me that he was not interested in testing psychics, and only changed his mind as a result of meeting Inga when I brought her back.

#

My decision to skip a semester and go to Antarctica led to my break-up with Coral. She had planned our wedding for the week after I graduated, and persuaded her favourite uncle to offer me a job in advertising. When I went to tell her that Trask had offered me a place on the expedition, I expected her to be as excited as I was. Instead, she looked at me in a stunned sort of way, and asked if I realized that this would delay our marriage by at least a year. I said this wasn't true; we could get married whenever we liked—even before I set out. But she simply didn't see my point. As far as she was concerned, I was throwing away my career for a romantic daydream.

What amazed me was that she even bothered to try to influence me. It made me suddenly aware how little we had in common. Up until that moment I had believed I was in love with her—I certainly felt she was one of the most attractive girls I'd ever met. But, the moment she tried to persuade me not to go to Antarctica, I fell out of love. When she said, "If you go, we're through", I said, "OK, we're through", and as I walked out of the room was amazed that I didn't feel the least pang of regret. I think that, if Trask had not invited me to join the expedition, I would have made my way to Antarctica on foot.

In effect, Trask had invited me along as the office boy or gopher. When my grandmother asked me what I was supposed to do, I said I didn't know. In fact, I have never worked harder than in those three months between July and early October when our plane took off for Little America. I used to arrive at Trask's apartment—at the top of the building above the lab—at eight in the morning, and find him dictating to his secretary a list of all the things I had to attend to.

The secretary, Charles Schmidt, had been with him for fifteen years—ever since a female secretary had been indiscreet about one of his inventions to a new boyfriend of hers who had turned out to be a private detective hired as an industrial spy. Trask was determined never to let it happen again. I was sworn to secrecy about the real purpose of the expedition. As far as the press was concerned, our purpose was oil exploration. Even Trask's friend Colonel Leroy, of the US Air Force, who obtained the permission to use Little America as a base, was not told the true reason. Trask knew that if the press found out, we'd be pursued by a planeload of reporters.

He also told everybody who knew about the laser experiments to refer to the device simply as "the supercharged laser". Under no circumstances was anyone to breathe a word that we were using the Vassilievskies.

The Vassilievskies, of course, had to be told, since they were—to put it mildly—a crucial part of the operation.

#

Although the second ruby crystal had shattered, the first one was still working. But it was obviously less than half as powerful as the one that the whole family had "charged", and now Trask had them working on rubies seven days a week. For this he paid them far more than they had ever earned as an acrobatic team; he also moved them to a suite in the Waldorf-Astoria.

One of my tasks was collecting the cylinders, and I often had the opportunity to see how the family worked. They sat in a darkened room, the ruby on a small round table, nesting in the middle of a piece of green velvet that was one of Natalia's old ballet costumes. All four sat around it, placing their fingertips on the crystal and staring intently. The room became totally silent. Then—it seemed to me—the ruby became brighter. When that happened, they all simultaneously released their breath and relaxed. And the ruby was ready to be taken back to the laboratory.

On my third day there, Pavel said: "Why don't you come and help?" I thought at first that he was joking, until he drew up another chair. I said, "Are you sure that's a good idea?", but he merely gestured at the chair. So I sat down and joined in. I frowned at the ruby, and tried to summon the same sense of "power behind the eyes" that could make clouds dissolve. Looking into the ruby was a strange experience, for after a few seconds I seemed to be somehow drawn into it, until it filled my consciousness. Moreover, there was a strange sense of resistance—I can only compare it to wading through water. Then the red glow became brighter, and I felt the resistance disappear. When I released my breath and relaxed, I felt as tired as if I had climbed a dozen flights of stairs. It was far harder work than dissolving clouds.

On the first day I did this, Bill Ruggles tested the ruby, then shook his head. "It seems weaker today." Instead of punching a hole through a block of metal, it took about ten seconds to drill through it, making a faint sputtering noise. Naturally, I wondered if I was responsible. But, after several more attempts, I realized this was untrue. Some days, the force exerted by the Vassilievskies was so powerful that it took only a minute or so to "change" the ruby; on other days, it might take ten minutes or so. I also noticed that, the quicker it took, the more spectacular the results, and the more likely the ruby was to fly apart.

I should add that I never told Trask, or Bill, or even my father, what I was doing. I had a feeling that this should be my secret.

#

So were the dreams.

Most nights I came back to our apartment late—I quickly fell into the habit of all Trask's employees, and began working all round the clock. Generally I fell asleep as soon as my head touched the pillow. But usually I woke up at three or four in the morning, and lay there on my back, experiencing a pleasant, peaceful sensation, like lying in a boat on a slow river on a summer day. Then, as I drifted back into sleep, I began to experience the "dream force", a glow of expectation, like sitting in a theatre waiting for the curtain to go up. Then I plunged into a world of dreams, sometimes delightful, sometimes strange, sometimes weird, sometimes even frightening—yet always fascinating. Even the frightening dreams were not nightmares, for I experienced no real sensation of fear—except once, when I dreamed I was in a world of intelligent snakes for whom human beings were a special delicacy. The dreams were like a form of entertainment, organized by some dream master with an endless stock of incredible tales.

Naturally, I dreamed again and again of Antarctica and Windy Gap. The dreams were always the same. The snow was bright and sparkling, like the snow on Christmas cards, and the place was magical, like a scene out of some fairy tale about the Snow Queen. The sky was always beautiful—sometimes green, sometimes blue, sometimes pink. Somewhere over to the east there was the giant crater that Admiral Byrd had flown over, but I never saw it; it was merely there in the background, a part of the mythology of this wonderful place. Some of these dreams were so real that there was a sense of coming home, as if I were returning to the scene of a previous life.

I had a feeling that, in some strange way, I had inherited my grandfather's dream about the future. What puzzled me was that it had happened only after I had become fascinated by Antarctica.

#

The day we set out was bright and clear. We were flying from an airfield near Poughkeepsie in a transport plane that belonged to the American Air Force—so great was Trask's influence with the present administration. The airfield had been chosen for the sake of avoiding publicity—no editor in

America could suspect that anything important could be happening around Poughkeepsie.

From the moment I'd woken up that morning I'd had that happy, bubbling feeling that I used to feel as a child when my father loaded up the car and we prepared to set out for Florida.

During most of the ten-thousand-mile flight to the other side of Antarctica—which lasted for almost twenty hours—the feeling stayed with me. There were moments when it seemed too good to be true; but I had only to concentrate my attention and experience the curious sense of power behind the eyes to know what this was no illusion. The next morning, as we flew over that endless white landscape between the Weddell Sea and the Ross Ice Shelf, the excitement was almost intolerable. It seemed incredible to be looking down on the land that might have been the cradle of civilization. But I knew that whether or not we found Hapgood's pre-Ice Age civilization was in a way unimportant. What was important was what I had learned in the process of looking for it.

My first sight of Little America was a disappointment. Standing in the icy west wind, I looked around at this endless flat white landscape, illuminated by an enormous red sun resting near the horizon, and thought: "My God, is this all?" Then I had to galvanize myself into activity. Anyone but Trask would have allowed us to retire to bed after a twenty-hour flight. But he was a demon of energy, and he expected everybody else to be the same. Our team of eight, which had spent five hours loading the plane, now had to unload it (with some help from the servicemen). We were not finished until late that afternoon—when, of course, the sun was still hovering near the horizon, and everything looked exactly the same as when we landed—except, of course, that it was now on the opposite horizon.

I have no complaints about the warmth of our welcome, or the hospitality of Colonel Leonard ("Lefty") Leroy. And I suspect that the personnel were so glad to see strange faces they would have welcomed us if we had been one-eyed cannibals with filed teeth. The party went on until after midnight, and even Trask was persuaded to drink a glass of brandy and water. But, when the meal was over, I noticed Trask and Leroy seated in a corner, talking seriously, and knew immediately that Trask was finally telling him the truth about why we were there.

It was not until a few moments later that I noticed that I had known, with total certainty, what they were talking about.

We were up after a few hours' sleep, for there was a great deal to be done. The materials for our living quarters had been sent on ahead by helicopter, but only the storage shed had been erected; we had to do the rest ourselves—assuming the weather permitted. After an uncomfortable six-hour flight in transport helicopters, we landed at the foot of Mount Holyoake at four in the afternoon. The temperature was several degrees below zero, and the sky had turned grey. Even with the help of the team Leroy had lent us, it took seven or eight hours to erect the huts. Trask worked as hard as anyone, although he had chosen two of the team—Chet Morison and Elmo Jarnefelt—for their sheer size and strength, and our cook, Dave Eng, who in New York worked in the laboratory as a kind of unofficial security guard and caretaker, was bigger than either of them. We ate dinner at two o'clock in the morning—it might as well have been midday as far as the sun was concerned. My own small, bare hut contained nothing but a camp bed, a chair and my unpacked luggage, although the fan heater—powered by atomic batteries developed by Trask—kept the place agreeably warm.

#

A few hours later I woke up suddenly with a strange sense that I was not alone. The daylight in the room made it clear that I was mistaken. I closed my eyes, and again experienced the feeling that there was someone else present. I sat up on my bed and peered out of the window; as far as I could see through the ice crystals, there was no one out there.

There were still three hours to breakfast, so I decided to go back to sleep. But, as I lay there in that deep silence, broken only by the almost inaudible sound of the fan heater, I became aware of something that made me turn on my back and open my eyes.

I had suddenly—and with total certainty—become aware that I was not there by chance.

I knew, of course, that a certain chain of events had brought me there—a chain that began with the visit of Admiral Byrd to the Winchester Geographical Society in 1930, and that included my grandfather's visit to this place where I was now lying in bed. But I was not there through some complex logic of events. I knew now that I was there because I had been summoned there.

And now whoever—or whatever—had summoned me was establishing contact.

I lay there for perhaps half an hour, waiting for something to happen. During all this time, I continued to feel that I was not on my own. A Scottish aunt of mine had once told me how she had slept in a haunted room, and awakened with the sensation there was someone in the room. But she said that the room was freezing cold, and that she had a feeling that there was a "presence" watching her from the end of the bed. She had rushed out and spent the night in an armchair downstairs. But my room was warm, and I felt no sense of alarm—just the undeniable certainty that I was not alone.

Then I relaxed, and, as I drifted into sleep, I felt the "dream force" take over.

This was not a lucid dream, so I cannot remember its exact details. All I can remember is that urgent sense of someone communicating with me, but failing to make me understand. In a sense, it was rather like Trask's lecture—simply above my head. Something—someone—was trying to tell me something about travelling through space, but it made no sense. As far as I could understand, it was space itself that was moving, in a kind of stream. But, when the stream encountered something solid, like a meteor, it flowed into eddies around it, and turned into waving tentacles, like water flowing over a stone.

This force had encountered our earth, and had been attracted by its living aura. The earth itself was alive, but in a dull, unconscious way, like someone deeply asleep. But the mountains, standing out above the earth, were more alive than the rest. So this space-force entered into the mountains, making them more alive.

And at this point I began dimly to understand. Mountains, of course, were the "primal beings". It seemed perfectly obvious. Mountains were attached to the earth from which they sprang, so they could draw upon its vitality. This is why the most primitive religion was the worship of mountains, for ancient man sensed that the mountains were alive. It is no figure of speech to talk about the "roots of the mountains". They have roots, like trees or plants, and the roots draw upon the living force of the soil.

All this brought with it a most wonderful sense of awe and happiness. It was like great music or great poetry. I was being told something that made sense of life and of the universe. And in my dream, it all seemed perfectly clear and obvious—for example, this was why hermits lived in caves on the mountains: they drew strength from the vital aura of the mountain. Why should we be trapped inside our bodies and our minds, like prisoners in a cramped cell, when we could share the life of the mountains?

At this point something woke me up—I think it was somebody slamming the door of the store room, which we had converted into a kitchen and dining room. But I didn't want to wake up. I wanted to go on dreaming. Within a few seconds I was asleep again. And the "communication" continued, confirming my certainty that this was not a dream.

I was seeing the primitive earth as it was before the simplest living organisms made their appearance. The seas were hot, and covered with thick mist. Every valley was full of mist—only the mountains stood out above it. But the water could also absorb the living force. As the seas cooled, the mist vanishing, they began to absorb sunlight, and to swarm with tiny green creatures, like the algae on a pond.

And now the mountains began to mould this life into more complex forms. They literally began to create living creatures—tiny wriggling groups of cells. The larger groups of cells absorbed the smaller ones, making themselves bigger, becoming the first predators.

But of course these tiny organisms were not in charge of their own life force; they could easily be destroyed. Only the mountains were independent, indestructible.

Millions of years passed, and the soil in the valleys absorbed the sunlight, and began to produce bright green moss. The mountains guided the development of this moss, so that it put down roots, and began to grow into more complex forms, like grass and ferns.

It was at this point that the mountains began to understand the disadvantages of being rooted to the same spot. The earth and the seas were now teeming with life. Only they were unable to move. So now they developed the power to concentrate their life into "eddies", and then to mould the crude matter around them into organic forms. The simplest of these forms was the limpet that sticks on rocks by the seashore. This is made of a tough, durable flesh, with a consistency not unlike leather, protected by a rock-like shell. The first embodiment of independent life on earth—life that has no fear of destruction—was a giant limpet that could move about on its retractable base . . .

#

I was awakened by the gong summoning us to food. I could see from the window that the sun had moved westward along the horizon. As I dressed, I found the room oppressively hot—and then realized that this was because my body was so cold. I had to plunge my hands into hot water to warm them.

I wondered if I should tell Trask or Bill Ruggles what I had "seen". The answer came back immediately, almost as if a voice had spoken in my head, and that answer was no. Thinking about this, I saw it was common sense. What could I tell them?—that I had been dreaming about the origin of life on earth? They would wonder why I thought it so important.

Outside, I was startled by the cold. During the "night" the temperature had dropped by about ten degrees. Before I reached the dining room my face and fingertips felt frozen.

We ate a large breakfast of ham, eggs, tomatoes and hash-brown potatoes, with orange juice and coffee. Trask was in brilliant form, talking with marvellous fire and enthusiasm. He was often silent and withdrawn, almost morose, but this morning he was obviously full of excitement, and he made the rest of us feel it.

We set out about eleven o'clock. Unlike the IGY expedition, we had no dog sleds—only one huge snow tractor with a trailer, brought from Little America. This carried the sonar equipment and two "laser guns", which looked less like guns than cannons. I walked behind with Trask, Bill Ruggles and Elmo Jarnefelt; we were all wrapped in furs until we looked like polar bears. Under this we were wearing electrically heated track suits, designed by Trask. But the heating did not extend to our boots, and soon my feet were freezing. The ground underfoot was solid ice, and we had to tread cautiously.

The scenery was magnificent, with Mount Holyoake towering above us, the Robertson Plain stretching eastward to Mount Faure, which was clearly visible in the transparent air, and the Rockefeller Range glittering against the sky in the northwest. The sky overhead was dark blue.

The head of Windy Gap was a mile away, to begin with partly hidden behind the 45-degree slope of Mount Holyoake. What surprised me was my sense of familiarity. Usually a place is quite different from your anticipation of it, but this looked exactly as I had imagined. And when finally we rounded the slope and looked southwest along Windy Gap it too looked precisely as it had in my dreams.

I was not surprised. I now knew beyond all doubt that I was not there by accident. This feeling—that destiny was working in my favour—filled me with a glow of confidence and certainty, the total conviction that we were on the point of some major breakthrough. I could sense intuitively that everyone felt exactly as I did.

The snow tractor had halted about a mile along Windy Gap, in exactly the place I had expected and just as I had known it would. This, I knew, was the place where, in his dream, my grandfather had seen the "cyclopean" city. Chet Morison was already working with the sonar, while Bill Ruggles was setting up the laser in the back of the trailer; at this distance it resembled an astronomical telescope. Trask, wearing a tartan scarf and a baseball cap, looked not unlike a games coach in charge of an ice-hockey team.

The most important part of our equipment was the portable atomic-energy generator; "portable" was only a theoretically accurate description of something that weighed a quarter of a ton and took two men to handle it.

As we arrived, Chet Morison, without speaking, handed Trask the computer simulations. Trask studied them, handed them back, then said: "OK, let's get started."

We all moved to the rear of the snow tractor. The atomic motor was humming softly, almost silent—although it could produce enough current to light a small city. At the last moment, Elmo Jarnefelt, who was going to film all this, called: "Wait a moment. This thing is affected by the cold."

We waited in silence for perhaps five minutes. Nobody spoke. At that point, there was nothing to say. Then Jarnefelt said: "It's rolling."

Bill Ruggles said: "I'll try her on half." That meant fifty per cent of the possible energy output.

Almost instantly, the intense ruby beam, three inches wide, knifed out of the laser gun like a bar of red hot steel and struck the ice. There was a violent hissing that made us all jump backwards, and suddenly we were engulfed in steam. Then there was an explosion, and even more steam.

Trask shouted: "Turn it off."

As the steam cleared, we all ran forward to look. What we saw was an anticlimax. At first, there was no sign that anything had happened. Then, at the point where the laser had struck the ice, we saw the small hole, still steaming like a geyser.

Somebody said: "What was that explosion?"

"The steam trying to escape. It forms pockets—like trying to cook an egg in a microwave oven."

It was disappointing. That enormous volume of steam and the noise that went with it had produced merely a three-inch hole, which was slowly widening as steam continued to hiss out of it.

Jarnefelt, walking a few yards beyond the hole, said: "Look, the ice is cracked here. The explosion did that."

Bill said: "Thank God I didn't try it on full power. It would have blown us sky-high."

And now, suddenly, we could all see the problem. The laser could cut through the ice to any depth we liked, but it would convert that ice into high-pressure steam. Even now, this was falling back on us in the form of freezing rain. And we would still be left with only a three-inch hole.

Trask, never one to be discouraged, said: "Let's try one more, and see what happens. And move the beam around like a water jet."

This time we stood well back. Again there was a deafening hiss, and we were enveloped in a cloud that soon became as thick as pea-soup fog. Because it was a windless day, the mist simply surrounded us. We were quickly soaked by the condensing droplets. There were several explosions, one so violent that Bill jumped backwards and fell off the trailer. The steam roared out of the hole in the ice like the jet from a fire hose.

The result, when we finally examined it, was more satisfying than before—the hot steam had enlarged the mouth of the hole to more than two feet. But, as we stood looking, the partially melted ice collapsed inward like soft snow. In effect, cutting a hole through ice was like trying to cut a hole through water—the heat would cause the surrounding ice to collapse inward.

It seems absurd that none of us had foreseen this. But I think we all had the same attitude—let's try it and see what happens.

We were soaked to the skin, and it was obvious we had to get back and change before we froze to death. We piled into the trailer and Chet drove us back at thirty miles an hour. We spent most of the drive bumping violently up and down like peas on a drum, but were too cold to care.

I struggled out of my clothes, which were now like stiff canvas, and turned up the heater. Dave Eng brought me hot soup, which soon restored me to normal. After that, I dressed in dry clothes, and—since my room was filling up with steam as the wet clothes dried out—went across to the dining room.

Trask was sitting alone at the table, drinking orange juice—he never took stimulants like tea or coffee. To my surprise he looked cheerful. "Well, Matthew, what do you think?"

"That we have to wait for a windy day."

"Right. The wind will solve the problem of the steam. Second, we have to stick to the surface, and cut down at an angle against the face of the mountain. I calculate it should take us about a week to reach those blocks."

He had worked out on a sheet of paper the number of calories it would take to dissolve ten million tons of ice, and decided that, at full strength, the laser could evaporate more than a hundred thousand tons a day. Having seen the amount of steam generated in less than half a minute, I could believe it.

His optimism was infectious. And what he said was obviously true. Since there was no point in drilling down into the ice, we had to concentrate on evaporating its surface over a fairly small area. And if the wind carried away the steam, there was no reason to anticipate any further problems.

That afternoon, the wind sprang up. This time, only Trask, Bill Ruggles and myself went to Windy Gap, leaving the others to work on the huts—electric light still had to be installed, and the hot showers. The wind chill factor sent the temperature down to ten below, and all three of us kept in the shelter of the trailer, whose high sides made it windproof.

Bill directed the beam at the surface, at an angle of no more than a few degrees. The result was spectacular—there was a hiss, and the surface of the ice turned into clouds of white vapour, to be carried away by the wind, which must have been blowing at fifty miles an hour. It was very satisfying to see the great clouds carried away until they turned to water droplets and disappeared. We went to survey the result at close quarters, and were impressed. Because the angle was so small, the superheated steam had dissolved the ice above it, so there was a trench about a foot wide and up to two feet deep up to the point where it vanished from sight. The power of the laser was awe-inspiring—it felt rather like unleashing a small atom bomb.

Next Bill turned the trailer at an angle and fired towards the mountainside. Again, it gouged out a foot-wide trench that went on into the rock for ten feet. By the time we had made half a dozen similar trenches, our progress was obvious. The laser had also made a ten-foot-deep cavern in the rock, but, by using the laser in short bursts of ten seconds, Bill prevented it from cutting deeper. We had no desire to cause the side of the mountain to collapse.

It was an oddly exhausting activity—releasing such savage and destructive bursts of energy. I was almost deaf from the explosive hiss. The same thought occurred to all three of us—that used as a weapon of war, the supercharged laser would make ground attack obsolete.

Bill began to move the beam back and forward like a fire hose, and the result was even more satisfying—the ice simply dissolved away. Soon we had a hole fifty feet deep and a hundred yards wide, with several feet of water in the bottom. But, as we paused to drink hot soup, we could see our new problem. The hole looked enormous, big enough to hold a dozen buildings. But fifty feet was only a fiftieth part of half a mile. If we were to go fifty times deeper than this we would have to keep moving back until we were on the far side of the valley. To dissolve this much ice, even with a supercharged laser, was like trying to drain a lake with a bucket.

The alternative, of course, would be to cut a wide tunnel down into the ice, at an angle of perhaps thirty degrees. But this would obviously be dangerous, for the explosions of steam would crack the ice, and the whole tunnel might simply collapse—with us inside it. And, at an angle of thirty degrees, a tunnel that reached a depth of half a mile would have to be at least a mile long. It would take months.

Trask had another suggestion. If we simply concentrated on cutting a hole straight down into the ice at an angle of sixty degrees or even more we could probably reach a depth of half a mile within days. It would be necessary to make sure that the hole was at the side of the blocks we were looking for—otherwise we might destroy them. Then, once we had our hole, the laser could be taken down to the bottom, and could begin to cut sideways into the ice. It would be dangerous, but workable.

Another problem, of course, was that steam rising from a depth of half a mile would not necessarily reach the surface—much of it would turn to water, and run back into the pit. And, if we vaporized the water with the laser, it would simply do the same thing all over again.

I must admit that, when we returned to camp at six o'clock, my optimism had started to dissipate, and even Trask looked grim. The amount of work we had done was tremendous. (When the others walked down to look at it, they were amazed.) But, compared to what remained to be done, it was absurdly small.

Later that evening Bill brought more bad news. Towards the end of the afternoon, even I had noticed that the results were growing less spectacular—it seemed to take longer bursts to achieve the same amount of evaporation. I had assumed that this was because my senses were becoming accustomed to the explosions of steam. But, checking with the laser's inbuilt computer, Bill verified that it had been working at less than fifty per cent of its potential. For some reason, the ruby crystal was losing its strength.

This was not as serious as it might have been. To begin with, Bill had anyway been using the laser at less than half power. Second, we still had nine more ruby cylinders. Even using them up at a rate of one a day, they should cut through half a mile of ice.

#

That night I slept normally and deeply—so deeply that I cannot remember any dreams. But when I woke up I was once again full of energy and optimism.

Today there was again a strong wind, and the temperature was lower than ever. Again, only the three of us went to Windy Gap, while the others worked back at camp.

We moved the tractor back another fifty feet, and continued to deepen the hole. It was slow work—now the hole was so large it was harder to see results. Moreover, the laser was fast losing its strength. When, an hour later, it shattered into a dozen pieces, Bill simply replaced it and continued.

At one o'clock we were tired and cold, and decided to let the others take a turn. Back at camp, Trask was half an hour late for lunch. When he finally came in, he told me that he had been speaking to Leroy in Little America. He had come to the conclusion that, however many crystals we got the Vassilievskies to charge in New York and then flew down here, the chances were we would run out at some time of greatest inconvenience: much better to bring the Vassilievskies here in person to manufacture more supercharged crystals on the spot, as required. Accordingly, he had told Leroy to telephone them and ask them to fly down to join us.

Leroy had said: "What if they refuse to come?"

And Trask, with his usual confidence, had replied: "They can't refuse. There's too much at stake."

Trask proved to be wrong; an hour later Leroy radioed to say they had refused. Rodion had told him they were happy in New York, had started a job in the Copacabana, and didn't want to fly to Antarctica. Rodion, I had often noticed, was stronger-minded and less obliging than the others.

Trask said: "Get him back on the phone and let me talk to him."

While we waited, he said: "Come to think of it, you know them better than I do. *You* talk to him."

But it was Inga who came through on the crackly line. When I explained the problem, she said: "But I don't understand. You must have more than a dozen."

"No, we have nine."

"Is that not enough?"

"It might be. It might not. Can't you persuade them to come?"

"I don't think so. We have just started work, and the act is a great success. We don't want to let down the management."

With Trask's eye on me, I did everything to persuade her. It made me unhappy, for I could understand why she hated the idea—why should she want to change New York for Antarctica, which, I could now see, would strike her as the most boring place in the world?

She promised to try, and I said we would contact her that evening.

When I talked to her again a few hours later, she told me that her brothers refused to come. But the act could do without her for a few weeks, and, if it would help, she would come alone.

As she said this, I wished she was in the room so I could hug and kiss her. There was something very gentle and kind about Inga. I began to suspect I might be in love with her.

Trask was nodding enthusiastically, so I told Inga we would arrange her transport right away—Trask had a friend, the head of a business corporation, who owned two private jets and owed him a favour.

A few hours later, when the team returned from Windy Gap, we learned that the second laser crystal had shattered, and that they were now on the third.

#

That evening, before I went to bed, I began to experience a curiously relaxed and dreamy feeling. I knew what this meant; soon after supper I excused myself and went to my room. As soon as I closed my eyes, I experienced again the sense of not being alone. It was so clear that I could *feel* the presence that pervaded the whole room. There was a strong tide of peace and serenity; yet I felt no desire to sleep. I simply lay on my back with my eyes open, and waited for something to happen. It was exactly as if I were waiting for someone to speak.

For perhaps a quarter of an hour, nothing happened; but I felt myself settling into a more and more deeply receptive state. Finally I was so relaxed that I could hardly detect the beating of my heart.

Next came a rush of great warmth and happiness which seemed to be flowing into me, not originating inside me. I interpreted this as an expression of gratitude for what I had done. It was a delightful sensation, yet I experienced a certain impatience. What I now wanted to know was precisely what I was supposed to have done to deserve gratitude.

Another ten minutes or so went past. I began to feel sleepy, and closed my eyes. I immediately experienced a sense of approval, as if this were what the invisible "communicator" wanted. I relaxed still more deeply, and began to experience the pleasant glow as the "dream force" invaded my consciousness.

What followed was quite unlike my "dream" of two nights before. This was not at all like any dream, but was a series of insights, exactly as if someone were speaking to me without words.

I must emphasize that the communicator did not "tell" me what I am now going to explain, except in the sense that a book "tells" you something you want to know. It was already there, laid out for me, like the maps of the ancient sea kings the Library of Congress laid out for Hapgood. All I had to do was choose what I wanted to know.

Within seconds, everything that had happened made sense. The "communicators" were not ghosts from Plato's Atlantis. They were creatures like ourselves—except that they were far more intelligent and possessed far greater powers than human beings. Moreover, they had been on earth for millions of years—so long that their name for themselves was "the First Ones".

Then what had happened to them? What were they doing under the Antarctic ice? It was clear that they themselves did not know the answer to this question. They had been struck by a cold so extreme that there was no question of escape. Even the Antarctic, where the temperature is often fifty degrees below zero, had never known such cold.

Strangely enough, I was in a better position to understand it than they were. In *Earth's Shifting Crust*, Hapgood had discussed the mystery of the Beresovka mammoth, discovered in the frozen bank of the Beresovka River in Siberia in 1901. It was removed by building huge fires to thaw the ground. Examination of its stomach revealed fresh buttercups that had not had time to digest. The mammoth had somehow been frozen instantaneously. Hapgood had approached the Birdseye frozen food company to ask how they would freeze a mammoth so that even its stomach was frozen solid, and they admitted that they would find it almost impossible, for there is no known method of freezing something organic of that size so quickly. Even in the coldest deep freeze, it would take days.

Hapgood had described how the winter in northern Canada can arrive so suddenly that a lake in which one has just been swimming can freeze over in hours. But even that could not explain how intelligent creatures could be caught so unprepared that they were unable to escape.

My own conviction was that there is only one way to explain how mammoths could freeze within minutes, or even seconds. Only the cold of outer space could produce this effect. For example, a tremendous volcanic explosion could eject gas and magma far out into space. When pulled back to earth by gravity, it would be an icy gas whose temperature was close to absolute zero.

The truth is that scientists still know nothing about what causes the great ice ages; every theory so far has proved inadequate. All we know is that they can arrive so suddenly that gigantic animals can be frozen solid so quickly that their meat remains edible when they are unfrozen thousands of years later.

This, apparently, is what had happened to the First Ones. And it was the fact that they had a high resistance to cold that made them vulnerable. Their giant city had no form of artificial heating, for they were perfectly happy at temperatures well below zero. If the temperature dropped below that level, they simply induced certain biochemical reactions—not unlike our human ability to generate heat by shivering—which prevented them from freezing. The great cold that plunged their city close to absolute zero took them completely by surprise. Before they understood what had happened, their bodies had frozen solid. And still the temperature went on plummeting.

It would, of course, have killed a warm-blooded animal instantly. But the First Ones were not warm-blooded—they were a kind of giant limpet.

There is another factor that must be taken into account: far back in the remote past, they had *chosen* their bodies. If they had wanted to, they could have vacated those bodies and created new ones. But this would have involved a tremendous effort of creation, and there was no time for this. So the First Ones had been trapped in a tomb of ice.

There was nothing they could do but wait. One day, the great ice age would come to an end, and they would be free again.

It came to an end, of course, some 14,000 years ago. But by this time they were buried underneath a mile of ice in Antarctica. And since the beginning of the last ice age, about 100,000 years ago, Antarctica had moved further south—it had originally been three thousand miles closer to the equator. The Antarctic ice sheet vanished, and the coastal regions were populated by human beings who built ports.

But, for the First Ones, the thaw never came. Windy Gap was then, as it is today, one of the coldest places in Antarctica. And it remained—like other inland areas exposed to the west winds—frozen solid, although the ice sheet melted away until it was only a quarter of a mile thick. It must have seemed to them an appalling irony when the thaw stopped and the new mini ice age began in Antarctica, about 5000BC.

When men began to visit Antarctica in the 20th century, the First Ones' optimism rose—now it could be only a matter of time. You might say that the First Ones possessed a kind of broadcasting system: that is, their minds could reach out to other minds, particularly in a state of sleep. When my grandfather came with the IGY team in 1957, they saw him as the saviour they had been waiting for. It was they who sent him dreams of a civilization below the ice, and filled him with that sense of urgency and expectancy that I knew so well. When the sonar located the remains of their observatory, they had no doubt that their troubles were over. But they had reckoned without the caution of the academic temperament. (Their own minds worked on a principle of supra-logic which made this wariness quite incomprehensible.)

But they knew that, nevertheless, their long wait must be coming to an end. When I'd discovered Hapgood's book in my grandfather's library, and began talking about it to everyone who would listen, they saw me as their best hope so far, and began to concentrate on influencing me. That was why I woke every morning with this bubbling sense of optimism. The First Ones were "subsidizing" my vital energies.

And when Trask came to lecture at Columbia, they saw their opportunity. That was why, in spite of my intention of going home, I found myself coming back on campus. That was why, instead of rushing to the bar with the others, I went forward to speak to the lecturer who—to be honest—had left me slightly bemused and bored.

They knew that the moment Trask became intrigued by the problem of how to penetrate down through half a mile of ice nothing would stop him until he had solved it.

At this point, I felt that my brain had absorbed as much as it could take. As soon as this thought entered my head, I fell into a peaceful sleep.

#

When I woke up, it was already eight o'clock. As I showered and shaved, I was surprised by my own calmness. For there could be no doubt that, when I considered the situation coolly and logically, it pointed to one absurd yet inescapable conclusion: that I was the most significant member of the human race ever to have existed.

After all, I was the first to learn of the existence of this age-old tragedy. Without me, this expedition would never have happened. And there could be little doubt that, when the First Ones were freed from their icy tomb, the history of the human race would enter a new phase—its most important so far. As a child I had often fantasized about what would happen if Martians, or some infinitely wise race from the stars, landed on earth and took over its leadership—how war and crime would vanish overnight, and how men would finally learn the secret of happiness. And now, incredibly, it was about to happen—and I had been chosen to play this decisive role in the transition to a new future.

As I ate breakfast and watched Trask drinking his decaffeinated coffee, I was surprised by the sensation of affection and loyalty that I suddenly experienced. Trask was not the kind of person who inspired obvious affection—there was something oddly detached about him, something slightly inhuman. Yet, now, I was aware that his name and mine would be linked in all future history, I began to feel that we were as closely linked as family members.

But of course there was no question of telling him what I had learned—he would probably think my mind had collapsed. Sooner or later, he would learn what I had. Then would be the time to tell him of my own knowledge . . .

#

That morning I returned to the site of the excavation and was impressed by what had been achieved in twenty-four hours. Recognizing that the laser would have to be moved down into the ice as the hole deepened, Chet Morison's team had started to cut a trench across the valley, with a gradually sloping ramp on one side. This meant that there was a wall of ice on the far side—already more than fifty feet tall. But it also meant that the snow tractor could descend to the bottom of the ramp, and continue deepening the hole above what I now knew to the remains of an observatory.

This also had the advantage of sheltering us from the wind, which blew that day in gusts of up to sixty miles an hour. The steam rose straight into the air, and was blown away before it could even begin to condense.

By the time we returned in the early afternoon, the hole was nearly two hundred feet deep—two hundred and fifty feet below the original ice level. That was about a tenth of the total distance to the valley floor, and an eighth of the distance to the observatory ruins. Chet Morison's team would deepen the ramp by at least another fifty feet. At this rate, we might achieve our objective within two—possibly three—weeks.

At six o'clock that evening Bill Ruggles told me that Inga had landed at Little America an hour ago, and was already on her way by helicopter. At half-past seven, Chet Morrison's team returned an hour later than expected—the work had gone so well that they had stayed on. The ruby showed no sign of losing its strength. They had given up only because the wind had dropped, and was no longer carrying away the steam. As they sat drinking coffee, I was struck by their air of immense optimism—and realized that, like me, they were being "subsidized".

#

Soon after nine, the clattering of the helicopter sent me rushing outside. I hardly recognized Inga as she climbed down the steps swathed in furs, her face peering out of a white fur hood, looking rather like a Russian doll. I had forgotten how small she was. When I bent to kiss her, she shyly turned her cheek, then said with concern: "But you are cold."

163

The pilot also delivered a dozen ruby cylinders.

Dave Eng had cooked Inga a meal, but she said she was not hungry. I sat by her and watched her toy with it, and helped her by eating two sausages. The others occasionally glanced across at her with obvious curiosity—with the exception of Bill Ruggles, no one had any idea who she was or why she was there, although they had all seen her back at the laboratory. Trask had not appeared—he was in his room, working on a calculation, and no one wanted to take the responsibility of disturbing him.

When she had eaten, and settled in her cabin—Elmo Jarnefelt had moved in with Dave Eng to make room for her—I asked her if she was tired; when she said no, I suggested going for a walk.

As we tramped across the hard-packed snow, I asked her what she thought of it. She said: "It is very beautiful—like Siberia. But I don't like such places."

We walked on in silence to the end of Windy Gap. The sun, on its circular path around the horizon, had reached its westward limit, and lay there framed between the mountains, making them look bleak but very beautiful.

We stopped, and I looked down at her face. She seemed preoccupied. I asked: "What is it?"

She shook her head, and her face became troubled. "I don't know."

"Would you like to walk further?"

"If you like."

But, half a mile down the valley, she stopped. "I would like to go back now."

"Are you tired?"

"No."

I did not press her to explain, and we walked back in silence. It was quite different from the meeting I had envisaged, in which I had intended to tell her about the First Ones, and ask her advice on when I should tell Trask. Now, for some odd reason, there seemed to be a barrier between us, and the mere thought of telling her aroused a strange feeling of resistance inside me, as if this was somehow the wrong time and the wrong place.

Back in the dining room, Trask had emerged from his seclusion—typically, he had not even noticed the sound of the helicopter. When he learned that I had not told Inga about the progress we had made, he immediately swept her off into a corner of the room to bring her up to date. I saw my presence was unnecessary, and went back to my room.

I felt jumpy and tense, unable to relax. I lay down on the bed, and began to place myself in a state of relaxation. It took nearly half an hour to confirm my feeling that there was something wrong—some kind of obstruction. But, as soon as I felt the onset of the "dream force", I knew nothing had changed. The First Ones were still there, still glad to communicate. Yet I could sense a mood of caution. They had waited so long for this moment. Now it was so close, they were afraid there would be something to prevent it.

A knock at my door made me jump as if a bomb had exploded—this is one of the dangers of sinking into a near-trance state. With my heart thundering in my ears, I hastened to open it. It was Inga, still dressed in the fur uniform that made her look like something out of a Russian fairy tale.

She was holding a slim brown paper parcel—obviously a book.

"I am sorry. Your father asked me to give this to you."

"Ah, thank you." As she turned away I said: "Won't you come in?"

"Are you sure I am not disturbing you?" She sounded very formal.

"No. Please come in."

As she stepped inside she said: "Ah, it is very cold in here," and I suddenly realized I had forgotten to switch on the heating. Oddly enough, I had not even noticed the cold in the room. Now I hastened to turn on the fan heater, then smoothed out the bed, and asked her to sit down—the room, of course, was very bare, with only the bed, one chair and the trestle table.

"Did you not notice the cold?"

"No." It seemed strange that she should pursue something so unimportant. "Why?"

She looked at me strangely for a moment, then seemed to make up her mind. She said in a firm voice: "There is something about this place that I do not like. I cannot stay."

"You can't stay!" I was aghast.

"No, I must leave. And you should leave too."

"But why?"

"There is something bad. That is why I could not walk down the valley. Here it is better because of the mountain." She gestured out of the window.

"But what's wrong?"

"I don't know. But I noticed it as soon as I stepped out of the plane. There is something very bad here, something dangerous."

I looked at her closely.

"What do you know about this?"

"Only what I feel. And I feel frightened."

I stood up and walked up and down the room. The situation seemed absurd—worse than that, insane.

I sat down and pulled my chair closer to her.

"Look, I have a lot to tell you. Please listen to what I have to say. Then make up your mind."

She gazed into my eyes quietly, without speaking. As she did so, I experienced again that feeling I had known ever since meeting her—an odd kind of intimacy, almost as if we were brother and sister. In that sense of intimacy, the disconcerting feeling of reluctance I had been feeling seemed to evaporate.

If I had been trying to explain to Trask, or even my grandfather, I would have had to start with assurances that I was not insane or on drugs. With Inga it was unnecessary. She knew I would speak only the truth.

I began by telling her about that feeling of electrical excitement I had experienced the day I found Hapgood's book in my grandfather's library, and about how I felt it incredible that something so important could have been ignored. And as I told her about my dream on the night I had met Trask, and my certainty that I was going to play a major part in rediscovering the lost civilization, I found myself wondering why it had taken me so long to realize that all this was being engineered by alien and yet benevolent forces.

Then I went on to tell her about what I had learned since arriving in Antarctica—how I had been in communication with the First Ones, and learned about the strange catastrophe that had buried them below half a mile of ice. As I described all this, I was certain she would now understand and sympathize with these creatures who had been entombed for perhaps a hundred thousand years, like miners trapped in a tunnel under a mountain, trying to attract the attention of the outside world.

Yet, when I had finished, she sat silent, staring at the floor. I said finally: "Well?"

She said: "I understand what you feel."

Her reaction baffled me. "Yes, but what do you think about it?"

"I think you are wrong. There is something . . . bad about this. There is something wrong."

I almost exploded in exasperation. "Why? What do you mean?"

She shook her head. "I don't know. I just feel it."

"But what could there be wrong? These poor devils have been down there for thousands of years. Are you saying we should leave them there?"

She shook her head, obviously miserable.

I said: "Try to give me some idea of why you think they're bad."

"I am not saying they are bad. I can only tell you what I feel."

"Please try to explain."

Inga was not an articulate person, but she made an effort.

"You say they are like miners who have been trapped. But have you read the story in the Arabian Nights about a fisherman who finds a genie in a bottle, and lets it out?"

That stopped me short. What she said certainly made sense. I had seen a movie as a child in which someone opens the bottle he finds on a beach, and a wisp of smoke comes out, then gets bigger and bigger until it turns into a man a hundred feet tall, towering above him as a human being towers above a mouse. Her comment made me aware of something I had not thought about before—that the First Ones would certainly have all the magical powers of the genie in the Arabian Nights. Once they were out, there would be no going back. Human history would be changed forever.

But would that be such a bad thing? Throughout recorded history, human beings have been doing terrible things to one another. Even now, living in a world whose technology could provide for the needs of the whole human race, and ensure prosperity for everyone, they are still more concerned with killing than with peace and happiness. The Old Ones might stop them murdering and tormenting one another.

I was deeply troubled. It seemed impossible to imagine what harm could come through releasing the First Ones from their prison.

I said: "I'll have to think about it. You probably need some sleep."

She smiled palely. "Yes, I am in truth very tired. You want me to go?"

"No, not unless you do . . . "

She said: "Can I stay here?"

"Stay here?" I stared in astonishment.

"I don't want to be alone."

I made an attempt to reassure her. "But you have nothing to be afraid of."

"I would like to stay here." She said it politely but stubbornly.

"Well . . . all right. You can have the bed."

"No. I will sleep on the floor."

We argued it out. Finally it was agreed that I would fetch her eiderdown and pillow, and sleep on the floor. Luckily, no one saw me staggering along with an armful of bedding.

When I got back, she was already in bed, her furs on the floor. I made up my own bed, closed the curtains, and lay down on the floor. When I said goodnight there was no reply—she was already asleep.

But I had no desire to go to sleep. There was too much that I needed to understand.

To begin with, why did Inga want to sleep in my room? She was not likely to be physically attacked. Was it simply a child's desire for safety and reassurance? That seemed unlikely. In the few months I had known her, she had always struck me as a self-controlled and adult personality.

Second, what was she afraid of? When I told her about the First Ones, I had expected her to understand immediately, to realize that she had merely sensed their presence below the ice, and that she had nothing to fear. Yet whatever was troubling her was clearly as strong as ever.

At this point, I realized that Inga was having a bad dream—she was moving in her sleep and making faint noises in her throat. It made me think of my grandfather's dog chasing rabbits in its sleep. I got up quietly, stood by her, and placed a hand on her forehead. It was very cold. I expected her to wake up, but she remained fast asleep. As I stood there with my hand on her forehead, she slowly relaxed. When she was breathing normally again, I shook her gently, but she continued to sleep. Either she was indeed very tired or she was in some kind of a trance.

Back amid my bedding on the floor, I decided the most sensible thing to do was try to make contact with the First Ones. Perhaps they could make me understand what was troubling Inga. I lay on my back and spent ten minutes relaxing deeply. But this time the "dream force" refused to come. It was like dialling a telephone number and getting no reply.

And now I heard Inga's breathing becoming irregular once more. Again I stood by her and placed my hand on her forehead—again surprised by its cold. This time it took longer. I made myself relax deeply and tried to transmit a sense of reassurance, and finally her breathing became even. I noticed that her forehead also became warmer.

#

I dozed for an hour or so. Towards morning the wind sprang up from the southeast. Our camp was sheltered from the west winds by the mountain, but these were blowing from the Ross Ice Sheet, and made the windows rattle, while a draught made it apparent that the hut had not been bolted together tightly enough. The noise made it impossible to hear Inga's breathing.

At about five o'clock, just as I was beginning to doze, I was jerked awake by a sudden sense that something was wrong. I went to look at Inga and found she was hardly able to breathe. Her breath came in gasps, and her face was grey. I pulled my chair across to the bed and laid my hands on her forehead; it was like ice. My attempts to soothe her had no effect—ten minutes later, she was still breathing as if she had pneumonia. Finally, I pulled back the bedclothes, climbed in beside her, and held her tightly against me, pressing my cheek against her face until my own felt numb. She was fully dressed, and her body felt very thin. I had the feeling that, if I could convey some of my warmth to her, I could awaken her from the nightmare that seemed to be convulsing her. It took a long time—it seemed an hour—but at last I had a feeling that she was aware of me, in some dim, unconscious way. Her breathing slowly became calmer, then returned to normal and her face became warm again.

At the same time, the wind dropped and the morning became very still. I went back to my own bed on the floor, and lay there on my back. But, though I remained alert, I had a feeling that her nightmares were over.

Once again I tried to relax and contact the First Ones, but it was still impossible. At that point I decided to try another method. I stretched my body until all the muscles were tense, and tried concentrating hard. The effect was interesting. I began to feel the same odd sensation of power behind the eyes that I had experienced after dispersing clouds.

It was so strong that I went to the door and looked outside. From horizon to horizon, the sky was grey. Now the wind had dropped, everything was still. I selected an area of cloud, focused my attention on it, and then concentrated hard. There was an odd sensation of force behind my eyes—rather like the sensation we experience when pushing against a stalled car to get it into motion. In spite of this, nothing seemed to be happening to the cloud. Yet the sensation was so satisfying that I went on trying. Then I noticed a swirl of cloud at the spot where I was concentrating. Suddenly, it parted, and I could see the blue sky beyond. A few seconds later, the hole had filled again. But now I know why it had taken so much effort. This was not a single cloud I was trying to disperse, but a whole bank of them, perhaps a quarter of a mile thick.

It brought a surge of deep and intense satisfaction. I had realized that I didn't need the First Ones to "subsidize" my vital energies. I could do it myself, by the use of the right kind of concentration.

There was a sound behind me, and Inga was looking out of the door.

I said: "How are you feeling?"

"Well, thank you."

"Did you sleep well?"

"I think so." She yawned. "Now I must go back to my room."

I carried her bedding back to her own hut. Fortunately, there was still no one around.

As I left her—making herself coffee—I said: "Do you still want to leave?"

She wrinkled her nose.

"Perhaps. I hate it here. Will you come too?"

"No. I have to stay until the job is finished."

She thought for a moment, then said: "Very well. I will stay too."

After the vehemence of the previous night, her casualness puzzled me. But I was too glad she had changed her mind to press her about it.

#

Back in my own hut, I made coffee, then lay down on the bed. It was strange that, after a night with so little sleep, I felt so wide awake.

I noticed the brown paper parcel sent by my father, and tore it open. It contained a fairly bulky paperback called: *H.P. Lovecraft, A Centenary Appreciation*, published by Brown University Press. My father had scrawled in the front of it: "This might amuse you." I had heard vaguely of Lovecraft, but had never actually read him—I had an idea he wrote horror stories, and these have never appealed to me. This book consisted of a number of critical articles on Lovecraft, and a selection of his fiction. My father had also added a parenthesis: "See p. 347."

Page 347 proved to be a story called "At the Mountains of Madness". Then I saw why my father thought it might amuse me: it was set in Antarctica.

The opening sentence read: "I am forced into speech because men of science have refused to follow my advice without knowing why. It is altogether against my will that I tell my reasons for opposing this contemplated invasion of the Antarctic . . . "

The narrator was a scientist from "Miskatonic University" who had taken part in a recent Antarctic expedition—he seemed to have the Byrd 1929 expedition in mind. The author of the story had obviously gone to a great deal of trouble to learn all about Antarctica.

In Lovecraft's story, a polar expedition finds a range of mountains higher than the Himalayas. An advance party discovers a cave containing barrel-shaped, leathery beings with tentacles and membranous wings, frozen solid. At this point, the advance party loses radio contact with the base. The narrator leads an expedition to find out what has become of them. They locate the camp, but everyone is dead, "torn and mangled in fiendish and altogether inexplicable ways". There is no sign of the barrel-shaped creatures with wings and tentacles.

The camp lies in the shadow of mountains whose "witchlike cones and pinnacles" remind them of a "Cyclopean city of no architecture known to man". The narrator and his party investigate, and discover that it is indeed a ruined city. On the walls of one of its immense buildings they discover sculptured reliefs that tell them the story of its builders: how the barrel-like beings—the Old Ones—came from a remote star system in Precambrian times and colonized the earth, creating human beings and animals as food . . .

The slaughter at the camp, they learn, occurred when the Old Ones were attacked by the sled dogs, and defended themselves. In the confusion that followed, all the men and dogs were killed. The narrator concludes:

Poor devils! After all, they were not evil things of their kind. They were the men of another age and another order of being . . . That awful awakening in the cold of an unknown epoch—perhaps an attack by the furry, frantically barking quadrupeds, and a dazed defense against them and the equally frantic white simians . . . poor Old Ones!

I began reading with a kind of amusement which soon turned into an odd sense of unreality, as if someone were playing an absurd practical joke. What I was reading seemed a kind of grotesque parody of the story of the First Ones, but written in the style of 1930s pulp fiction.

The knowledge of Antarctica seemed so precise that I wondered for a moment whether H.P. Lovecraft might be the pseudonym of somebody who had accompanied Byrd on that expedition. A glance at the Introduction soon convinced me this was not so—Lovecraft was a shy recluse who spent most of his life in Providence, Rhode Island, wrestling with poverty, detesting the modern world, and writing horror stories as a kind of defiant escapism. He died of cancer in 1937, at the age of forty-six, and his stories were kept in print by his friend August Derleth, who ran a small press in Wisconsin.

The first essay in the book was by Derleth. And, on the very first page, I was electrified by this comment:

From his earliest childhood, Lovecraft experienced incredibly vivid dreams—in his own words, "strange cities, weird landscapes, unknown monsters, hideous ceremonies, Oriental and Egyptian gorgeousness, and indefinable mysteries of life, death and torment". Many of these he introduced direct into his stories . . .

And now, suddenly, I felt I understood. That was why Lovecraft's story sounded like—as he would have put it—"a grotesque and blasphemous parody" of the history of the First Ones. His was one of the minds they had reached in their attempt to make the world aware of their predicament.

I went on reading, now fascinated. Another story, called "The Shadow Out of Time", is about a professor—naturally, from Miskatonic University—who falls into a trance that lasts for years, although as far as his colleagues are concerned he has merely become an unpredictable eccentric. His alter ego studies magical works in the university library. Then, five years later, he awakens from a deep sleep and is once again his former self. But he suffers from nightmares in which he sees a strange city of

dark cylindrical towers . . . built of a bizarre type of square-cut basalt masonry and tapered slightly towards their rounded tops. Nowhere in any of them could the least traces of windows or other apertures save huge doors be found.

As I read this, my scalp tingled. It all sounded uncomfortably like the city of my grandfather's dream.

A few paragraphs further on he speaks about dreams of a place where "the skies were almost always moist and cloudy . . . The far horizon was always steamy and indistinct, but I could see that great jungles of unknown treeferns . . . lay outside the city."

Again I was reminded of my grandfather's dreams.

The professor also begins to study "forbidden" books, like the *Necronomicon* and von Juntz's *Unaussprechlichen Kulten*, and learns that, according to ancient knowledge, mankind is not the first intelligent race on earth. "Things of inconceivable shape . . . had reared towers to the sky and delved into every secret of nature before the first amphibian forebear of man had crawled out of the hot sea three hundred million years ago." And only fifty million years before the advent of man, there had been a Great Race, "in whose vast libraries were volumes of text and pictures holding the whole of Earth's annals . . . " These creatures, he learns, can travel mentally into the future, enter the mind of some other being, and displace it, while the "displaced mind" is sent back to dwell in the past. By this time, it is obvious to the reader that this is what has happened to the unfortunate professor.

The members of the Great Race are immense cones "ten feet high and with the head and other organisms attached to foot-thick distensible limbs." They moved around like huge limpets, by expanding and contracting their bases.

Years later, the professor is invited on an archaeological dig in the Western Desert of Australia, where are vast ruins of square-cut blocks. Wandering among the ruins, he finds the entrance to a tunnel, which leads to an underground city which seems strangely familiar. He finds himself in a library, whose "hieroglyphed shelves" he recognizes. He takes down a book, and in the light of his torch sees "queerly pigmented letters" written in English in his own handwriting. This is where he had spent his "missing years".

"The Shadow Out of Time" was Lovecraft's last story, written in 1935, shortly before he died of cancer. And here, as in "At the Mountains of Madness", it is obvious that he feels considerable sympathy for the Old Ones. These are not horror stories—in fact, there is an obvious conflict between the horror-story framework and the actual content of the story, which is closer to science fiction. I am not surprised that Lovecraft died when he did. He must have known that he had outgrown the feelings from which he had created his life's work.

But what fascinated me most was this mythology of the Old Ones. It was obvious that Lovecraft had received insights very like my own, and in some ways even more detailed. Here, I felt, I might find a clue to what was puzzling me about those beings under the ice.

#

But there was no time now—I had to find out what Trask wanted me to do today.

He was sitting in the corner of the dining room, talking to Inga. As I took my breakfast and went and joined them, he flashed me a welcoming smile, then went on talking to her—he was explaining how, when we all got back to New York, he wanted her to cooperate on a series of tests to try to determine what she had done to the ruby laser crystals. Inga was nodding, her eyes lowered, but I could sense that she was less than enthusiastic—in fact, that the whole idea bored her.

Trask, on the other hand, looked happier than I had ever seen him. A naturally introverted man, he was never a great communicator. But this morning he was full of excitement and optimism. I suspected I knew the reason.

When he paused for breath, I asked him what he wanted me to do today. He said he would like me to stay behind with Inga while she tried her transformative techniques on another ruby. This was what I had hoped he would say.

After breakfast, I returned with him to his room, and collected two of the ruby cylinders the New York laboratory had sent the previous day. Half an hour later, as Trask was leaving on the snow tractor, I took these—and my only chair—to Inga's room.

She was already sitting at the table. She hardly glanced at me as I sat down opposite. When I asked her how she felt, she gave a very faint smile, and made a movement of her shoulders.

The table was covered with a dark blanket. I laid one of the cylinders on this, then drew the curtain so the room was in half-darkness.

"Ready?"

She sighed. "Yes."

She placed both hands on the ends of the ruby, and I placed mine over hers.

After a few seconds, there was the familiar sense of being drawn into the crystal, as into a bright red universe. Within moments, it had filled my consciousness. Once again there was that strange sense of resistance, like wading through water.

Now my mind and hers were united together in the joint effort. If Pavel, Rodion and Natalia had been there, it would have taken only a few minutes. But there was obviously something wrong. Although my own powers seemed exceptionally strong, hers were obviously weak. When we took a break, at the end of five minutes, she was obviously tired. We made coffee, and she told me about their engagement in a New York night club, and how they had made more money in a week than they made in a year as a circus act in Russia.

We decided to have another try. But something was puzzling me. Last night, she had been so vehement that there was "something wrong". Now it was as if she had totally forgotten about it.

As we gazed into the crystal, and our minds were joined in concentration, I did something I knew to be wrong: I deliberately probed her mind to find out what she was feeling. It was wrong because I was ignoring her right to privacy. She recoiled instantly.

"No."

I said: "What are you hiding from me?"

"Nothing."

"Then let me see."

She said: "There is nothing to see."

"Then why not let me see?"

"There is nothing to see."

But when I took her hands and placed them on the ends of the crystal, she made no resistance. I placed my hands over hers and gazed into the red universe. Then, as we concentrated together, I did again what I had done before. She flinched, but made no attempt to resist.

Quite suddenly, I was behind her eyes. I had ceased to be myself, and was looking at the world from inside her body. If I had looked up, I would have stared into my own eyes, as if looking at myself in a mirror.

Now I knew she was telling the truth. She was hiding nothing from me. But that did not mean there was nothing to hide. When I thought about the First Ones, there was a strange feeling of resistance.

I withdrew my mind, and looked into her eyes.

She said: "Well?"

"You are right. There is nothing to see."

We sat there quietly for a few minutes.

She said: "Shall we continue?"

I said: "No. I don't want to do any more at the moment. I'll tell Trask you were tired after your long journey."

She nodded gratefully, glad of the chance to escape further effort.

I stood up. "If you need me, I'll be in my room. Why don't you rest?"

"Thank you."

But it was not her tiredness that had made me decide to stop working on the crystal. As our minds joined together in concentration, it would have been impossible to conceal from her what I suspected. And that was the last thing I wanted.

The first time I had probed her mind she had resisted—naturally, for we all wish to preserve our inner privacy. But the second time, she had allowed me inside her mind. And although she had ceased to resist, I was still aware of resistance.

That resistance was connected with my attempt to probe her feelings about the First Ones. Like some traumatized child, she had induced a kind of amnesia about something that terrified her. If I allowed her to suspect this, I would only be plunging her into even deeper anxiety.

But, as I returned to my own hut, I had no doubt in my mind what had happened. While she had been asleep in the night, something had invaded her mind. I say "something" because at this stage I had no idea of what it was. But I found it impossible to believe that the First Ones were responsible. All I could know for certain was that her mind had been seized and taken over. This is why her face had become so icy cold; the "something" had plunged her into a deep trance state. My presence there had made it more difficult for them, for—as I now realized—I had instinctively sensed a strangeness.

That was why Inga had insisted on staying in my room. She had sensed instinctively that she was in some kind of danger.

Inga had been born into Soviet Russia in the Brezhnev era, and life had been hard. Her father—whom she worshipped—had died after a long and painful illness, and her mother's death had been hastened by lack of food. There were many things Inga preferred to forget, many memories she refused to allow into consciousness. So it was not difficult to manipulate her mind when she was in trance. In effect, she had been hypnotized, brainwashed. And for the moment I felt it was safer to leave her that way.

#

Back in my own room, I decided to make another attempt to establish contact with the First Ones. I lay on my bed and allowed myself to sink into a deeper and deeper state of relaxation. Yet, no matter how much I relaxed, nothing happened. Again I felt that something was obstructing me.

After a quarter of an hour or so, I surrendered and picked up the Lovecraft book. I had a feeling he might be able to offer me a clue.

The longest piece in the book was an essay by Fritz Leiber called "Lovecraft and Speculative Fiction". And it was here that I found what I had been hoping for: an account of Lovecraft's mythology of the Old Ones.

According to Lovecraft, the Old Ones came to earth before the continents began to form, more than a thousand million years ago. They were barrel-shaped and had five membranous wings. They had erected cities on earth and under the sea, and had created life for food. They also, said Leiber, created hypnotically controlled protoplasmic masses called shoggoths, who were their servants. These shoggoths eventually evolved mental powers that made them extremely dangerous to their creators. Lovecraft, maintained Leiber, was obviously against the shoggoths and in favour of the Old Ones.

The next arrivals on earth were cone-shaped beings, half-animal and half-vegetable, like the Old Ones.

Next came a "half-polypus race" called the Blind Beings. It was these Blind Beings who built "windowless basalt cities", and who preyed on the cone-shaped beings.

Then the Great Race came from space, "from transgalactic Yith", took over the bodies of the cone-shaped beings, and drove the Blind Beings into caves under the earth.

After this, during the Carboniferous era, there was a "serpent race" called the Volusians.

Then, about a hundred and fifty million years ago, there was a great revolt of the shoggoths against their masters, which the Old Ones eventually won.

The glacial ages of the Cenozoic era—our own era of mammals and human beings—"worked great hardship on the Old Ones, who were driven out of their cities by the shoggoths".

After this, Leiber spoke about Lovecraft's "future history", which was typically pessimistic, and obviously irrelevant to my enquiry.

What was I to make of this tangled tale? Back in New York, I would have dismissed the whole thing as the fabrication of a neurotic romantic. But, under the circumstances, such a dismissal was impossible.

Lovecraft knew more than he suspected. He had obtained much of his material from dreams, and obviously made any changes that he felt increased the dramatic effect. But he knew about the First Ones, even though he added the absurdity of membranous wings (why should anyone need wings to fly through empty space?), and he knew about the great "windowless cities"—which he said were built by the Blind Beings.

The "serpent-like Volusians", I noted, were a reference to creatures invented by his friend Robert E. Howard. So they could be dismissed. But how much of the rest of Lovecraft's "mythology" was true?

I was struck by the number of references to the shoggoths. To me, these "hypnotically controlled protoplasmic masses" sounded authentic. When a race is the master of the earth, it needs servants. And robots made of protoplasm would be ideal. I imagined them looking a little like jellyfish, except that they would be almost shapeless.

But why should the shoggoths rebel against their creators?

It seemed to me that I could make a good guess. A mass of crawling protoplasm would not make a particularly good servant, no matter how obedient. If it was to be truly useful—for example, in building cities—then it would have to be turned into something with arms and legs, something that could move things and lift them. And it would need to be given a brain that could make intelligent decisions. In fact, it would need to be given some degree of freedom. In effect, the Old Ones would have to build Frankenstein monsters.

And I already knew the next step—from my own experience. An ordinary animal is basically a robot; it reacts to stimuli like a penny-in-the-slot machine. It accepts the fact that it is made of matter, and that this matter is subject to illness and death. In fact, it accepts its own limitations.

But human matter differs from animal matter in one basic respect. Human beings have always had strange and inexplicable ideas about "spirit" and "God" and "eternity"—some timeless realm of being beyond the material world. They believe that they are something more than the matter. These strangely potent convictions have driven them to create monasteries and cathedrals, and religions in which men can strive to free the spirit from its bondage to matter.

I had discovered, by a seeming accident of circumstance, that I could make clouds dissolve. I had learned that, after making them dissolve away, I experienced a peculiar feeling of power behind the eyes. And my introduction to laser technology had made me aware that the mind itself can be made into a sort of laser. When its powers are brought to focus, and made to march in step like a platoon of soldiers, they prove to be far greater than we could imagine. I had caught only a glimpse of these possibilities. But it had taught me to recognize that human beings are quite mistaken to think of themselves as animals. The unknown powers of the mind mean that they are potentially gods.

What had happened, I was fairly certain, was that, like me, the shoggoths had reached a point where they discovered the powers of their own minds. And at that point they rebelled against their creators. Those placid Old Ones, half-animal and half-vegetable, moving slowly on their retractable bases rather like giant snails, must have struck their servants as boring and outmoded relics of the past, like slow-witted old men. The shoggoths dreamed of freedom.

What I found hard to understand is why the Old Ones did not simply offer the shoggoths their freedom, and allow them to go their own way. But perhaps by that time the bitterness of the shoggoths was too great. Or perhaps they didn't give the Old Ones a chance—perhaps they simply attacked . . .

All this came to me as I lay on the bed, reading Leiber's essay. Yet it was not mere speculation. I had an odd feeling of *knowing* it.

And it also seemed to me that I now knew the truth about what lay under the ice. I had been assuming that only the Old Ones were waiting for their freedom. Now I was certain I was mistaken. Leiber—quoting Lovecraft—had said: "The glacial ages of the later Cenozoic worked great hardship on the Old Ones, who were driven from their terrestrial cities by the shoggoths . . ." My grandfather had seen one of these cities in a dream—a city of windowless towers. And it was almost certainly one of the cities that had fallen to the shoggoths.

Of course, the shoggoths might have been destroyed by the catastrophe that had trapped the Old Ones in a frozen tomb. But in that case what had terrified Inga so much? What was now "obstructing" my attempts to establish contact with the Old Ones? The shoggoths had to be the answer.

What were they trying to achieve? That was also obvious. Until yesterday they had had nothing to fear. All they had to do was wait until help arrived. Sooner or later, their freedom was inevitable.

Now that Inga had arrived, all this had changed. She had to be silenced.

And what about me? Since I knew the truth, I was the greatest threat of all . . .

I must admit that for a few minutes the thought made my heart beat unpleasantly fast. To calm myself, I went to the door and looked out across the white, flat landscape at the sun hanging above the horizon. It all looked pleasantly normal. I could hear the sound of pots and pans from the kitchen as Dave Eng prepared lunch. And from the end of Windy Gap great clouds of steam billowed on the wind, then turned into hail that lashed down on the ice. It was obvious that the rescue operation was going according to plan.

That realization filled me with a sense of urgency. Somehow, this operation had to be stopped—at least until we had time to assess the situation. But how? What would Trask say if I told him I had something important to tell him, and then warned him that he might be letting a genie out of a bottle? He would think I had gone insane—particularly if I explained that the genie was out of an H.P. Lovecraft horror story.

The thought made me smile—and made me aware that, in spite of everything, I was still feeling curiously optimistic. I could simply not believe that our expedition constituted a serious threat to the future of the human race. Ever since I had met Trask, I had experienced a sense of buoyant optimism, a feeling that something marvellous was going to happen. I found it impossible to believe that it was all some delusion. And now, as I looked at the reflection of the sun on the ice, I still had a deep inner certainty that all was well.

#

Half an hour later the snow tractor returned. As Trask jumped off the back, I went to meet him.

"How's it going, sir?"

"Very well, Matthew—excellent. We've gone down another fifty feet. What about you?"

"Not so good. Inga's too tired to do anything."

He looked concerned. "That's too bad. She needs time to recover. Tell her to rest as long as it takes."

As he started to go towards the dining room I said: "There's something else . . . "

He turned back. "What else?"

"It's not just that she's tired. You're going to think this sounds absurd . . . but she feels that what we're doing is dangerous."

"Dangerous?" He looked at me with total bafflement. "What do you mean, dangerous?"

I said: "She thinks there's something down there."

He shrugged impatiently. "Of course there's something down there—the remains of the oldest civilization on earth. Haven't you explained?"

"Yes, she understands that."

"Then what's worrying her?"

"She says she has a feeling of . . . evil."

"Evil?" He stared at me blankly, and I realized that he didn't even begin to understand.

I tried another approach.

"She says that, if we go ahead, we'll be releasing a kind of genie from a bottle."

I saw immediately that I'd said the right thing. As a scientist, he knew all about releasing genies from bottles—the atomic bomb, atmospheric pollution, destruction of the ozone layer.

He thought for a moment, then said: "Do you know what she means?"

I decided to duck that question. There was no point, at this stage, in trying to tell him the truth.

"No, sir."

"All right. Bring her to lunch and I'll ask her myself."

But when I told Inga she shook her head.

"I don't want to go."

I knew there was no point in trying to persuade her—I could sense that the thought of talking about it filled her with anxiety and insecurity. I said: "I'll tell him you're asleep."

To my relief, there was no need to lie. When I joined Trask in the dining room he was looking unexpectedly jolly, and on my telling him Inga didn't feel hungry he merely nodded. It was obvious that his incorrigibly active mind had already moved on to other things. As soon as I sat down opposite him—with my frankfurters and chips—he said: "I've been a fool. We should have brought that girl with us in the first place."

"Yes?" I wondered what he was talking about.

"She could have told us where to start. She can sense what's under the ice."

Now I understood. Trask had seen her locate coins hidden under cups and perform various others feats of extra-sensory perception. He now went on to tell me how a dowser had led him to the site of one of the biggest oil finds in the Midwest. It was still financing his researches.

Windy Gap was basically a glacier—a slow-moving torrent of ice. And the parts of a glacier move at different velocities, the centre moving fastest. If there was a city under the ice, then it had probably been torn apart. We might spend another three weeks getting down to the floor of the valley and then find nothing. What Trask was hoping was that Inga could tell us if we were wasting our time.

"Do you think she'll feel well enough to come along this afternoon?"

The thought made my heart sink, but I said: "I'll go and see how she's feeling."

Inga was asleep when I got back. As I peeped in the door she woke, sat up in bed, rubbing her eyes, and looking so pale that I hardly had the heart to tell her why I'd come. But as I sat by her bed, wondering how to begin, she said: "I know. Dr Trask wants me to come."

I had forgotten she had flashes of telepathy.

"How do you feel about it?"

She gave a faint shrug.

"Since he has brought me all this way, I cannot refuse."

I had an idea. "Why don't you and I go ahead and take a look at the place? I'll see if I can borrow the Snobile."

#

The Snobile was a cross between a sled and a miniature tractor, used for carrying small loads around the camp. Dave Eng was using it to move frozen food when I located it, but he let me take it.

I had never driven it before, but it was simple enough. Wheels with snow tyres projected only a few inches below sled runners, so that if the snow was unexpectedly deep it could not sink in. It worked off long-life batteries and made a high, whining noise.

Both wrapped up to the eyebrows, we set out at twelve miles an hour—about the speed of a bicycle—following the tracks of the snow tractor.

The vehicle bumped and rolled, throwing us both from side to side, but it didn't bother me. I had a watery feeling of foreboding in the pit of my stomach, and the bumps were a welcome distraction.

It was a calm, bright afternoon, with a clear sky, and the wind had dropped. I braked the Snobile within a few feet of the edge of the trench. This now extended about halfway across the valley, being roughly three hundred feet deep at the north cliff face. At the far end it was merely a ramp sloping down into the trench. The chief danger, obviously, was that the snow tractor would slide down the ramp and end up at the bottom of the hole, so the slope had been made very gentle. I anticipated that, by the time the hole was half a mile deep, the trench would have to extend right across the valley.

We walked across and looked down into the hole—a terrifying sight. The thought of what it would look like when it was six times as deep made me feel dizzy.

I looked at Inga, and was shocked by her paleness.

"Are you all right?"

"I would like to sit down."

We went back to the Snobile, and she almost collapsed into the passenger seat. She sat with her eyes closed, looking very ill.

"Shall I take you back?"

She shook her head, then rested it on the back of the seat. I sat beside her, afraid to speak. Finally she opened her eyes.

"What is it?"

She said: "This place tastes of death."

"Death?" That startled me.

"Can you not feel it?"

I looked at the white snow, glittering in the sun that lay behind us, and shook my head. To me it looked bleak but rather beautiful.

She said: "Take off your gloves."

Wondering what it was all about, I did as she said. She slipped off her own fur gloves, then made me turn towards her and took both my hands.

Suddenly, I understood.

I had been making the obvious mistake—looking at the landscape and trying to imagine what lay below it. I should have been looking inside myself.

As soon as she took my hands the watery feeling in my stomach increased and turned into something like nausea. At the same time I became aware of something like a very unpleasant smell—the most horrible smell I have ever encountered in my life.

I say "something like" because I was perfectly aware that it existed only in my own mind. I knew that, physically speaking, I was breathing in the new-leather smell of the Snobile and that of the joint of smoked bacon that Dave Eng had been carrying in the passenger seat when I borrowed the vehicle. The "other" smell was somehow inside me, like an unpleasant memory that was so clear that merely thinking about it made it come back.

It was like rotting flesh, but far more nauseating—so nauseating that I knew if I gave way to the temptation to cough I would end up being sick.

Then I began to understand what Inga meant about the taste of death. This whole valley seemed to be full of it—an appalling sensation of cruelty and evil. Something horrible had taken place here—not once, but many times.

The sensation became so sickening that I had to let go of her hands. It was rather like turning your face away from an accident with a gruesomely mutilated corpse. Even then, it persisted for perhaps half a minute before it slowly faded.

Now I understood why Inga looked so pale. She had been aware of this ever since she'd arrived.

There was no point in trying to put it from my mind. I wanted to understand it. So I suppressed the queasiness in my stomach and reached out to take her hands again.

Now it was not merely the smell that I was aware of, but the cruelty. This is what was so frightening. It brought back an afternoon when I was in fifth grade, when we had been studying Christopher Marlowe's *Tamburlaine the Great*, and I had been sufficiently curious to go and look him up in the library. Tamburlaine had been a Mongol, a descendant of Genghis Khan, and he was an insane sadist. On one occasion he had two thousand prisoners bricked alive into a living mound; on another he had three thousand beheaded and their heads built into a pyramid. The book gave me nightmares for weeks afterwards. Now the nightmare seemed to come back, but amplified to a point that made me feel physically drained.

Inga took her hands out of mine, but this time the nightmare refused to go away. I had tuned in to it, I suppose you could say, and it was inescapable.

I climbed out of the Snobile to get some fresh air, knowing that for the rest of my life the smell of smoked bacon and new leather would bring back this nauseating odour of death. Now I had braced myself against it, it was slightly more bearable. But the stench remained appalling. I cannot describe this, but it might convey some idea if I say that it was like a combination of meat that has been allowed to go rotten, a public toilet that has not been cleaned for years, and an oddly sweet burning smell, like some kind of plastic. It seemed incredible to me that I had ever been unable to smell it.

I longed to get away from the place, but knew this was impossible. We had to wait for the snow tractor. So I began to walk across the valley towards its south side. This only made the smell worse. I tried walking back toward the camp, and this did improve it slightly. The further I got from the place, the better it seemed to be.

I was amused at the thought of how Lovecraft would have described all this. He would have said something like: "My mind reeled into an abyss of blasphemous horror . . ." In fact, it was not at all like that. What was so unpleasant about the place was not blasphemous horror but just sheer nastiness. And, as my mind recovered its balance, I realized there was no point in being sickened by it. In the long history of mankind, the earth has seen some appalling cruelty. Yet man remains basically decent, and civilization goes on. We have to face it and move on from there.

Inga came and joined me. The cold had brought a little colour to her cheeks.

I said: "Well, what do you think of it?"

"Of what?"

"Are they digging in the right place?"

She looked down at the trench and said drily: "They will find what they are looking for."

It was odd that she could tell what lay under the ice. I asked: "What's down there?"

"The remains of a city. And a graveyard under the city. But I think it contains more than graves."

There was no need to ask what she meant. As she spoke, even I could feel it. There was something down there, and it was aware of our presence. It would have been pointless to ask whether it was benevolent or otherwise. Is an octopus lurking in an underwater cave benevolent, or a python lying along the branch of a tree? I suppose your attitude would depend on whether you happened to be something it liked for dinner.

I pointed at the hole. "What will they find down there?"

She frowned, and lowered her eyes.

"It is . . . some kind of science laboratory . . . "

"An observatory?"

She looked at me with surprise.

"Yes, an observatory."

I pointed across the valley.

"Why does it feel worse over there?"

She frowned and shook her head. "I don't know."

"Come and see."

Walking towards the south side of the valley cost me an effort; I was soon reeling from the stench, and tempted to hold my breath, although I knew this would make no difference. Finally I could go no further and was forced to stand still.

"Well?"

Her face, too, was wrinkled with disgust. "Yes, it is very bad. It is . . . a place of torment."

"Torment?" But she seemed unable, or unwilling, to elaborate. "I mean, is it dangerous?"

To my surprise, she shook her head. "No. I do not feel it is dangerous."

"And where is it?"

"Where?" At first she did not seem to understand me.

"Is it under our feet?"

"No, no." She pointed. "It is down there, in the side of the mountain."

She was indicating a place slightly to the north of where the landslide had happened.

"How far down?"

She considered, then said: "Perhaps a hundred feet."

"No more?"

"No."

And even now, it was obvious that she had not grasped the significance of what she had said.

I heard the sound of the snow tractor coming towards us. It was late—the time was now about half-past three.

I said: "Will you tell him that?"

"Yes." But she was obviously puzzled.

A few moments later the tractor arrived, and Trask jumped down, wearing his tartan scarf and baseball cap. He told us they had been delayed while he contacted Little America via satellite.

"Anything happening?"

I said: "Inga's found something."

"Good. What?"

"She thinks we've started in the wrong place."

I left her to do the explaining.

She pointed across the valley. "You should have started there."

Trask said: "Why, what's there?"

"There is something about a hundred feet down."

I felt almost guilty at the look of delight that crossed his face.

"A hundred feet. What is it?"

"I don't know. I can't tell. Some kind of a cave in the face of the cliff."

Trask beamed at her, then at me. Then he turned to Bill Ruggles. "Get that thing over there."

Bill, who had not been close enough to hear the conversation, looked dismayed. "Over there? You're going to start all over again?"

Trask nodded. "That's right."

Bill knew him well enough not to argue.

Inga and I climbed into the Snobile and followed the tractor. The centre of the valley had less compacted snow than the sides—the wind carried it away as soon as it settled—and the Snobile was inclined to skid on the ice.

The tractor stopped. Trask came back to the Snobile.

"Tell us where it is."

She got out and pointed. "Somewhere down there."

They turned the tractor and positioned it with the laser pointing at the face of the mountain, which at this point was almost vertical.

While Inga and I watched from inside the Snobile, Trask got into the trailer and helped Bill and Elmo adjust the angle of the laser. She stared with a kind of horrified fascination as the ruby beam stabbed into the ice like a spear, and steam hissed into the air. The breeze carried it away up the valley. But now there was far less steam, for Trask was directing the beam at an angle of about forty-five degrees, so it cut down through the ice, which then collapsed on top of it, and was in turn dissolved away. The method was sensible. The superheated steam melted the ice above it, which in turn reduced the amount of steam. Instead of wasting the heat in the steam, Trask was putting it to practical use. The violent explosions of trapped steam hastened the process.

It was good for me to concentrate on the laser; I noticed that doing this seemed to diminish the stench. After a few minutes, I worked out why this was. If I concentrated hard, narrowing my senses, it somehow decreased my sensitivity. Inga had made me "open up" to the psychic atmosphere of Windy Gap; if I wanted, I could close my mind again, by focusing my senses and exerting my will. This produced exactly the same effect as dissolving clouds—a sense of power behind the eyes.

Inga's psychic abilities were, of course, far greater than mine. But they had the disadvantage of being beyond her control. She could not close her mind, as I could. At the same time, I could not open my mind as she could. When I tried it as I sat beside her, doing my best to relax into a state of receptivity, my mind seemed to jam like a door that refuses to open.

This brought me an interesting insight. Ever since the Vassilievskies had taught me that I could dissolve clouds, I had experienced a wonderful sense of optimism and strength—the feeling that I had discovered a secret of which the rest of the human race was unaware: the secret that we can *make things happen*.

What I could not understand was why the Vassilievskies were unaware of it—after all, they had taught it to me.

Now, sitting next to Inga, I saw the answer. Their powers were natural—they were born with them. So they took them for granted. I had *discovered* mine. I was like a poor man who inherits a fortune and who because of his previous poverty feels far richer than a person who was born rich.

And, as I looked at Trask, supervising the operation in his baseball cap and tartan scarf, I saw that he was also in the position of someone who has been "born rich". With his terrific energy and vitality and purpose, he used his "secret" powers quite automatically, without ever being aware that he was making things happen. Trask could have dissolved clouds if he wanted. But, even then, I doubt whether he would have understood the secret. He would have thought it was some natural power that we happen to possess, and would probably have thought it was far less interesting than inventing a new kind of transistor. He would not have understood that it is the most important discovery that human beings can possibly make: a discovery that can enable them to take charge of their fate and become masters of reality.

I had talked to Anton Voronski—the man who had been testing Inga when I met her—about some of his experiments with psychic powers. And I had remarked that it seemed to me amazing that most scientists refuse to accept the existence of abilities like extra-sensory perception and psychokinesis when the laboratory evidence is so overwhelming. Voronski replied: "That is because it is not strong enough. You see, most people can use only about two per cent of their psychic powers."

I asked him to elaborate.

"Look, if I put two cards face-downward on the table and ask you to guess which one is the ace of spades, you will stand a fifty per cent chance of guessing correctly. If I repeat the experiment a thousand times, you should guess correctly exactly five hundred times. So if you *consistently* make five hundred and twenty or so correct guesses out of a thousand, that proves you possess ESP. But that is not going to convince the sceptics—they will find some reason to dismiss it. Now it is my experience that two per cent is the average level of ESP. Most people have thought about their Aunt Mildred on the morning they receive a letter from her—but they assume this is chance. They fail to realize that they are using their natural ESP."

I now saw that Voronski had handed me the vital clue. When you do something in a mood of happiness and expectation, it nearly always turns out OK. That is because you are putting that "extra two per cent" into it. You somehow know it's going to come out right. When a racing driver is in good form, he knows he's not going to have an accident. Yet he doesn't realize that he is using his two per cent of "secret powers", the same powers I used to dissolve clouds.

As I thought about this I began to feel again a marvellous sense of happiness and optimism. For I saw that I had stumbled on the answer to the most important problems of human existence. People don't realize they possess "hidden powers", just as a few centuries ago they didn't realize that the blood circulates around the body. When we are "accident prone", and things keep going wrong, we don't realize we are *making* them go wrong, by making negative use of "hidden powers".

If the whole human race understood about these hidden powers, man would become a completely different kind of creature—a kind of superman.

At this point I was brought back to the present by a billowing cloud of steam that surrounded us and plunged us into a kind of white darkness. When it cleared, I saw the laser had stopped working. I walked over to the trailer to see what was happening and—as I expected—found that the crystal had shattered. For some reason, its power always increased before it burned out.

I also took the opportunity to look down into the hole. It was only about twenty feet wide, but already more than sixty feet deep. The rock of the cliff face had fused into a shiny blue colour where the laser had struck it. The ice sloped down to the cliff face at an angle of about thirty degrees, and the bottom of the wedge-shaped hole was full of steaming water.

I spoke to Trask, but he didn't even hear me; he was so absorbed in what he was doing that he was totally oblivious to the outside world. I sensed that nothing would distract him until he found what he was looking for.

Back in the Snobile, the heater made it oppressively warm. I asked Inga: "Would you like to go back?"

She shook her head. "No. I want to see what they find."

"It may be hours—or perhaps even tomorrow . . . "

But I knew it wouldn't be tomorrow. When Trask got the bit between his teeth he didn't give up until he had what he wanted.

The new ruby cylinder was unusually powerful; once again, we were enveloped in a cloud of steam that left the windshield covered in drops.

"What do you think they're going to find?"

She shook her head. "I don't know."

I reached out and took both her hands in mine. This immediately brought back the sickening stench—I found it hard to understand how she could stand it. And the sense of evil and cruelty was overpowering—it felt like being trapped in a nightmare.

I asked her: "Have you ever known anything like this before?"

"Yes. I once visited Babi Yar, where all those people were massacred. That was a little like this. But not as bad."

"Was there the same stink?"

"No. Just the smell of fear and misery."

What was troubling me was who had died. The Old Ones? Or the shoggoths? Or both? Whichever it was, I could sense great hatred as well as cruelty. This battle had been long and bitter. Yet I found it impossible to believe that the Old Ones were capable of cruelty . . .

To try to escape this sense of struggling in a nightmare, I let go of her hands and concentrated my mind until—as abruptly as a bursting bubble—the feeling of helplessness suddenly vanished.

The relief was enormous. Able to think clearly once again, I began to reflect on the problem. If I had been in a bottle for a long time, what would I want to do when I got out? I would begin by thanking those who had released me, and find out what I could do for them. I would want to try and understand them and make them understand me . . .

Or would I? I recalled my image of a human being towering above a mouse. How would I feel in a world of intelligent mice? The answer, I had to admit, was: probably rather bored. Grateful and benevolent, perhaps, but bored.

That was a disturbing thought. The next one was even more so. It struck me that, whenever civilized man has discovered a simpler, more primitive society, he has destroyed it. I am not now speaking about the Spaniards who invaded Mexico and enslaved the Aztecs, or the white Americans who drove the Indians off their ancestral lands, but even the modern students of anthropology who have discovered unknown tribes in the heart of Borneo or Sumatra. For all their good intentions, all their determination not to impose their "civilized" values on the natives, they have always devastated the culture they were trying to preserve, just as surely as the early European explorers decimated the Maoris of New Zealand by bringing smallpox.

The Old Ones might be entirely benevolent. But could they avoid bringing disaster on the human race, merely by being more powerful and intelligent? With a sinking feeling, I suddenly realized that this reflection changed the whole perspective of what we were doing.

#

To shake off these doubts and perplexities, I went to see how the work was progressing. Trask and the others had pulled back the tractor to cut into the ice at a less steep angle, but even so it was now at least thirty degrees. Elmo—who was now controlling the laser—would point it at the bottom of the slope, releasing a hissing cloud of steam and a shower of sparks as it struck the cliff face. Then, when the hole had been deepened by ten feet or so, he would concentrate on the ice of the slope, cutting away its surface until it ran straight and level up to the cliff face. Then he would lower the angle of the laser, and cut another ten-foot hole.

The problem, I could see, was that the slope would soon be approaching sixty degrees. When that happened, they would have to pull back again, and evaporate thousands of tons of ice in order to make it less steep. It was now nearly seven o'clock in the evening. At this rate, it would take until midnight.

I was about to turn back to the Snobile when Elmo lowered the angle of the laser and plunged us into an exceptionally choking cloud of fog. I paused, waiting for the sharp hiss and the shower of sparks as the beam struck the cliff. But this time there were no sparks. Yet, from where I was standing at the eastern edge of the hole, the steam seemed to be thicker than ever. I called out to Elmo to hold on. He switched off the beam and, as the vapour cleared, I saw that the laser had gouged deep into the cliff face, creating a cavity that looked as if it had been made by a huge dentist's drill.

I ran back to the Snobile, where Inga had fallen into a doze, and shook her. "Come and look." I took her by the hand and led her to the edge of the hole.

Trask asked her: "Is this what you meant?"

She shook her head, still dazed with sleep. "I don't know. I think so."

Elmo said: "Shall I go down there?"

Even I could see that he would break his neck on the sheer slope of ice.

Trask said: "No. We'll have to get ropes."

Bill Ruggles had a better idea. "If we move the laser to one side, we can cut grooves in the ice."

That is what we did. The laser was taken to the eastern edge of the hole, so it pointed across the slope. Then it was turned down to a tenth of its power, and a series of parallel grooves were cut across the ice. It took half an hour, but finally we had a series of shallow trenches, between six inches and a foot deep, at intervals of a few yards.

Trask was the first to lower himself over the edge; Elmo and Bill Ruggles followed. I saw that Inga was hesitating.

"Don't you want to see?"

She shook her head. I was too excited to stay with her, and followed the others.

We should have spent more time cutting the grooves; although they prevented us from sliding like a toboggan to the bottom—and probably breaking both legs against the cliff—they were themselves as smooth as an ice rink, while the span of the ice in between them meant we landed in each one with a jarring crash that knocked the breath out of us. By the time I reached the bottom my face was scratched and I had lost both gloves.

The others were peering into the hole, which was six feet wide and perhaps ten feet deep. It was difficult to tell whether it was a cave or merely a kind of hollow in the cliff face. Trask finally gave orders to return to the top, a scramble that was even worse than the one coming down. At least I recovered my gloves on the way.

Trask told Elmo to deepen the hollow with a low power beam, and to widen it at the same time. Ten minutes later the steam cleared to reveal a projecting ledge, and we knew we had found a cave.

I must admit that I was tired—my lack of sleep was catching up with me. Inga seemed oddly listless and indifferent. But Trask was obviously driven like a demon by a tremendous suppressed excitement—if we had all insisted on returning to camp, he would have continued alone.

Once again we scrambled down the slope—Bill Ruggles made this part of the task easier by producing ice axes with spikes on the back that bit into the ice. Going the last twenty feet or so was the most dangerous, since it involved dropping down onto the ledge. It would have been safer to leave it until morning—we were all too tired to pay proper attention to caution—but no one would have dared suggest it.

Finally, we all stood in the cave entrance. The roof stretched high above us—about twenty-five feet—and the ice had been melted to a depth of perhaps a dozen yards. It was extremely dark—since we were at the bottom of a hole—and a downward-sloping wall of ice still blocked the cave itself.

We all had the same thought—that perhaps, after all this effort, we had found merely an empty cavity that had filled up with water and frozen. Then Elmo gave a shout. He was shining his torch at the ice to the right of the cave. Embedded in it, at a depth of a few feet, was an object that looked like some kind of artifact. Trask shone his powerful light on it—the ice was as clear as glass—and gave a chuckle of satisfaction. What we were looking at was an axehead—an enormous axehead about three feet across.

Bill and Elmo used their ice axes to chop their way in to it. When it had been freed and dragged into the cave entrance, we could see it was big enough to fell a mammoth. The surface was blackened, so it was impossible to tell what kind of metal it was made from, but its sheer weight suggested iron or bronze. Moreover, on the far side of the hole that had held the haft, there was a broken surface, as if this had once been a double-headed axe like the ones found at the Palace of Minos in Crete.

As we looked down on it, we all recognized that we had made one of the major archaeological discoveries of the century. It was one of those moments when a shared emotion seems to unite a group with a kind of telepathy.

Bill said: "Congratulations, Dr Trask. You've done it again."

Trask smiled modestly. "Only with your help." He looked around him. "I think this deserves to be called the Cave of the Giants."

While Bill took a photograph of Trask and Elmo, with the axehead propped up between them, I picked up Trask's torch and went to investigate. Since the laser had cut down at an angle, the face of the ice sloped backwards, forming a miniature cave, about eight feet deep. I crawled into this and shone the torch into the clear ice. Although it was difficult to be sure, I had the impression that I was looking through a wall of ice—when the torch was moved, the light seemed to be reflected off another surface a few feet away.

I called Trask, and handed him the torch. He confirmed my impression that only a few feet of ice divided us from the inside of the cave.

The simplest method of gaining access would have been the laser, but unfortunately it had already reached its limit—we were going to have to lower it by several feet to enable it to reach deeper into the cave. To do this we would need more manpower, and Trask called the camp on his radio to tell Chet Morison to join us. Meanwhile, Elmo began hacking into the ice just above floor level—cautiously, in case he caused the ice above to collapse. (If it had, it would have squashed him like a fly.) Bill and I removed the chunks of fallen ice by hand. When it became clear that the ice was stable, Bill and I added our efforts to Elmo's. Up above us, Trask and Chet Morison were using the laser to create a slope leading down to the ramp, but it was going to be a long, slow business.

Then, as all three of us hacked into the ice, it began to look as if the laser would be unnecessary. We had created a tunnel about six feet high, at its entrance, and six feet wide—some of the chunks of ice we brought down weighed more than a hundredweight.

Our blows had made the ice opaque, so we could no longer calculate how far we had to go. But we all knew it could not be far, and chopped away with increasing energy, each hoping to be the first to break through.

In fact, it was Elmo. A tremendous underhand blow caused a hole to appear just above the height of the floor. We all began to cheer and laugh aloud.

Trask called down to ask what had happened, and, when we told him, came scrambling down at a dangerous pace. By that time, a few more blows had enlarged the opening until it was three feet across.

Bill leaned in and shone his torch—then came staggering back.

"God, it stinks!"

As the nauseating stench came filtering out, we all fell back to the mouth of the cave, where there was clean air. Chet Morison began to retch.

I was the first to recover. Since I had been smelling it most of the afternoon, I was already more or less accustomed to it. Besides, the stench was by no means as foul as it had been when Inga had first held my hands—this might have been nothing worse than an unclean butcher's shop in which the blood had turned putrescent.

I picked up Elmo's torch, went back to the hole, and shone it through. The powerful beam shone on the rear wall of the cave, about fifty yards away, then on something that looked like animal carcasses piled against it. I stayed there for several minutes, playing the torch around the cave's interior, before deciding it was safe to climb in through the hole. Controlling my nausea by concentrating, I took a few steps across the level floor.

Trask's voice said: "My God, what are they?" His own light shone over the carcases.

I already knew the answer to his question.

"I think they're called shoggoths."

He climbed in through the hole.

"How do you know?"

"Lovecraft wrote about them."

"Lovecraft?" He had obviously never heard the name. "Who is he?"

"A writer who had nightmares."

Trask was advancing across the floor, and I admired his courage. These things filled me with the same sense of nastiness that I had experienced earlier in the day, and I felt no desire to approach any closer. Finally, shame led me to suppress my revulsion and follow Trask.

He asked: "But what are they?"

"Frankenstein's monsters."

"Oh, nonsense . . . " Then his voice trailed away.

He was looking down at one of the carcasses that lay halfway across the floor. It was headless, and one of its upper limbs was missing—the limb was lying nearby on the floor.

A shoggoth is almost impossible to describe, since it lacks the symmetry of a human body. They are big—even without its head this one was twelve feet tall. It has six limbs, the lower ones squat and powerful, like a caricature of an ape, the upper ones long and sinuous, more like tentacles. But the "tentacles" also have smaller tentacles, giving them the appearance of some kind of root. The whole body has a disorganized lumpy appearance, like some grotesque potato that bears only a freak resemblance to a human being.

I bent down and touched the grey-green flesh. I expected it to be frozen solid, like a carcase in a butcher's freezer, but it yielded slightly under my finger, like some kind of leather or plastic. This was clearly quite dissimilar to human or animal flesh, and I recalled Leiber's comment that the shoggoths were made of a mixture of animal and vegetable matter. The substance that had leaked out of the severed neck looked like yellow pus.

Elmo startled us by shouting: "You'd better come out—this ice is cracking."

But before we could even start to move it had happened—the immense block of ice above the entrance came crashing down, shaking the whole cave. Our blows had weakened its hold on the roof above, and we were lucky it had not collapsed at the time.

As far as Trask and I were concerned, this made no real difference—we were in no danger. No doubt we could have clambered up over the ice and crawled through the gap at the top. But that would have been both hazardous and pointless, since all we had to do was wait for the laser to free us in due course.

Bill Ruggles shouted to ask if we were all right. Trask called: "We're fine—just get us out when you're ready." Then he turned his attention back to the corpse.

"What is it—a kind of Abominable Snowman?"

"As far as I know, it's a kind of artifact. You could say it's a robot."

"You mean it was never alive?"

I had to admit: "I'm afraid I just don't know the answer to that."

Trask was advancing to the back of the cave. We passed what looked like two more bodies, then realized it was one body that had been torn in half. This shoggoth was immense—it must have originally been twenty feet tall. It had a head—a kind of bulbous mound rising out of humped shoulders—and it also had eyes, a series of yellowish globes that ran around the mid-part of the head. These seemed to have eyelids at both the bottom and the top, and most of them were closed. As far as I could tell, there was no mouth, and the only thing that looked like a nose was a hole just below the eyes. Strange entrails, like bunches of blue rope, projected from its upper half, and the lower half was correspondingly hollow. I found myself wondering what force could have torn such a huge creature in two like a rag doll.

Against the rear wall of the cave there were at least two dozen carcases. They lay in a tangle of limbs, as if they had been driven like leaves in some tremendous gale. It reminded me of a photograph I had once seen of a pile of corpses in a German concentration camp at the end of the Second World War.

Trask, his voice sounding incongruously brisk and businesslike, said: "But, if these were robots, who made them?"

"According to Lovecraft, the original inhabitants of the earth—the Old Ones."

I was aware that it sounded absurd, and that under normal circumstances Trask would have wondered about my sanity. But, faced with these grotesque carcases, I could see that he would have believed me if I had told him they were Martians.

The strangest thing about the shoggoths was that they were all unlike. Every one of them was in some way different from the others. Some had barrel-shaped bodies, with the middle limbs growing out of the sides. Some were broad and flat, and had eyes like rectangular slits. One even had two heads. I felt that they resembled vegetables rather than animals—some kind of root vegetable, like a swede, or even a Jerusalem artichoke, with its knobbly and unpredictable appearance. In some, the lower limbs even resembled taproots, tapering to a point. I had the impression that these things had been created almost arbitrarily, like plasticine figures moulded by a child.

Trask asked: "How do you think they died?"

To me the answer seemed obvious.

"I think they were killed by the Old Ones."

"Any idea why?" I had the feeling he felt compelled to go on asking me questions, even though he knew I could only guess at the answers. In this case, I did know the answer.

"Because they were in revolt."

"And where are these Old Ones now?"

I pointed downward.

"Somewhere down there, under half a mile of ice."

It took him some time to absorb this. I could see he was stunned, and could imagine what he was feeling. He had expected to discover the remains of a maritime civilization dating from about 7000BC. Instead, he was looking at the remains of a tragedy that had taken place before *Homo sapiens* had appeared on earth.

He asked finally: "How long have you known about all this?"

"The Old Ones? Ever since we came here."

"How did you know?"

This was no time or place to explain, so I said: "I just felt their presence."

"And Inga?"

"Yes. She can feel them too."

Again he was silent. He said finally: "How do you think these Old Ones died?"

It seemed pointless not to be honest with him.

"I don't believe they *are* dead."

"Not dead?" He was not as startled as I expected. Or perhaps he simply had more self-control. "How can that be?"

"Don't forget these beings are not human." I pointed at the carcases. "In the same way these things are not human."

"Yes, but nothing could remain alive under half a mile of ice."

"Some fishes do."

"That's merely for the winter. Nothing could live that way for thousands of years. It contradicts all the laws of nature."

I nodded at the carcases. "But so do these."

He shook his head. "That simply doesn't follow. What you say is not logical."

I observed a tone of irritability, and decided not to contradict him. Instead I tried to turn it into a joke.

"I think I'm going to freeze if I stay in here much longer."

The cave was like a refrigerator. It had been cold outside, but the sun and the steam from the ice had kept the temperature around freezing point. In here it must have been twenty below. And we had already been trapped there for about half an hour.

Trask went to the debris of fallen ice that blocked the entrance, and called: "Anything happening there?"

Elmo's voice came back.

"They're nearly ready. You'd better stand well back."

We retreated to the rear of the cave and stood against the wall. One of the creatures, which had lost two of its limbs, lay a few feet away from us, the yellow pus-like substance forming a pool around its body like a melted ice cream. I noted between its lower limbs—which were sprawled apart—a gaping hole that seemed to be surrounded by thicker flesh, like a mouth, while inside there were a few elongated white spines that looked as if they might be teeth. I pointed it out to Trask, who knelt beside it and shone his torch into it.

"Yes, it seems to be some kind of mouth. I wonder if these things gave rise to the legend of troglodytes . . . "

It struck me as ironic that, after half an hour, we were both taking these creatures for granted, when the first sight of them had been such a shock.

As I stood there in the semi-darkness, one thing suddenly became clear to me. These twisted carcases explained the sense of evil that Inga had felt as soon as she arrived. I could imagine the same kind of butchery taking place all over the valley—shoggoths being slaughtered like cattle, but with a deliberate cruelty that sprang from rage and vindictiveness.

In that moment of insight, I was also forced to face the truth that I had been trying to ignore since Inga took my hands: that the Old Ones were not the wise, benevolent creatures I had assumed—and that Lovecraft came to believe they were. They were capable of the same kind of brutal ferocity and sadism that had shocked me when I read about Tamburlaine. Perhaps, of course, it was justified. Perhaps the shoggoths had treated them in the same way. But, looking at these horribly mutilated corpses, one thing was clear: the Old Ones were monsters.

#

A hissing sound told us that the laser had been activated. They must have been using it on low power—otherwise the beam would have cut straight through the ice. What happened now was that the ice was suddenly illuminated from inside, as if by a red sunset, then began to collapse. At that point, the cave filled with steam. We both began to cough. Then the laser turned off.

Elmo's voice called: "Are you OK?"

We both shouted yes. Moments later, the ice reddened again, and more steam surged around us. It was by no means an unpleasant sensation, for we had both been frozen to the bone, and the steam turned the cave into something like a sauna. I noticed water flowing across the floor, then my feet began to feel warm. I knelt and put my finger in it, then snatched it away—the water was near boiling point.

I looked around for something to stand on, but there were no ledges or fallen rocks. Reluctantly, I clambered on to the nearest body, and felt rubbery flesh yielding under my boots. I almost fell, and had to lean back against the wall of the cave. The steam made it impossible to see what Trask was doing.

Elmo shouted: "Are you all right?"

Trask's voice called: "Yes."

"Just once more."

I noticed that the stench of rotting flesh had suddenly increased, and I felt my boots sink into the body underneath me. At that point I realized it had no bones. The shoggoths, like the Old Ones, were a kind of mollusc.

Again the cave filled with hissing steam—this time far more of it. Another wave of hot water flooded across the floor. Then Elmo's voice—suddenly clear—shouted: "Where are you?" We heard his footsteps splashing through the water.

I shouted: "Be careful." It had suddenly struck me that he might stumble into one of the shoggoths, and that it would be an extremely unpleasant shock. A moment later I knew it had happened—Elmo gave one of the most appalling screams I had ever heard.

To my right, Trask sounded as if he were choking.

I called, "Dr Trask!", but there was no reply.

I decided I had better go and see what was happening.

As I tried to climb off the shoggoth, I felt something grip my ankle. I looked down and saw that a tentacle was winding around my leg, and that the yellow eyes of the creature I had been standing on were staring up at me.

At that point I too began to scream, and to kick out frantically. I yelled even louder as another tentacle wound around the other leg, gripping with frightening strength. I bent down and struck out with the torch at one of the yellow eyes. It squelched like jelly, and as one tentacle released me I fell sideways, tearing my other leg free, and ran for the door. In my panic I cannoned into somebody—perhaps Elmo—and kept on running until I tripped and fell heavily onto the ice outside the cave. I was scrambling to my feet when I realized that Bill Ruggles was blocking my path. When he asked, "Where's Dr Trask?", I pointed frantically behind me.

As Bill ran into the cave, shouting Trask's name, I was suddenly ashamed of my panic, and went after him. Then I saw why Trask was not answering. He was being gripped by a tentacle that had wound around his neck, and his face was purple. All around him, the mass of shoggoths was heaving and struggling like a giant heap of maggots, as if those underneath were trying to push their way out. Even the shoggoth that had been torn into two halves seemed to be moving, and the headless one was crawling on all fours. Incredibly, the severed limb was writhing like a blind snake.

I saw Bill slash with his ice axe at a tentacle that wound itself around his ankle, then drop the axe to grab the tentacle around Trask's throat with both hands. I ran forward to help him, seizing the fallen axe and hacking at a tentacle that had wound around his waist, and another that seized my leg. For a despairing moment, I had a sudden conviction that we were all going to die.

Then Bill was dragging Trask across the floor towards the cave-mouth, and somebody was helping him, and I tore myself free, leaving a boot behind, and ran for the door, and sprinted up the slope towards the tractor as if I were running downhill.

Bill and Chet Morison arrived moments later, dragging Trask with their hands under his armpits. In the confusion that followed it was difficult to tell what was happening, except that Inga flung her arms around me, and then quickly let go as she realized I was covered from head to foot in a kind of yellow slime.

The flash of the laser almost blinded me—I was standing within six inches of the end of the barrel—and another great cloud of steam hissed up to the sky. Elmo was pointing it towards the cave and, to judge by the shower of sparks, he must have turned up the beam to maximum strength.

I sat down on the ground, my teeth chattering, suddenly feeling very weak. Inga was trying to pull me by the arm, shouting in my ear: "You must come back." But I shook my head. I just wanted to be left alone.

It was impossible to see through the billowing steam, but I thought I could discern one of the shoggoths trying to climb up the slope before dissolving like melting wax as the laser hit it. Then, to my bewilderment, Elmo raised the beam so it pointed up the mountain. I understood his reasoning only when an avalanche of snow and ice began to crash down into the valley. A piece of flying ice cut my cheek, and I suddenly accepted the wisdom of returning to the Snobile.

I tried to climb into the driver's seat, but Inga refused to let me, and took the wheel. Then, bumping and lurching, we drove up Windy Gap at a speed that made my head bang against the canvas roof.

I was still shivering violently, and the foul smell of the slime was so disgusting in the restricted space that I had to fight against being sick. As soon as we stopped in front of my hut, I crawled out on all fours, and vomited on the ice. Then I went and lay down on the floor of my hut and, refusing all Inga's attempts to make me undress and climb into bed, fell asleep.

#

When I woke up, she had covered me with the eiderdown and placed a pillow under my cheek. My head was splitting apart, and I felt as if I had the worst hangover of my life.

When I looked at my watch, I was amazed to see that it was eleven o'clock in the morning. The room was full of the horrible stench of the slime, and I pulled off my clothes and threw them outside the door. Everything in the camp seemed quiet, and there was no one around. I took a shower, scrubbing my hands and face to remove the slime, which had set into a kind of gelatine—it clogged up the shower outlet. Then I threw the pillow and eiderdown back on the bed, climbed in, and fell asleep again.

Inga woke me up at five in the afternoon with some coffee. I still felt oddly weak, as if I had been poisoned, but I succeeded in drinking the coffee. At least the stench had decreased.

I asked her: "What's happening?"

"Nothing. But Dr Trask is in bed."

"Is he all right?"

"Yes, but he cannot speak."

Trask, it seemed, had been vomiting all night, and was now asleep. It looked as if Bill Ruggles had been just in time—Trask had been unconscious when they dragged him out of the cave, and Chet had had to apply some kind of heart massage before he began to breathe normally.

I said: "What about the cave?"

"It is sealed up."

"Did you see the things inside it?"

"No. But I heard about them. Were they the Old Ones?"

I stared at her in amazement. "The Old Ones? Of course not. They were their servants, the shoggoths." Then I realized that she knew nothing about Lovecraft or the shoggoths, and had to explain.

It was as I explained that I suddenly began to understand. So far, I had had no time to think what it all meant. Now I found myself asking myself questions that had not struck me at the time—and realizing that the answers were even worse than I had suspected.

I had not asked myself, for example, what the shoggoths were doing in a cave nearly half a mile above the valley floor. Now I realized that it was a prison—a virtually inaccessible prison, with a sheer drop below and a sheer cliff face above. It could be reached by the Old Ones, because they possessed a kind of limpet-like base that was intended for clinging to rocks. But, for the shoggoths, it was escape-proof.

Why should the Old Ones want to torture them? That answer came to me only later—as I lay awake in the middle of the night. The shoggoths were virtually unkillable. Like worms and lizards and other primitive organisms, they could simply re-grow damaged limbs or amputated parts. I now recalled that the shoggoth who had been torn in half was taller than the others—it had obviously continued to grow even after it was too badly damaged to repair itself.

How could "unkillable" creatures be kept in a state of subjection and, if necessary, punished? There was only one answer: by sheer cruelty, by inflicting hideous damage. I could not forget that, even after its head had been torn off, one shoggoth remained alive.

In that case, was it really cruelty? On reflection, I could not doubt it. These things must have had some ability to feel pain, since pain is a safety mechanism without which a living creature would perish. To subdue their virtually indestructible creations, their masters had turned cruelty into a science.

There was a price to pay. It is impossible to become an expert in inflicting pain without turning into a sadist. This is what had happened to the Old Ones. In their ruthless Darwinian world, there was no room for benevolence. The Old Ones slaughtered and tortured the shoggoths, and the shoggoths—when they got the opportunity—probably slaughtered and tortured the Old Ones. That was why the valley reeked of cruelty.

That was also why the human race could never afford to release them. Nature had sealed them in a tomb of ice, and there they had to stay. If, at some future date, the polar ice caps show signs of melting away, then our descendants will have to face the problem, and make up their minds about whether to destroy the creatures or establish some kind of cooperation pact. But the latest long-term projections suggest that the polar ice caps will remain frozen for at least another hundred thousand years. Perhaps by that time the Old Ones will no longer be the most intelligent creatures on earth.

#

Later that evening I felt well enough to go to the dining room and eat a bowl of soup. After that, I went in to see Trask. He was sitting up in bed, and his face was covered with petechial haemorrhages. His voice was weak and hoarse, but I soon sensed that he was more vigorous than he looked.

He began by reaching out and shaking my hand. "I want to say thank you."

"For what?" I was astonished—I was still feeling guilty about leaving him behind in the cave.

"You were right and I was wrong."

I said awkwardly: "It's nice of you to say so." But I felt this was all a mis-understanding.

Trask said: "Tomorrow we're all going back to Little America."

"Are you sure you're well enough?"

He shrugged impatiently. "Of course. And I don't want to stay in this place an hour longer than I have to. But, before we go, I'm going to have to ask you to promise you'll keep silent."

"Of course."

"I mean really silent. With your father, your mother, your grandfather. You understand why?"

He went into a paroxysm of coughing, and I had to persuade him to stop talking. In any case, it was unnecessary for him to explain. I knew exactly what he meant to say: that if this leaked out it would mean worldwide publicity and worldwide curiosity. Within a year or two, perhaps sooner than that, there would be another expedition to Windy Gap—and this time they might let the genie out of the bottle.

That, thank God, has not happened. Now, forty years later, Trask is dead, Elmo Jarnefelt has just died in Finland, Bill Ruggles is a retired multi-millionaire, Dave Eng has brought a farm in Ohio, and Chet Morison owns a fishing fleet in San Diego. And for the past ten years Inga and I have lived in the flat above the laboratory that used to belong to Trask.

#

And why do I tell this story when it might be best to keep silent? Be-cause I need to explain how I could leave Windy Gap with a clear conscience.

When, on that plane journey back to America, I told Trask about the Old Ones, he was appalled at the thought of leaving intelligent creatures trapped beneath the ice—perhaps for another million years. Yet when I had told him the whole story, he agreed that there is no alternative.

The truth is that we had no right to make the decision to release them without first consulting the best minds, the keenest intelligences, of our own race. And when they had considered the problem objectively, I believe that they would have agreed we made the right decision.

For let us suppose for a moment that the Old Ones are the basically benevolent, trustworthy, kindly creatures I had assumed, and that we could rely on their integrity not to use their power and intelligence to enslave mankind.

Try to imagine what would have happened if we had released them, and they had indeed proved to be as wise and humane as I thought. By the law of superior vitality and dominance, they would soon have become the trusted advisers of mankind, and, in a short time, our rulers. And we, of course, would have been delighted to leave our worst social problems in their hands. All human beings long for a father-figure, someone to advise and protect and look after them. There would be no more wars, crime would vanish, and the wealth of the earth would be distributed wisely and justly . . .

But mankind would also have lost the gains of ten thousand years of social evolution at a stroke. For evolution consists of the power to control ourselves, to govern ourselves, to take the consequences of our own actions. The aim of human evolution is for every individual to achieve a high degree of self-mastery.

At present we are children, and our purpose is to grow up. And this can be done only by taking responsibility, and above all by learning to concentrate. Dr Johnson once remarked: "The knowledge that he is to be hanged in a fortnight concentrates a man's mind wonderfully." I had learned that man possesses an "unknown power", and that the key to unlocking this unknown power lies in concentration.

You may reply that placing our practical problems in the hands of benevolent father-figures would give us even more time to learn to concentrate. Unfortunately, this is not the way evolution operates. Human history has been virtually a non-stop crisis—ice ages, floods, earthquakes, predators, wars—and we have achieved our present level of consciousness by continuous struggle. Without struggle and effort, man tends to slip into laziness and mediocrity.

I am totally convinced that we are now on the point of an evolutionary leap to a higher phase—a phase in which we shall recognize that the power to control our own destiny lies in the mind itself. And the key to the "unknown power" lies literally behind our eyes.

So even assuming the best possible scenario, in which the Old Ones proved to be benevolent and trustworthy, their introduction into the human story at this point would be a disaster. In effect, humankind would be back in the nursery.

But, having thought endlessly about those events of that last twenty-four hours in Windy Gap, I cannot believe we would have been confronting this "best possible scenario". In retrospect, it is clear that the Old Ones deceived me. They set out to convince me they were kindly creatures, far too intelligent to be capable of brutality or ruthlessness. The cave of the shoggoths taught me otherwise—that they are as impatient and ruthless as any tyrant in human history, and that they react just as badly to any attempt to thwart their will. I believe that the human race would have come to hate the Old Ones just as much as the shoggoths did.

I also believe that the Old Ones sensed the coming change in human consciousness, and that it increased their sense of urgency. They wanted to escape before mankind grew beyond their control. Only chance—and the arrival of Inga—thwarted them. I believe—and Trask agreed with me—that the human race would be stupid to consider taking that risk again.

#

We returned to find New York in the grip of the worst winter for twenty years. Yet, in comparison with the South Pole, it seemed pleasantly mild. Strangely enough, no one ever showed the slightest curiosity about what had happened in Antarctica. Colonel Leroy accepted Trask's word that it had been a waste of time. Trask's shareholders accepted that he had failed to find oil. And the press did not even bother to try and interview us.

The only loser, in retrospect, is Hapgood. His lost civilization still lies under the ice of Antarctica, and, since his book has been out of print for over half a century, it seems unlikely that civilization will ever be found.

www.ingramcontent.com/pod-product-compliance
Lightning Source LLC
Chambersburg PA
CBHW020445270626
47155CB00022B/1608